D0396735

HOT property

HOT property

Michele, Samantha,
and Sabrina Kleier

HARPER
1817
An Imprint of HarperCollins*Publishers*
www.harpercollins.com

This novel is a work of fiction. Any references to real people, events, establishments, organizations, or locales are intended only to give the fiction a sense of reality and authenticity, and are used fictitiously. All other names, characters, and places and all dialogue and incidents portrayed in this book are the product of the authors' imagination.

For information, address HarperCollins Publishers, 10 East 53rd Street, New York, NY 10022.

HarperCollins books may be purchased for educational, business, or sales promotional use. For information, please write: Special Markets Department, HarperCollins Publishers, 10 East 53rd Street, New York, NY 10022.

FIRST EDITION

Designed by William Ruoto

Library of Congress Cataloging-in-Publication Data has been applied for.

ISBN: 978-0-06-112766-3

11 12 13 14 15 OV/RRD 10 9 8 7 6 5 4 3 2 1

This book is dedicated to our guardian angel Jonathan Kleier. Jonathan, you helped us write this book and now you are immortalized forever. This is all for you. We miss you every second of every day.

Love You,

The Family

HOT property

CHAPTER ONE

Kate

Carnegie Hill Classic

BACK ON THE MARKET—Five-room totally renovated prewar co-op. 2 spacious bedrooms, 2 baths, FDR, WBF, sunny, bright tree-lined views in this pet-friendly building steps from Central Park, shops, museums $2.3 million.

Don't get her wrong—she *knows* how lucky she is. Kate Chase is twenty-nine, bright and attractive, the daughter of devoted and generous parents, one of three children who are as close as any siblings could possibly be. Sometimes, in fact, it's difficult for people outside the family to understand exactly how close Kate and Isabel and Jonathan are—how they would almost always prefer to spend time in each other's company than in anyone else's. The three of them grew up together in a classic nine on Park Avenue—one of those spacious, high-ceilinged prewar apartments designed by Rosario Candela in 1928—just around the corner from where she and Isabel have been living since Isabel, three years younger than Kate, graduated from college. Their parents, Elizabeth (named for Elizabeth Taylor, her own mother's favorite movie star) and Tom, own Chase Residential, a wildly successful mom-and-pop boutique agency that specializes in the sale of high-end apartments throughout Manhattan, and the world they so comfortably inhabit affords all of them the great luxury of never having to worry too much about money. At least not if they don't want to. Kate and her sister work alongside their parents in the family business (their brother, Jonathan, twenty-one, is a junior at Emory), and oh what a glamorous business it can be, ornamented by a sprinkling, here and there, of celebrities from the entertainment business, professional athletes, chefs with their own TV shows.

Kate knows the family legend well: how Elizabeth started buying real estate young. When she was twenty-two, she and Kate's father purchased their first home, a maisonette on 76th and West End Avenue (the building used in the original *Stepford Wives* and, coincidentally, the very building where Kate sold her first exclusive. When Kate went to pitch it with her mother, in fact, Elizabeth talked their way into giving Kate a peek at that lovely little maisonette, and was able to point out where her water broke and where Kate's cradle had sat by the window).

When Kate was seven weeks old, the Chase family sold the maisonette and moved across town to 92nd Street. (Elizabeth was always an Upper East Side girl; the West End Avenue apartment was a "blip" that they sold for a huge profit when they moved a couple of years later.) When Isabel was born, they sold 92nd Street (that one, on the east side, doubled in value thanks to a wise real estate decision, Tom's upgrades, and an improving market) and moved to the nine-room on Park Avenue, where they are still today and will be forever.

But at this moment Kate's thoughts are elsewhere, focused on Scott, her boyfriend since the summer after her junior year at the University of Pennsylvania, someone with whom she's had a long and tumultuous history, an on-again, off-again relationship that sometimes makes her wish they'd never been introduced that night at Smokey Joe's near campus—a bar they always said reminded them of Cheers, where'd she'd gone with a couple of girlfriends for lemon drop shots (their college favorite). Scott, who'd already graduated and come back to visit friends, had been standing at the bar with a couple of fraternity friends, one of whom, Michael Prescott, would later become her sister Isabel's boyfriend. Though her junior year feels long ago now, Kate remembers that night she and Scott met, and how, even in that hot, noisy bar where Neil Diamond's "Forever in Blue Jeans" was playing on the jukebox, they had an impassioned conversation about Al Filreis, an English professor they'd both adored, a shy, middle-aged man with a Vandyke beard who lectured quietly but brilliantly about Shakespeare's early plays. At some point, she recalls, Scott left his friends, and she left hers, and the two of them strolled along Locust

Walk through the College Green and beyond, ending up at Franklin Field, Penn's football stadium, where Scott pressed her against the wall and kissed her so sweetly and so ardently that she felt herself falling for him right then and there. After that first, lingering kiss, Kate opened her eyes to look at him. Very tall, with thick dark hair, a perfectly sculpted nose, gray eyes, a probing, even haunting gaze. He was very handsome, sort of like a young Richard Gere, she thought, and very intense. But when he smiled his incredibly charming smile, his eyes crinkled at the corners and two deep dimples punctuated his cheeks. He didn't smile all that much, but when he did, Kate felt herself swooning.

Tonight, though—a warmish Sunday evening in mid-April—after a dinner of empanadas with smoked chipotle salsa, grilled chicken marinated in fresh lime, and one too many margaritas in Maz Mezcal, a loud, darkened Mexican restaurant off Second Avenue, Scott leans across the table to grab the check, examines it under candlelight, and sighs so heavily that despite the ambient noisy chatter, Kate is able to decipher what lies beneath that sigh—obvious impatience, but also pent-up frustration with himself, and maybe even with her.

"What is it, Scott?" she asks him.

He shakes his head at her.

"I'm guessing it's not that the chicken was too burnt for you?" she says. Anyone who eats with Kate knows that she always orders her chicken very well done, almost burnt, she always tells the waiter. She knows what's coming.

"Kate," Scott begins, "listen, I just—"

"Not again!" Kate interrupts him quietly. "Don't. Do *not*." Her bright brown eyes, delicately mascaraed, fill with angry tears. She folds her manicured hands into fists, but keeps them in her lap. "I can't believe you're going to do this to me again," she says.

"I'm really, really sorry," Scott says, but he can't even look at her as he talks, his eyes focused, she sees, on the check, which he smoothes with the flat of his hand over and over, as if trying to calm himself. "So, um, you know what, I just don't think it's good that I keep going back and forth in my mind about us. I think this could really hurt you. And that's why . . . maybe I need to take a step back—maybe a few steps back, and, I mean, I think we should take a breath and just not see each other for a while."

Why does he keep doing this to her? And why does she keep letting him? What's wrong with her that she would allow herself to be put on hold like this again and again, never knowing if he's going to return, never knowing if Scott will ever be willing to enter into a grown-up relationship? She's already mentioned the idea of couples therapy to him in the past in a desperate bid to save their relationship, despite the fact that the Chase family doesn't really believe in therapy. Clearly she is grasping. . . .

"Not see each other for a while?" Kate hears herself say, knowing it's pointless to ask him about couples therapy again. "What does that mean? A week? A month?" She allows herself to hide behind the curtain of her shining brown, pin-straight hair, wanting to conceal her lovely, delicate-boned face from Scott—whether he's looking at her or not—so he won't see her weeping.

Scott shrugs. "I just don't know," he tells her now. "I wish I did, but honestly, I have no idea what's gonna happen with us. I don't know what else to say, Kate." He looks at her.

She's heard this from him more than once in the nearly seven years they've been seeing each other, on and off and on again, and each time it stung more than the last. She picks up the linen napkin draped across her lap and wipes her eyes with an unused corner. "You can't do this to me, Scott," she says, but she knows, even as she speaks, that this is a lie. He *can* do it, and will do it, because it's he who controls the relationship, and because he is, in his way, the most juvenile, unsettled thirty-two-year-old she's ever encountered. He lives with his friends in Brooklyn, and not one of them has a job that requires a wardrobe of suits and ties. Instead, Scott and his friends work as DJs at deafening, overheated clubs, or at magazines that seem always in danger of folding, or at Web sites in danger of being permanently shut down. Like Scott, almost all of them are from well-to-do families, and attended Ivy League schools. But though in their early thirties, they still seem indecisive, directionless, still uncertain of what they want to accomplish in this world.

Unsettled, indecisive, and directionless though he is, Scott is beyond handsome, not to mention impressively well-read, utterly charming when he wants to be, and the love of her damn life. If only she could see some of that charm right now, just a smidgen of it, well, that would make her feel just the slightest bit better.

Silently, Scott walks her several blocks back to her apartment. She's hoping that he'll suggest coming upstairs—so she can try to change his mind, of course—but to her further disappointment, he doesn't.

"Okay, I guess I gotta go," he says as they approach the awning of her building. He tips his face downward and kisses the top of her head with a lovely gentleness that, over the years, she's grown intimately familiar with and that she won't ever forget.

Tears spring to her eyes again; even though she's furious with Scott, she has to admit there is still something incredibly seductive about him, and also something so appealingly sweet that she just can't resist him.

Except that she is going to have to, until he comes back to her.

"Come on," Scott is saying, "please don't be angry at me. You know this is the way I am; I just need time to figure out what I want."

"You've been figuring out what you want since the day I met you," Kate says. "You're nearly thirty-five," she adds, and immediately regrets it when, a moment later, she sees the stricken look that crosses his face.

A neighbor who lives down the hall is out walking his Yorkie; the man, whom she knows only slightly, is smoking a cigarette while his dog Muffin, whom she knows well, stops as Kate bends down to put his nose in Kate's hands and lick Kate's fingers before sniffing around the flower beds. (She thinks about how cruel it is to smoke around a dog—or any other animal, for that matter.) Kate reaches over now and punches Scott's arm sharply; the hug he gives her in return is accompanied by a kiss, an urgent, deeply romantic one, before he turns and leaves her outside the entrance to her building. "I hate you," she murmurs, and then instructs herself not to watch as he lopes down the street and away from her in his faded jeans and black suede Nikes, his shoulders slightly hunched, leaving her feeling, yet again, utterly bewildered. And terribly lonely. It's the sort of loneliness that all the well-meaning, generous-hearted love from her family can't help. At least, that's how it feels at this moment.

She and her sister Isabel and their mother are three savvy businesswomen, but they are also old-fashioned romantics who will always believe in the sanctity of true love. And that, Kate tells herself as she rides upstairs in the elevator, is what will sustain her, whether or not Scott ever decides to come back to her.

She drops her Vuitton Speedy bag onto the table in the entrance hall, ignores the copies of *Vogue* and *New York Magazine* that arrived in yesterday's mail, walks across the large soft, white rug, and sinks into the delicious purple velvet Shabby Chic armchair in the living room across from the big built-in bookcases that are spilling over with her favorite novels from her and her sister Isabel's days as English majors at Penn. They have saved every book they ever read, from Edith Wharton's *Age of Innocence* to her favorite Henry James story, the novella *Daisy Miller*, to D. H. Lawrence's *Sons and Lovers*, which they both read the spring of their junior year on the lawn of Horace Mann with their favorite English teacher, Dr. David Schiller. This is the cozy home she so happily shares with her sister: a two-bedroom, two-bath that is a mini version of her parents' apartment on Park Avenue. The kitchen and bathrooms have been made to look old-fashioned again with the white subway tiles her father helped them pick out, along with the tea-for-two deep soaking bathtubs and the white wooden medicine cabinets. The windows look out onto the back of the building, facing south, a lovely glimpse of leafy trees that—green and covered in buds or snow-covered—Kate loves seeing when she awakens every morning. The view is just like the trees she woke up to every morning in her bedroom on the third floor, facing Park Avenue. She loves, too, all the framed photographs everywhere in the apartment, photographs of all her happy moments with her family; pictures of her and her brother and sister as children, all in the bathtub together in the Park Avenue apartment, Jonathan's blond curls damp from the water she and Isabel had splashed on him, Kate and Isabel in giant clear shower caps with red, blue, and yellow appliqué flowers; Kate in a purple nightgown ornamented with rainbow-colored hearts, eight-month-old Jonathan held tight in her arms, smiling gleefully with a finger in his mouth; a photograph of all three children posed on the boardwalk at Atlantic Beach, Isabel in a white lace dress, Jonathan, age five, in a pink sport coat and madras bow tie, Kate already a teenager in a short black lace dress. The happiest, most uncomplicated times, the best days of their lives, perhaps.

Though Kate has been told again and again that she resembles Natalie Wood, she's never been completely aware of how attractive she is, with her glossy, dark brown hair and, in summer, that rich tan that settles on her petite body. Like her mother and sister, she lives in the color black, which she makes pop with lots of gold jewelry, particularly vintage Chanel pieces layered on necks and wrists (more is more when it comes to jewelry for the Chase women) and the occasional jolt of dramatic turquoise or brilliant pink. Her sparkling, slightly ironic smile is always highlighted by lipstick; her mother taught her at a young age to never show up in "public" looking pale and drippy. "You never know who you may run into," she told her girls. When Kate strides through the city in her five-inch Louboutin boots or tight pencil skirts, men look. She and Isabel have, in the past, been known to be party girls, especially at Dorrian's on the Upper East Side, where they love the jukebox. (She and her sister have been going there since college, sneaking in with their older cousins' IDs; they've always been old-fashioned in that way, liking what was familiar and returning there again and again. And they'd always enjoyed being at Dorrian's with people they knew from both high school and Penn;

even the bartenders and bouncers have known them forever. But recently Isabel seems to be spending more and more time with her boyfriend Michael, and Kate wouldn't think of going out like that without her sister.)

She considers calling her mother and Isabel now and telling them about this latest breakup with Scott. But she knows that they think he's going to take forever to grow up, and that each of them will probably say she should move on and start dating other people because he isn't getting his act together anytime soon. And that's something she just doesn't want to hear at this moment. So, strange as it is to keep anything from them, Kate decides that for now, anyway, she will keep it to herself.

It's 11:30, but she's too riled up to go to bed. She turns on the flat-screen TV mounted on the wall and watches an old episode of *Seinfeld*, one of her favorites; in it, Elaine is dating a man who insists on being called "Maestro" at all times, even though he's merely the conductor of the Police Benevolent Association Orchestra. What a pretentious drip! "Oh, get over yourself!" Kate yells to the actor on the TV screen. He reminds her of a fortysomething client she once had, an utterly self-important plastic surgeon who insisted that Kate call her "Dr. Powers" even after they'd spent months looking at apartments together. Even worse, her husband, an equally obnoxious man who clearly worshipped her, referred to her as "Doctor" as well, saying to Kate, "Dr. Powers and I will meet you at eleven o'clock in the lobby of 1136 Fifth Avenue, as previously discussed." What pretentious jerks, the two of them! And after six months of taking them all over Carnegie Hill, looking at one $5 to $7 million apartment after another, they ended up right back where they started, in their rental on East End, because, despite what Kate had told them, had *warned* them, Dr. and Mr. Powers refused to believe that they just didn't have the financials to get past the co-op boards in the choicest buildings on Park or Fifth.

"Get over yourself!" Kate repeats, shaking her head at the TV screen, at Elaine's insufferable boyfriend. But of course she's talking to herself as well, and she knows it.

When her cell phone rings, she almost decides she's feeling too wrung-out and despondent over Scott to answer, but then sees that it's Lorelei Lyne, one of the brokers from Chase Residential.

"Hi there," she says, and is surprised to hear that Lorelei—a twice-divorced, middle-aged broker who's been in the business more than twenty years and is quite a tough cookie—is actually weeping. "What is it?" Kate urges. She slips off her high heels and tucks her legs underneath her.

But Lorelei is sobbing so hard, she can't even speak. Hearing those sobs, Kate feels like crying herself. *I don't want to keep hurting you*—a simple half dozen words that have punctured her heart.

"Lorelei," she says, changing the channel on the TV, "what happened?"

"Let me pull myself together," Lorelei says; Kate can hear the click of her cigarette lighter and the long, drawn-out exhaling of smoke that follows.

"Are you smoking? Lorelei, I thought you were quitting," Kate says instinctively, as if there's a forty-eight-year-old in the world you can talk to like that, even if it's for her own good. She can picture Lorelei with the cigarette protruding from her mouth, lounging on her bed dressed in nothing but a leopard-skin push-up bra and a matching slip, her long black hair arranged around her cleavage like armor; in truth, Lorelei's become kind of slutty, and perhaps a little desperate as well. Since her second divorce—this time from a husband she made sure was arrested on two counts of criminal nonsupport for failing to pay alimony and child support—she's been scrambling harder than ever to get those commissions and also to find a "reliable" man for herself.

"Oh, I'm smoking, all right," Lorelei says. "Chain-smoking's more like it. The more Xanax I take, the more divine the ciggy," she says, and inhales deeply, looking, Kate imagines, like Mrs. Robinson in *The Graduate.*

"Now you're making me nervous," Kate says. "What's going on?"

"It's Rodney Greenstein."

"Oh, no, *now* what?" Greenstein is one of the city's wealthiest men, and a beast through and through. Kate's mother sold him and his string of ex-wives several multimillion-dollar apartments over the years, but the man's behavior had grown increasingly intolerable. Whenever Elizabeth took him to the handful of triple-mint Fifth Avenue co-ops that had recently struck his fancy, she'd found herself down on yet another vast marble floor, picking up the trail of sugar-dusted crumbs left in Greenstein's wake—all from those damn E.A.T. crumb cakes he brought as his mid-morning snack, nibbling on them with his hairy fingers that were either too chubby or too careless to contain the crumbs, so they followed behind him like the trail in "Hansel and Gretel." Once, Kate knows, when her mother suggested that Greenstein might actually try and catch his crumbs in a napkin or leave the crumb cake in the entrance gallery for after the showing, he glared at her and took a big crumbly bite. According to Kate's mother, it hit her then that Greenstein delighted in seeing her on her knees in her pencil Ralph Lauren skirt or charcoal gray pants, scrambling after his crumbs. If only he weren't one of the biggest sharks in finance, a billionaire whose appetites—for money, real estate, and sex—are legendary. But, as she has told Kate and Isabel more than once, Elizabeth was absolutely unwilling to sell her soul for a commission no matter what the price, because Greenstein was just too vile. So she passed him off to Lorelei Lyne, who would work with anyone.

"He's going to make an offer on 740 Park," Lorelei tells Kate now. "You know, the twelve-room duplex, with the double-height living room and the—"

"Twenty million?" Kate interrupts. "With four bedrooms?"

"Oh, yes, and it's a serious offer," Lorelei says.

"Well, that sounds fabulous, so why are you crying, and why'd you call me, not Mom?"

"Your mother's not picking up her cell."

"Oh, she's charging her phone," Kate says. She and Isabel have a ritual of talking with their mother at the end of every night, just to check in one last time before bed. And then first thing the next morning, as well—always a quick call to discuss the weather, and what outfits and jewelry they'll wear to work.

"And the problem is what Greenstein wants from me," Lorelei is saying, lighting another cigarette.

"What do you mean?" Kate is up now, walking toward the refrigerator (she's always been a late-night nibbler), though she knows perfectly well there's nothing in it but some expired mayonnaise, some shiny plastic take-out packets of mustard and ketchup, a couple of bottles of pinot grigio, and a few bottles of Poland Spring and Vintage seltzer, which she and Isabel have delivered by the case from FreshDirect. That's it. And in the freezer nothing except a half-filled ice tray. She is craving some delicious raspberry or lemon or coconut gelato from Sant Ambroeus on Madison, but why bother to have any food at home when she and Isabel have almost all their meals with their parents, in the apartment they grew up in just around the corner on Park?

"What I mean," Lorelei continues, her voice wobbly again, "is that Rodney Greenstein wants something I'm not sure I can give him. I mean, I could, but I don't want to . . ."

"Lorelei, what are you saying?" Kate says, walking back into the living room, settling back onto the sofa, and plucking a sour apple Charms pop from the apothecary jar on the end table. It's not gelato from Sant Ambroeus, but it's something. And these particular lollipops—which she buys by the dozen at Dylan's Candy Bar—are her favorite.

"Oh, my God!" Lorelei moans.

"Lorelei, please tell me what happened," Kate says. She picks up a copy of *Vanity Fair.* On the cover is a photograph of Michael Douglas looking really gorgeous; beneath him are the words

It's Still About Greed and . . .
MONEY

"He wants me to give him a b.j.," Lorelei says in a whisper. "If I don't, he won't buy the apartment."

"WHAT?"

"He won't buy the apartment unless I give him a blow job, it's as simple as that, okay?"

"Are you kidding?" Kate says, thinking how ironic it is that she's sucking a lollipop. "Please, please, *please* tell me this is a joke."

"If it were a joke, do you think I'd be in hysterics?"

At least Kate's half forgotten about Scott and her broken heart; at least there's that. But what a night, Kate thinks, and contemplates calling her mother's landline and waking her up to tell her everything. And to get her advice. But maybe her mother would appreciate it if she handled this turn of events regarding Greenstein on her own. She's twenty-nine years old, after all; she can do this. "Okay, look, Lorelei," she says, biting down on her lollipop.

Lorelei continues. "Because if I lose this sale, this $600,000 commission for us, I'll kill myself!"

"Lorelei," Kate assures her, "you're a smart grown woman, and you know what you should do—you don't need me to tell you." Running her fingertip along the bottom of one of her upper molars, Kate discovers a tiny chip.

"You *have* to tell me what to do!" Lorelei says. "I'm unraveling!"

"Listen, Lorelei, when you first started at Chase Residential and Mom told you that good brokers get down on their hands and knees to close a sale, you do understand that she was not being literal, right? So get it together and let's never, ever mention that we had this conversation."

"All right, fine," Lorelei says, sniffling. "Thanks." For a moment they sit on their ends of the line in companionable silence. "Hey, Kate? Don't you think I should at least be a little flattered that one of the most powerful guys in the whole city wants a blow job from me?"

Oh, dear! What is WRONG with this woman?

Kate forces herself to be patient. "Lorelei, what he asked you to do is disgusting! I don't care what he's worth, he's completely and totally vile, and it's not one bit flattering that he demanded a blow job from you, okay? And my mother would tell you the same thing if you asked her."

"Okay," Lorelei says, but she doesn't sound convinced.

"Lorelei, please tell me I don't need to worry about you," Kate says. "Can you promise me you aren't going there?" Gazing at the framed movie poster of *High Society* on the wall above her dining room table, Kate takes in the sight of the strikingly beautiful Grace Kelly in an elegant floor-length ballroom gown, flanked on either side by Bing Crosby and Frank Sinatra, and, in the background, Louis Armstrong poised with his trumpet at his lips. Kate and her family adore those old romantic comedies where, in the end, and with a wonderful inevitability, everything works out just as you know it was meant to. Even the names of the characters give Kate a small thrill—Tracy Samantha Lord, C. K. Dexter-Haven, George Kittredge. One of the reasons Kate and Isabel's apartment is filled with framed old movie posters is because Tom, in his past life as the president of the major advertising agency he founded with two partners, did the campaigns for Showtime, which he named, and dozens of films, including *E.T.* and *Back to the Future*—Jonathan even has the license plate from the movie up on his wall at school. The girls loved when their father was in advertising; he had two floors of offices at 777 Third Avenue (Elizabeth always said, "What a lucky number!"), and they would go and draw in the art department, and sit on their father's lap and help him edit copy. And the holiday parties they had (usually catered by Shun Lee Palace)! One of Tom's biggest clients had a pet monkey who played cards, and who for many years was the surprise guest at the parties. But their favorite thing was that Tom did the campaigns for Loews Hotels and Princess Hotels, so that in addition to the family always being sent to fabulous places, like the Southampton Princess Hotel in Bermuda, Kate and Isabel, ages seven and four, modeled in their brochures, the two little girls standing at the far end of the beach in matching purple bathing suits with stripes of rainbow down the sides, snorkel masks on their heads, flippers on their feet, and braids in their hair. Kate was toothless, with wet brown bangs across her forehead, and Isabel had a mop of curly blond hair.

"Okay, I promise," Lorelei is saying now in a tiny voice, and hangs up.

Kate's purple cell phone, which she keeps with her along with her BlackBerry at all times, rings again an instant later; it's her client Alexa Walden, whose brother had been in high school with Kate at Horace Mann—where Kate and Isabel have served on the alumni council since they graduated and attend monthly meetings for benefits and fund-raising, often at the divine head of school Tom Kelly's house in Riverdale. Alexa's husband is an investment banker who's done exceptionally well at Goldman Sachs. So well, in fact, that they'd been looking for nearly six months now to upgrade their postwar apartment at 1025 Fifth and move to a prewar on Park or Fifth.

"We heard back from the co-op board," Alexa says; she sounds miserable, as if she's just suffered an unbearable loss. Or in her case, more likely, as though she just received a rejection letter stating that her five-year-old, Chloe, has been denied acceptance to the $36,000-a-year kindergarten of her choice.

"What do you mean?" Kate says, sitting up. "They called you?" Clients almost never heard from co-op boards before their brokers did.

"I told them I was desperate to hear and asked them how soon I would find out. And then I just went ahead and gave them my cell phone number and begged them to call me directly. And you know what: they turned us down!" Alexa wails. "I *loved* every bit of that apartment—the wrap-around terraces, that three-room master suite, that enormous entrance gallery, in my head I'd already arranged all my artwork. . . . It was fucking perfect!"

Kate sighs. "Oh, no, Alexa, what did you do?"

"Well, I don't know," Alexa says vaguely. "You have to fix this, Kate."

"Alexa, didn't we go over in great detail what you should look and act like at the board meeting? You said you took notes! Understated! That meant no Chanel bag, or huge diamonds; no labels, no spiked heels, no short dresses or low-cut shirts. I told you what Mom always says, 'When your own initials are enough'—like Bottega Veneta. . . . Remember, I even said look like Miranda on *Sex and the City*—remember I told you all that?"

"Well, I had to take the special-order Birkin with me, you know, the one with the saltwater crocodile skin and the diamonds in the buckle," Alexa reports. "But just because I was on my way to a cocktail party at 834 Fifth afterward, and I told the board that, I figured they'd understand—"

"Alexa, was there something else? I can't imagine they turned you down simply because of the way you were dressed," Kate says, though she knows that *of course* they could have. Knowing Alexa, who likes to dress low-cut and sexy, and in her strappy six-inch Louboutins and no stockings, her beautifully tanned face fresh from the Viceroy in Anguilla where she vacationed most recently, well, Kate can easily imagine the distaste with which the brittle, sixtysomething ladies on the co-op board viewed her, despite her impeccable financials. What they feared, Kate speculates, was the very thought of their distinguished husbands riding in the elevator for even two minutes with the likes of the sexy young wife of one of Goldman Sachs' most valuable players, Alexa licking her lips or rubbing her long red nail over one of her quilted Chanels. Alexa, as Kate saw tonight, is unable to control her urges.

"I remember you told me to keep my mouth shut during the co-op interview, and not to speak unless spoken to, but I just can't stand those awkward silences," Alexa confesses. "They're dreadful. So I made small talk here and there, but nothing serious."

Kate sighs, thinking, What's the point, really, when the deal has come undone and it's too late for a miracle. Though she does in fact know of a client who, having been rejected because of the scandals of her much-married, drug-rehabbed celebrity father, wrote a sweetly poignant letter begging for a second chance from a co-op board—a letter that ultimately warmed the board's icy hearts and got her client the $6 million apartment of her dreams. But that, of course, was a rarity. A co-op board is like the Harvard admissions office: once they turn you down, it's over.

What a hideous night it's been. (Speaking of which,

where is her sister? She's due back any minute now from Millbrook, a cute little town upstate in Dutchess County, where Isabel had gone for the weekend with Michael. It's almost midnight, and tomorrow's Monday.) Even when a client gets hoist by her own petard, Kate knows she must act sympathetically and behave like a lady.

"Oh, those terraces," Alexa says tearfully. "Will we ever find any like them? Kate, what have I done? I don't know why boards won't let you bring brokers to board meetings—I just know you would have controlled me!"

"I promise you, Alexa, we'll find you another apartment that you'll fall in love with. Now tell me you believe me. Okay? I want you to have a glass of wine and get a good night's sleep, and we'll start again tomorrow."

"Okay," Alexa says morosely. "Whatever."

"Speak to you tomorrow," Kate says.

She's about to call her brother, who's always up late hanging with his friends or girlfriend, and is always the perfect tonic when she needs cheering up. But there's another call on her cell phone now.

"Hi there," she says at the sound of Samantha Siegal's excited voice.

"Wait till you hear about my weekend!" Samantha is her oldest and, other than Isabel, closest girlfriend; she and Kate started at Horace Mann nursery school together more than a quarter of a century ago, and ended up as roommates at Penn fifteen years later.

Despite her slightly chipped molar, Kate selects another

lollipop from the apothecary jar and begins to unwrap it as Sam shrieks happily into the phone: Randy, her boyfriend since right after college, only a few minutes ago presented her with a sapphire-and-diamond engagement ring. Kate is, of course, one of the very first people Sam is calling, the very first person, in fact, after her mother, to hear the news.

So her oldest friend is engaged. And what comes immediately to Kate—before she even has a chance to congratulate Sam—is a line from *High Society*: "My dear boy, this is the sort of day history tells us is better spent in bed."

"I'm so excited for you," Kate hears herself say, her voice rising with each word, trying not to cry. "I couldn't be happier." And it's the truth, even though she feels so terribly lonely at this moment, lonelier, she's sure, than she's ever felt in this enviably lucky, privileged life of hers.

CHAPTER TWO

Isabel

Legendary Bldg off Madison

4 large bedrooms, 3 baths and EIK in the famed Carlyle House; private elevator landing, old-world details throughout—ESTATE SALE $5.9m.

Isabel is having an awful, everything-that-can-possibly-go-wrong-does sort of morning. It started when she slept right through her alarm and woke, disoriented, to find that Dixie, the delicious shih tzu puppy she and Kate had recently bought from a breeder in Pennsylvania, had somehow tumbled off her bed, chewed through the toe of one of the new Christian Louboutin pumps Isabel had kicked off the night before, and left a couple of puddles (surprisingly large, considering she's such a small dog) on the floor, one of which Isabel stepped in on her way to the bathroom.

This inauspicious beginning on the morning after her return from Millbrook was followed by the discovery that a carelessly uncapped Sharpie had left an indelible black scrawl inside her favorite champagne leather Bottega Veneta bag. Kate had woken up in a foul mood, responding to Isabel's inquiries with monosyllables. And then came a jerky, stop-and-start cab ride to her first appointment, which made the latté she'd gotten at Juliano's—the small neighborhood espresso bar her family loved for its coffee—and gulped in an effort to wake herself up churn miserably in her stomach. At this moment, Isabel laments that her family never hired a driver. (They did once, actually; his name was Leo, and two weeks after he started, the market crashed and Tom and Elizabeth had nowhere to be driven to, so Leo sat in front of their building or office waiting for them all day. A few weeks after that, they sadly had to let him go, and there was never talk of a driver again. Elizabeth thought she'd single-handedly caused the crash of 1987.) Isabel actually had to get off the phone with her mother—their usual first-thing-in-the morning phone call, delayed by Isabel having overslept—because she needed to close her eyes and put her head back on her seat to rest for a few minutes.

The cab weaves now through the downtown traffic on Park Avenue, which seems even heavier than usual this morning. The cab is still stalled by a red light when Isabel's BlackBerry buzzes. It's Alex Fein, an entitled, highly demanding, and frequently annoying client to whom she has shown no fewer than thirty-two apartments in the last three months. Alex is calling to say that she's *so* sorry to have to report this to Isabel, but she has—guess what!—found the absolutely perfect Fifth Avenue gem, with everything she has been dying for: the perfect layout, wood-burning fireplace, southern exposures, three full baths, enormous chef's kitchen, fully planted terrace facing Central Park. This would be great news if not for the infuriating fact that Alex, sneaky, treacherous Alex, bought this apartment direct, having been seated at the Food Allergy Initiative charity luncheon at Cipriani (much to Isabel's misfortune) next to the exclusive broker, who had yet to put it on the market and, after hearing Alex whine during the gazpacho soup and then most of the striped sea bass about her apartment woes, told Alex she must see her new listing. A disaster, Isabel thinks—and clicks off, furiously.

She seethes, recalling how Alex rejected apartment after apartment that Isabel showed her. "The hallway's too short," she complained about one, and "The lobby looks a little vulgar, don't you think?" she asked of another. "I'd have to use the service elevator if I had my dog with me?" (The one point Isabel herself agreed with—she, along with everyone else in her family, would never live in a building like that.) "What are these people thinking?" Alex griped about another co-op, stamping her foot (an Alex trademark). That was the way with Alex: in and out of taxi after taxi, apartment after apartment, and each time she managed to find some minute something or other to criticize—and to keep her from saying that all-important *yes.* (Once, after Isabel brought her to 32 East 64th Street, the doorman had taken Isabel aside and whispered, "She'll never get past the co-op board—those shoes, that handbag, that screechy voice!") "Nothing is good enough for her," Isabel told her mother. But she kept searching, taking Alex to apartment after apartment, saying, "This one has the most perfect layout, and every major room faces Park," or "This one needs a gut but has the best terraces in the world." Only to learn today that Alex—who routinely rejected apartments because she didn't like the pattern of herringbone floor in the dining room—"*No!*" she'd yell in her clipped, whiny voice—or the height of the towel bars in the master bath— "*No,*" everywhere they went, "*No!*"—has bought, in what seems like a split second, without her. Of course this is nothing short of maddening!

Well, she may be having a rotten day so far, but at least she knows she looks good. Although she is 5'3", Isabel has the presence of someone considerably taller. In part this is because she's always in heels—Manolos, Choos, and Louboutins stock her closet—but also because of her outsize personality: she's quick-thinking, quick-talking, and filled with a bubbly charm that her clients, friends, and family all adore. Her chin-length blond hair frames her attractive face, notable for her green-blue eyes and great smile. A few freckles ornament her cheeks and nose; although she tries to cover them with foundation and blush, her boyfriend finds them endearing. Her best friend from college, Nancy Scarlata, has always told her that she looks like Reese Witherspoon, and so many other people have echoed the observation that Isabel has begun to think perhaps it's true.

Isabel is thin and in perfect shape too, like her sister, despite the fact that the Chase sisters have never gone to a gym—their exercise comes from showing apartments all day long in high heels, and when they have time, speed walks and runs around the Central Park Reservoir. Her style at the office or out with clients is classic—she's partial to Ralph Lauren everything, like his cashmeres in gumball colors, silk shirts, and perfectly cut black pants or pencil skirts in black or dark gray. Her mother taught her and her sister that jeans are for weekends only, and by jeans she means slim-fit, gorgeous ones. Today she's wearing a kicky, pleated plaid skirt from Ralph Lauren, a clingy silk T-shirt, and lots of jewelry: three tinkling antique charm bracelets, a cluster of Chanel gold chains around her neck, including the Chase favorite, the Chicklet crystals, and her gold monogram ring—Tom gave each girl one on their fifteenth birthday and they never take them off. Like all the women in her family, she's obsessed with jewelry, and is especially in love with all the vintage pieces that she, Kate, and her mother share.

"Right here, please," she tells the cabdriver, pointing to the yellow brick and limestone Art Deco building at 50 East 77th Street. Isabel hands the driver the money for the fare, plus a generous tip. He seems pleasantly surprised, and wishes her a "really, really nice day," which is ironic because at only five minutes to ten, so much has gone wrong already. "You're welcome," she says to the driver, a slender man from somewhere in South Asia with the thin mustache of a teenager. He actually hops out and opens the door for her.

She steps into the spacious lobby of the Carlyle House. Her clients, the Bennetts, haven't arrived yet; good. She nods to the doorman, who knows her by now because she has sold and shown in the building many times, and takes a moment to primp in front of the large, gold-framed mirror. This is a fabulous building, she reminds herself; that despicable Alex Fein would have been lucky to get into a building like this, but Alex Fein is in the past. Isabel wills herself to stop thinking about her. The apartment she is about to show—huge master, three additional bedrooms, four and a half baths, a pair of dishwashers (one full-size, the other mini, holding just a handful of plates, glasses, and silverware) in the recently renovated kitchen—is fabulous, a fourteenth-floor jewel. Her phone buzzes, and she flips it open. "Hi Mom," she says. "No, not yet. They should be here any second." At the far end of the lobby, she sees Tara Chandler, the broker representing the seller, and she waves to her.

Tara is standing right by the door that leads into the Carlyle Hotel, which is adjacent to the residence. Isabel knows that owners here have easy access to the hotel lobby and are allowed to use the hotel's many amenities, such as the bar (with its wonderful mural by Ludwig Bemelmans), café, restaurant, lounge, Sense Spa, and concierge. Classic New York.

Just then, the lobby door opens again, and there is tall, scrawny Lawrence Bennett and his short, exceedingly pregnant-looking wife, Kimby, trailing behind, clutching the small hands of their four-year-old twins, Skylar and Carlin.

The little girls, dressed in matching pink-and-green floral smocked dresses and pink suede Mary Janes, remind Isabel of the way her mother used to dress her and Kate—always alike, whether in white dresses with smocking, or navy blue rompers with candy-apple-red Mary Janes and white tights, wheeling identical doll strollers, the girls always looking perfect and always identical.

"Gotta go, speak to you later," Isabel tells her mother, and moves toward Kimby, who is, in fact, not that far along in the pregnancy. But since she is having twins, she looks as if she might be ready to give birth next week. Lawrence, Isabel knows, is a newly anointed partner at a top law firm.

"Lawrence!" says Isabel, waving hello. She gives Kimby a quick peck on the cheek, and from her bag, she pulls out a pair of lollipops she took from Kate's jar and offers them to the twins.

"Gimme!" Skylar screams.

Kimby hesitates for a second before nodding. "Go ahead," she tells her daughters, and they both begin to pluck at the wrappers with eager fingers. "You're always so thoughtful," Kimby says to Isabel. "Let's hope all that sugar keeps them occupied through at least the kitchen and dining room."

Isabel introduces Tara Chandler to the Bennetts as they all get into the elevator to go to the fourteenth floor. In truth, it's only the thirteenth, but so many people are superstitious about living on the thirteenth floor that in this particular building, like many others, the architect eliminated it.

Some clients are even particular about that—they refuse to live on a floor that's called fourteen but is actually thirteen. Then of course there are clients who want to live on a high floor, because they feel that the simple gesture of pressing the top button in the elevator makes them feel "above" the rest of the building. Others only like low floors just in case they need a quick escape. Her client Sabrina Morningstar, who lived on the twentieth floor at 1120 Park and during the blackout a few summers ago had to walk down the twenty long flights with a six-month-old, a three-year-old, and a Havanese puppy, vowed never again to live above nine, despite the fact that her husband loved their reservoir view. Fortunately for Isabel, the Bennetts are not the least bit picky about the floor; they seem to have no feelings about the subject at all. The impending birth of a second set of twins makes them much more concerned about the size and number of bedrooms than anything else.

"I think you'll love this apartment," Isabel says confidently as they step out of the elevator that opens directly in front of 14B, the only apartment on the floor—one apartment per floor being a major status symbol in New York City. "Just wait until you see the kitchen. It's huuuge! Your housekeeper could cook for twelve children in there."

"We're stopping after four." Lawrence laughs. "Even if they *are* cheaper by the dozen."

Isabel laughs, more at his attempt at humor than because it's actually funny.

Tara slips the key into the lock, steps into the apartment, and then stands back, waiting for the magnificent light to take effect on the Bennetts. Instead, they are distracted by the sound of a loud yawn and feet shuffling along the herringbone floors. "Uh-oh," Tara says. She's warned Isabel that she is dealing with an extremely difficult seller, Drew Green, and that try as she might, she can't get him to leave during showings. And now Drew himself, a thirty-eight-year-old wreck, is stepping into the entrance gallery.

"Hey, ladies," he says. He nods in the direction of the Bennetts, who seem a bit surprised. And why shouldn't they be? They didn't expect Drew—tangled brown hair, sleepy brown eyes, wearing a noticeably ratty white terry-cloth bathrobe and battered slippers, and showing off a two-day growth on his chin and cheeks—to be there. Sellers are not expected to be home during a showing, let alone shuffling around like they just got out of a three-day bender in bed.

Tara says to Drew, "Aren't you supposed to be at work . . . or something?"

"Me?" He glances down at his coffee-stained robe, as if surprised to find himself wearing it. "I've just been glued to the computer," he explains. "Haven't had a chance to get dressed yet."

"Listen, Drew," Tara says. She's eyeing him worriedly now. "I need you to please accommodate us by leaving—we won't be more than twenty minutes, okay?"

"Damn straight he needs to leave," Lawrence says, and Isabel thinks how surprising it is that a partner at a distinguished white-shoe law firm like Lawrence would speak like this. Then, to Drew, he says, "Did you notice that my wife is pregnant? Well, she happens to be pregnant with *twins*, and time is of the essence here. It was hard enough to set up this appointment—we need to see the apartment *today*. As planned." He looks over at Tara, who takes Drew aside and says quietly, "Drew, you've got to get out of here. Right away. Please!"

"Okay," Drew says. And then, to the Bennetts, "Take a look around. Morning's the best time, anyway. By the afternoon, all that light turns the place into a sauna."

When it comes to reining in this reluctant seller, Tara is apparently useless, Isabel thinks. Drew continues, "And the new AC? It does work like a charm." Drew looks over at Lawrence. "But it takes a lot of juice. The electric bills? Through the roof! Oh, and by the way, the limestone floor in the kitchen is a disaster—you accidentally spill something like, let's say, balsamic vinegar on it, and it stays etched in the stone forever. That damn floor is impossible to keep clean, and I mean *impossible*."

Isabel is horrified, and she can tell Tara is too, though Tara can't seem to do anything other than trail behind them like an eager but ineffectual puppy. Drew is clearly trying to ruin this deal, and Isabel knows why, too—he does not, it appears, want to sell his late mother's apartment; he's made that completely obvious today. It's his two brothers who are so eager to sell, and since Drew can't buy them out, he's forced to go along with the family decision, Tara told her. Isabel gives him a cool, appraising look.

"Why don't you all go ahead into the kitchen?" she tells the Bennetts. "Tara and I just need to discuss something with Drew."

"I wanna go to the park," Carlin whines as the Bennetts start walking. "This is a stupid apartment!" She makes a loud, smacking sound with her lollipop, as if for emphasis. A drop of blue-tinged saliva trails from the corner of her mouth.

"You're a stupid idiot," her twin tells her matter-of-factly.

Isabel keeps her face in its frozen smile until she's alone with Tara and Drew. Then she turns to Tara. "Don't you think it would be a good idea if Drew left the apartment now?" she says sweetly. And then to Drew, "The damage is already done, so I think you can go now."

"Drew, you did say you'd be out of here first thing this morning," Tara reminds him; she seems to be drawing strength from Isabel's display of self-confidence.

"Really?" Drew says serenely. "Sorry. I must have forgotten." He rubs a hand, almost experimentally, over his unshaven face. "And anyway, what's the big fucking deal? I mean, you can still show the place. It's certainly clean enough."

"Drew, your presence here is making the clients uncomfortable," Tara says. When Drew doesn't reply, she adds, "Do your brothers know you're here? Because we both know how hot they are to sell this place. Maybe I should give them a call." She takes out her phone to show she means business.

"No no, don't bother them at work," Drew says quietly. One brother is a venture capitalist, the other a cardiologist; Isabel knows from Tara that Drew, who is a freelance photographer, is a little intimidated by both of them. "Fine, I guess I'll get dressed and take a walk around the block or something," he says grudgingly, tightening the belt on his bathrobe and loping off down the hall.

Tara snaps her phone shut.

"That was perfect," Isabel says softly as Drew walks off.

Then she and Tara walk into the kitchen, where the Bennetts are opening cabinets and remarking how nice two dishwashers would be; one could be devoted to sterilizing the new babies' bottles.

"So sorry again about that incident," Tara says, but the Bennetts don't look up.

"Nice kitchen," Lawrence says.

"Exactly as we would do one," Kimby adds.

"It *is* pretty perfect," Isabel says.

They spend the next few minutes in the square dining room and the entertaining space.

Drew is still banging around in one of the bedrooms. Carlin is chasing Skylar down the hall now, and Kimby awkwardly lumbers after them.

"Cut it out, girls!" she calls.

"Ow!" Carlin cries. She's collided with Drew, who has just emerged from one of the bedrooms. At least he's dressed—thankfully—in a pair of faded jeans and an equally faded green T-shirt.

"Hey, I'm sorry," Drew says, kneeling down to Carlin's level. "I didn't mean to hurt you, honey."

Carlin looks at him for a long moment and then suddenly starts to wail. "Ow, ow, OW!" Alarmed, Drew vanishes down the hallway.

"It's okay, baby," says Kimby. The two Bennetts murmur consoling words to Carlin while Skylar examines her tiny nails.

They hear the door close as Drew finally exits the apartment. Isabel hears Tara sigh. "Okay, finally he's gone! Let's go see the master suite—the bedroom wing is totally private, which is nice," she tells the Bennetts.

"Yes, it's amazing," Tara adds.

And indeed the room is vast, with a corner exposure, and is flooded with light. Although not renovated as recently as the kitchen, it's still exquisitely done, with creamy vanilla Venetian plaster walls, herringbone floors covered predominantly by a matching vanilla Stark carpet, all original moldings. Most of Drew's mother's furniture is still here, including a king-size bed with a tufted headboard and a down quilt covered by a raw silk duvet the color of the sea. Arranged at the center of the bed is a needlepoint pillow with the words "The Queen Sleeps Here" stitched in scarlet.

"Now let's go see the master bath," Isabel says. "All new, huge Infinity tub, and separate shower. All Cararra marble. Don't you love it?" She lets Lawrence enter first, and then she follows. Immediately, her nose wrinkles: the toilet, wide open and gaping, makes it abundantly clear that it has been used this morning—several times, by the look of it.

"Oh, gross!" Kimby says.

"Give me a fucking break," Lawrence says.

Tara flushes the toilet before following them out of the room.

"Don't even bother," Lawrence says.

"Drew obviously doesn't want us here," Kimby says.

"You think?" her husband says.

"I'm so sorry," Isabel says again, and then explains, "This is an estate sale, and sometimes there are major disagreements as to the sale—this is clearly one of them."

"Look, I could care less about that guy," Lawrence says. "He's not coming with the apartment, and you can be sure he won't be the one we would be negotiating with. I just don't care for people who totally waste my time like that."

"I agree. But he's gone now, so let's take a look at the other bedrooms," Isabel says, changing the subject. "They're all huge, perfect for the twins, and, when they're a little older, for sleepovers with their friends."

"I wanna see my room!" says Skylar, who, with her twin, has just emerged from under the bed, dust clinging to the hem of her dress like a spider's web.

Isabel says, "Wouldn't you love a great big room so you could spread out all your toys when you play?"

Skylar nods enthusiastically. "My Flower Fairies, my Twinkly Tiara, my stringing beads, my Barbies . . ."

"My Magnetic Mosaics, my Calico Critters, my Princess Puppets, my See and Spell!" Carlin chimes in. "My Barbies . . ."

Isabel remembers her own bedroom growing up, with the huge, hand-painted dollhouse her parents had commissioned for her.

"Let's see them," Kimby says, and taking each girl by the hand, leads the way.

They seem to love the first bedroom. Lawrence loves the view, the enormous closet where the girls can put their Barbie collections. There's no furniture in the room save a big overstuffed armchair covered in a blue-and-white gingham check. Carlin runs over to it and sits herself down.

"I said I wanted to go to the park," she reminds her parents. "You have to take us," she says, kicking the heels of her pink Mary Janes rhythmically against the side of the chair.

"Maybe," Kimby says; now both hands are resting on her rounded front. "We'll see."

"It *is* a good-sized room," Lawrence says, concession apparent in his voice. "Let's see the rest fast, I have to get to a meeting."

The next room is noticeably smaller than the others; Lawrence asks, somewhat testily, "Was this a maid's room? Because no child of mine is going to sleep in a maid's room," he adds, as if this were a fate too hideous to contemplate.

The room's appearance is not at all enhanced by the unmade bed and heap of clothing on the floor, including Drew's coffee-stained bathrobe.

"Look," Skylar says, pointing to an open laptop resting on the desk. "A computer." She turns to her mother. "Can me and Carlin play Strawberry Shortcake Amazing Cookie

Party while you and Daddy look at the rest of the rooms? Okay?" She trots over to the computer and touches the keyboard.

"Sweetie, that's not our computer, we can't touch—" Kimby begins, and then suddenly stops. Her voice sounds clotted and strange, so Isabel quickly shifts to follow her gaze. Skylar's touch has brought the screen to life, and there, plain as can be, is a naked woman with the largest breasts Isabel has ever seen. Her hair is an unnatural shade of purplish red and her eyes are closed; one hand is touching her pancake-sized pink nipple, while the other directs a huge penis toward her parted thighs.

"Who's that?" asks Skylar. She puts a fingertip to the screen and touches the woman's nipple, stroking it nonchalantly.

"Get your hand off there!" Lawrence shouts, and hustles his family down the hall toward the front door, Kimby waddling behind as best she can.

"Oh, well," she begins, with her hand on the doorknob. It looks as if she might be contemplating offering something further, Isabel thinks. But Lawrence is already at the elevator.

"Kimby!" he calls urgently. "The elevator's here. This place is too filthy, let's go right now."

And with that, the pregnant Bennetts disappear from the fourteenth floor, and possibly from her life forever.

As she searches madly through her purse for her cell phone, so she can e-mail Jonathan—who has just the right sense of wickedly dark humor for this—she sees Tara slinking toward her, shaking her head, and the two have no choice but to laugh.

Walking out of the Carlyle House into the beautiful April day, Isabel thinks for just one moment where she would be were it not in the family real estate business. Elizabeth's first hopes were actually for either Kate or Isabel to be not just a famous actress but a true movie star. Isabel, age three, was desperate to be a star, layering necklace upon necklace long before *Vogue* declared that "the look," while Kate daydreamed of being an architect and married by, at the latest, twenty-four, to a tall, dark, and gorgeous man named Gregory with whom, by twenty-six, she would have one daughter (Kim, as in Kim McAfee from *Bye, Bye, Birdie*) and a second (Scarlett, from *Gone with the Wind*) on the way. Elizabeth's biggest regret was that Isabel was born too late to play the starring role of Cee Cee as a child in the movie *Beaches*, based on the novel written by her best friend from childhood, Iris Rainer Dart. Although according to Iris, Isabel was far too pretty for the part.

So Elizabeth hired a photographer and took modeling shots of her girls wrapped around trees in Central Park. They went on go-sees for cereal commercials and to acting class, where they had to sing "Happy Birthday" with every different emotion possible. They took gymnastics and ballroom dancing (they loved these lessons because the white gloves they wore were very Kim Novak in *Vertigo*), and they watched *Gypsy* again and again and again. Kate of course was Louise and Isabel was Baby June, though as Elizabeth pointed out when the girls were older, "Louise grew up to be Gypsy Rose Lee, the most famous stripper in the universe, and Baby June grew up to be a housewife."

Isabel wound up getting the much-sought-after role of a Munchkin in *The Wizard of Oz* at the very prestigious Westbury Music Fair (the grade school equivalent of playing one of the girls on murder row in *Chicago*). But the moment her mother told her she would have to go on location on Long Island and miss most of the sixth grade at Horace Mann (a very important year, the last before children went from the elementary school to the "big" campus across the street), Isabel cried for a moment and then declined the role.

Her phone rings, snapping Isabel back into the present, and she scurries into a taxi to get to her office on Madison Avenue.

CHAPTER THREE

Elizabeth

Central Park West, 70s

Legendary Majestic 7-room co-op; sprawling terraces with sweeping Central Park views, 3 bedrooms, 3 baths. $6.3 million.

Well, I'll try to get hold of Teddy right now." Violeta, the receptionist at Chase Residential, hangs up the phone. In her third year at NYU part time, she is a Penelope Cruz look-alike who has inspired all the men in the office to linger at her desk before going to their own.

There's the click-clack of high heels and the sound of dozens of charm bracelets and Ippolita bangles clanging together—Elizabeth has arrived.

Violeta twirls her thick black hair into a low bun, poised to tell Elizabeth about Teddy.

Elizabeth flips one of her hands as if to say, "What?" her bracelets tinkling like coins. She's a beautiful woman whose features have deepened over time. Her smooth forehead, perfectly straight nose, deep-set dark eyes, and lovely smile have remained virtually unchanged since her twenties. A cross between Sophia Loren and Mary Tyler Moore, she hasn't had a stitch of work done, save for the occasional shot of Botox, and only started coloring her rich brown hair a year ago. Kate, everyone says, is her clone, although in truth, both of her daughters look exactly like her, though Isabel's blond hair and green-blue eyes set her apart.

"Who was that?" Elizabeth asks.

"It was the lawyer for Teddy's buyers."

"1148 Fifth Avenue?"

Violeta nods. "Teddy's forty-five minutes late for the walk-through, and no one's heard a word from him."

"What?" For a moment Elizabeth just stares at Violeta, then arranges both elbows on the tall mahogany sideboard that fronts Violeta's desk and cups her face in her palms. Teddy Wingo is the only broker at Chase Residential whose yearly business even approaches hers. And he knows as well as she does that a walk-through—the final opportunity a buyer is entitled to before the closing to go through the apartment and make sure that the property is exactly as it's supposed to be—is absolutely imperative. Without one, closings generally do not happen.

"We need to try and get hold of Teddy right now," Elizabeth tells Violeta.

Violeta presses one of her speed dial buttons. She pulls the receiver away from her ear. "Voice mail."

"I assume you tried his cell and e-mail?" This is most unlike Teddy, she thinks, and for a moment wonders if something is terribly wrong. "If we don't find him, I guess I'll have to go to the walk-through. So who's the attorney who called?" Elizabeth asks Violeta.

"Steve Matz."

At least the seller's lawyer is a cooperative one, Elizabeth reflects, anxiously watching Violeta's unsuccessful attempt to reach Teddy on his cell phone and then her French-manicured fingers tapping out a text. Once it's sent, Violeta looks up at her. "Is it a Gumley Haft building?" she asks, mentioning the real estate management company that Chase Residential is affiliated with. "In which case either Dan Wollman or Jim Stasio might know something, don't you think?"

Elizabeth considers this for a moment. "No, not ours. So why didn't I know Teddy had a walk-through today?"

"It's on your desk," Violeta tells her. "But remember, you were hardly in yesterday." The day before, Elizabeth had mostly been out of the office, supervising an open house on a new exclusive listing, a town house at 61 East 93rd between Park and Madison, an affair that involved catering and blitz marketing and required every bit of Elizabeth's attention on-site. To complicate matters, Elizabeth was never able to return to the office because the open house was followed by back-to-back showings and then a bidding war. Priced smartly at $9.9 million, the property had attracted three offers by five o'clock yesterday evening, two of them coming from best friends who were pitted bitterly against each other.

This wasn't the first time, of course, that Elizabeth had observed that the desire to acquire real estate trumped the bonds of friendship or that real estate in the city could be a vicious game. Real estate is, without a doubt, a family's biggest investment, and also the ultimate status symbol. Everyone in Manhattan wants to know what people are spending for their homes and where. In a crisis, people will sooner sell family diamonds, art, or furniture than give up their "address." (And of course what sort of home a person acquires reflects so much about him; income, taste, lifestyle.) She's observed, too, that someone battling a midlife crisis might move to a new location rather than look for a new love; instead of trading in his wife he'll trade real estate and move across town to a property that just might be more interesting than what he owned before. (Elizabeth had two clients, in fact, who within a year of each other moved from the same Park Avenue co-op to the same brand-new Tribeca condo, by sheer coincidence. One stayed married, the other did not.) And, too, until recently, co-op prices and the names of the people who bought them weren't public knowledge, which helped to make people even more obsessed with finding out who had bought and sold and for exactly how much. It became as much a dinner party or school benefit conversation as the subject of whether Brad and Angelina were adopting again.

"Well, then, you could've called my cell," Elizabeth hears herself reminding Violeta now. "Anyway, call Steve

Matz back and tell him I'll be at the apartment in twenty minutes."

Her cell phone rings. "I'm so annoyed!" she tells Kate.

"Oh no, what's the matter?"

"Teddy didn't show up at his walk-through at 1148 Fifth," Elizabeth says, and repeats the story to her.

"Well, that's kind of alarming," Kate says.

"And now I've got to go to the walk-through. I just got into the office and have a million things I have to do here, and I have to run right back out." Teddy's known all over town to be a womanizer (in Kate's words, someone who thinks he's a twenty-five-year-old womanizer), but one whose charm, gorgeous looks, midwestern calm, and appearance of unflappability have more than compensated for any lack of consistency. Elizabeth hired Teddy because he's well connected, a Yale grad with dozens of wealthy friends living in the city, so many of them buying and selling their homes every few years, it seems. But she finds him rather devious, always scheming for other people's listings—always with a dazzling smile on his face.

"Okay, I have to go, I'll call you later," Elizabeth tells her daughter. She stops in her office for a moment to pick up a piece of a board package she is working on and grab a few salty extra-dark special pretzels from the tub she keeps behind her desk (the family's secret stash) and then clutching her orange Birkin, walks back out to the reception area. Violeta is standing in front of her desk, holding out a manila folder.

"Is that going with me?"

Violeta nods.

Elizabeth lets out an elaborate sigh. "So when, exactly, was the last time you spoke to Teddy?"

"Yesterday around five o'clock. He'd just finished with his Venezuelan clients."

"The ones you think might be money launderers?"

"Well, I'm not going *that* far," Violeta says. "Teddy asked me what I thought of them, and I told him what I'd told you, which is that I didn't get a good vibe about them."

"I've got to go, but just tell me quickly what it was about these people that gave you a bad vibe, okay?"

Violeta's face reddens. "When they dropped by the office and I heard their dialect of Spanish and saw the name Carmona-Morillo, I thought to myself: *Not* good."

"But you're Argentinian—how do you know so much about Venezuelans?"

"Well, I'm from South America. And being South American . . ." Violeta hesitates. "Let's just say you learn to recognize the way certain women dress. The straightened hair, the designer clothing . . . it gives them away."

"Gives them away as *what*?" Elizabeth presses.

"You can just tell that the Carmona-Morillos recently came into a lot of money. *Very* recently," Violeta says with a whiff of imperiousness. Violeta is descended, in fact, from old Argentinian aristocracy that can trace its roots back to Spain.

Elizabeth's cell phone rings again, and she hears an unrecognizable male voice say, "I'm driving . . . I think I'm in a dead zone . . . I'm going to lose you—"

"Hello?" Elizabeth says, and then realizes the call has been dropped. In any case, she needs to get over to the walk-through right away, and with traffic it could take her twenty minutes to get to 96th and Fifth. She looks at her watch; it's a little before eleven now. "If we don't hear from Teddy by, say, twelve thirty or so, I'm going to have to go over to his apartment," she says.

Violeta looks startled. "Do you think that's a good idea?"

"What choice do I have? He didn't show for a walk-through on a three-and-a-half-million-dollar property. More than a little odd, don't you think?"

Violeta shifts uncomfortably and pushes a few strands of hair behind one ear. "You don't think something's happened to him, do you?"

There's a small knot of worry in her stomach, and yet Elizabeth shakes her head and makes herself say, "Probably a late night with one of his"—she makes a face—"numerous women, but I don't think anyone or anything would cause him to miss a walk-through. I'll call you after I'm done, okay?"

She's in the elevator, halfway down to street level, when she hears the opening notes from Billy Joel's "New York State of Mind" playing on her phone—Isabel's new ring-tone.

"I'm in the elevator, I may lose you," she tells her younger daughter.

"So, did you wear your new black-and-white Chanel beads?" Isabel asks.

"Why, was I supposed to?"

"For the brokers' lunch today at Gramercy Tavern."

"Oh, no. I wore them, but . . . you might have to go without me." Elizabeth explains Teddy's failure to show up at the walk-through, and there's shocked silence at the other end of the phone. The fact that Teddy does slightly more business than either Kate or Isabel has always bothered the girls a little bit, something they purposely play down because they know Elizabeth would only tell them, "He has far more experience than you do, girls, that's all."

"Anyway, the walk-through shouldn't take too long—come by after," Isabel says.

"Yes, but I have to reserve time just in case I need to go by Teddy's apartment."

"Why would you go there?"

"Because as of now, he's completely missing. Anyway, I'll call you later," Elizabeth says as she exits the elevator, and then the building. Phone still in hand, she hails a taxi. "96th and Fifth," she says to the driver, and then to Isabel, "I have to run—I need to make some calls before I get there."

"Bye, Mom."

As Elizabeth goes through her purse to find a pen, she comes across a photograph of her family: the three Chase women on the floor in their twenty-seven-foot living room on Park Avenue hysterically laughing, the girls opening their Christmas presents, Tom in the background cleaning up wrapping paper, Jonathan on a chair at his laptop not paying attention, their three Maltese—Lola, Roxy, and Dolly—blurry little balls of white fur. Cecilia, their housekeeper, who has been with the family since Jonathan was four, took the picture, Elizabeth remembers, and she had yelled, "Cecilia, don't get me in that, I look hideous!" But when they got the picture back from the store, Elizabeth loved something about it, something about how casual and happy her family looked, unposed, innocent. So she kept the photograph in her purse, of all she loved most.

Her phone rings—it's Laurel Rosenbluth, the seller of the town house at 61 East 93rd Street, wanting to know about the bidding. Laurel is always perfectly dressed in beautiful pantsuits, silk Hermès scarves, matching necklaces and bracelets she's collected over the years, and practical yet pretty pumps. Elizabeth has never seen her look anything less than perfect, her exquisite blue eyes beautifully shadowed and her cheeks filled with just the right amount of blush. Laurel Rosenbluth is a true lady. "They haven't budged yet," Elizabeth reports. "They both know they have to come up. I'm still waiting to hear from their brokers, Laurel. Hopefully by the time your tennis game is over, we'll have one far ahead of the other." As it is, the competing buyers have driven up the price of the town house over ask, something that happens less frequently now that the country has been besieged by a recession. Even the very rich feel that the ebbing financial tide in the country compels them to be a bit thrifty—and for those who are philanthropic, there's that need to give even more generously as a way to feel less guilty about continuing with their luxury lifestyle, like weekend trips to the Ocean Club in the Bahamas at over a thousand dollars a night.

Elizabeth considers herself and Tom lucky to have graciously weathered the economic downturn. Yes, the lower-priced apartments (under $2 million) have seen a noticeable dip in sales, but the properties at $3 million and above have managed to keep moving.

She starts to think about Teddy again—Teddy, who, with his palatial apartment in the Majestic on Central Park West, seems to silently run a very important part of Chase Residential's clientele: the show business players, who apparently like him because he is seemingly unimpressed by them, although Elizabeth knows he secretly loves their star wattage. He's very friendly with boldface names like André Balazs, Tom Brady, Gisele Bündchen, and Sarah Jessica Parker (the Chase girls' favorite). Teddy has also dated multiple models and has become obsessed with fashion—he always looks as though he has stepped off the pages of *GQ*. His annual earnings from commissions—over $1 million—allow him to dress incredibly well, and that is without the rather large inheritance he came into just after he turned forty.

But the most memorable trait of Teddy's is that he is truly a shameless womanizer. He goes through girlfriends like disposable pairs of contact lenses, and Elizabeth teases him about it all the time.

Vain womanizer that he is, however, Teddy is also a typical New York City workaholic. His days are divided between courting sellers for their listings, ingratiating himself with other brokers, and squiring clients around in his chauffeur-driven silver Mercedes. It's difficult for Elizabeth to admit this, but Teddy is the only broker in the office who's powerful enough in his own right to make her tiptoe around him. While she loves what he does for business, there is something slightly unnerving about it. Especially because things don't always add up about him: there's his knack for mysteriously winning over other brokers' listings and clients. Sure, selling New York real estate can be a cutthroat occupation, and yet Teddy always seems to be one step ahead of even the most artful bloodletters.

An hour and a half later, with the walk-through of the three-bedroom, two-and-a-half-bath, $3.45 million co-op finished, Elizabeth is sitting in another taxi, crossing Central Park, loving the daffodils and incandescent yellow forsythia. Teddy is still unreachable, and despite the fact that it's a lovely spring day, Elizabeth's feeling uneasy about the prospect of going to his apartment. She thinks for a moment that perhaps he has horrendous food poisoning, or a terrible hangover, but then why wouldn't he have made arrangements for someone to cover for him? As she sits in the park halfway between the east and west sides in bumper-to-bumper midday traffic, she thinks of how proximity to Central Park, even a sliver glimpse of its green from a 600-square-foot one-bedroom apartment, can vault a purchase price by six figures. A full view of the park, and the price rises by millions.

Elizabeth, meanwhile, loves her own apartment on Park Avenue and cares not a whit whether or not she has a Fifth Avenue address with a view. She much prefers Park Avenue—it's more convenient, less windy, and the islands in the center of it are her favorite part of the city—whether it's cherry blossoms and tulips in the spring, impatiens in the summer, or Christmas trees wrapped in lights in the winter. Central Park West, where she's headed now, has its own allure, especially to movie people who love the history and ceiling heights in the San Remo (and the fact that half the celebrities in New York have lived there), the magnificent rooms of the Beresford, where Jerry Seinfeld lives with his family, and, of course, the infamy of the Gothic Dakota, immortalized in *Rosemary's Baby* and of course as the home of John Lennon and Yoko Ono.

Her phone has continued to ring throughout the short ride, and she fields calls while nibbling a chocolate bar from the stash of candy in her purse, since she hasn't had even a moment for lunch. There's Kate, wanting to know how the walk-through went, Isabel, checking to see if there's any way at all Elizabeth could spare even a half hour for the brokers' lunch, because the ever mysterious writer Joey Arak from Curbed.com has arrived and may be interested in doing a piece on Chase Residential's $23.5 million palatial penthouse listing in the legendary Clocktower in Dumbo (the first time the Chases have ever ventured outside of Manhattan!). "Oh, too bad, wish I could, but I just can't," Elizabeth tells Isabel. Then there's the daily phone call from Bart Schneider, a very wealthy forty-year-old art dealer whose shrewdness for spotting talent has been praised by the *New York Times* but who insists that he needs to check in with Elizabeth every day, just to talk. He's considering several triple-mint apartments but can't decide which one he wants. Elizabeth isn't pushing him to make a decision, but the upshot is . . .

"Hi, Bart, I'm on my way through the park," she tells him.

"Oh, God, I'm just so stressed," he says.

"Why is that, Bart?" she dutifully asks, already anticipating his answer.

"I . . . you know, I need to say hi, that's all. It's just that I'm stressed about a lot of different things, and talking to you always seems to calm me down."

Is he the one person in New York City besides the Chases who doesn't have a therapist? she wonders.

As if reading her mind, Bart says, "You're better than a psychiatrist, Elizabeth. You're really good at calming me down. So tell me, how come *you're* so calm?"

Elizabeth laughs. "I'm not *that* calm, Bart."

"Well, you could've fooled *me*," Bart says. "Anyway, I know I'm obsessing about real estate when instead I should be paying attention to work, but do you think I'll ever be able to settle on one of those apartments? I mean, I just keep going back and forth, and back and forth, and—"

"Bart," Elizabeth says, "stop! You're going to drive yourself crazy, and me too. Why don't you come to the office one day next week, and we'll talk some more about the apartments. In the meantime, think about that duplex at 875 Fifth Avenue that I just know would be a fabulous home for you."

"You think so?"

"Yes, I do. But I really have to go, okay? One of my brokers is missing, and I'm on my way over to his apartment."

"Well, I won't keep you . . . ," Bart says reluctantly.

Elizabeth says, "Go online and look at the pictures of the apartments you're considering. And if there's any one of them you want to see again, just let me know."

"Okay, I guess I'll be in touch."

"Oh, I know you will," Elizabeth says, smiling to herself.

When the taxi pulls up in front of the Majestic, Elizabeth gets out, tilts her head back, and carefully counts up to the twenty-second floor, fixing her attention on Teddy Wingo's terrace, lined with cypress trees that he shuttles indoors and out depending on the season.

There's no sign of him.

She walks into the lobby. "How are you, Sergei?" she greets the doorman. "I'm here to see Teddy Wingo."

Sergei shakes his head. "Miss Elizabeth, I call him several times today. I have packages, dry cleaning. But he doesn't answer."

"How long have you been on duty?" Elizabeth asks him.

"Since seven this morning."

"Try him now, please, would you?"

Elizabeth waits while Sergei unsuccessfully buzzes Teddy on the intercom. Finally he puts down the phone and shakes his head again.

"Maybe he spent the evening out. Can you get hold of the night doorman?"

"He goes to sleep and turns his phone off," Sergei explains.

Elizabeth can't help but feel very concerned about Teddy. "I'm going to have to go up there," she tells Sergei.

"Do you have a key?" he asks her.

"No, but don't you?" she asks with a big smile.

The doorman stares at her for a moment, nods, and then begins looking up the key code in a worn grade-school notebook whose pages are filled with carefully written penciled entries. While he's busy, Elizabeth calls Kate. "Where are you?" she says when her daughter picks up.

"On my way back from a showing at 120 East End."

"I'm at the Majestic. Teddy's still missing. Can you come right over to his apartment now?"

"I had an appointment at two o'clock, but I'll make it later. It was just with Sol Howard to go over the board package for 45 East 72nd."

"Okay. I'm here waiting in the lobby."

"I'm in a taxi on Madison and, let's see, 70th Street, so I just need to get through the park," Kate says. "Let me call Sol and reschedule."

Elizabeth calls Isabel next, knowing she should still be at the brokers' lunch. Her daughter answers with lots of restaurant noise in the background. "I need you to meet me at the Majestic," Elizabeth says.

"What's up?"

"Well, Teddy's still missing. He hasn't answered the doorman all day. And he hasn't gone out. So I've got to go up to his apartment, and I don't want to do it by myself. I'd really like you and Kate to be here with me, okay?"

There's a brief pause. "Sure, Mom. I'll get there as soon as I can."

When Elizabeth gets off the phone, Sergei is holding out the key tentatively. The man's eyes are a startling deep blue, his face angular and very appealing in that Eastern European way. There is something about him that, oddly, reminds her of the actor Viggo Mortensen, who had been one of Teddy's clients for a second, though Teddy couldn't find anything to suit his reputedly eclectic taste.

"Well, I decided to wait for my daughters before going up," Elizabeth says.

"I will have to send somebody up with you," Sergei tells her. "One of the porters."

"Of course," Elizabeth says, and sits down in one of the faux Queen Anne chairs in the lobby. "Thank you so much again, Sergei." Her phone continues to ring. And ring: first it's Jolly, the groomer of her three Maltese, saying she can't come for their usual Monday-at-two appointment (can it be Tuesday instead?), then a client canceling an appointment for a showing because, after carefully looking at the floor plans on the Internet, he feels that at $19 million, it's absurd to have to walk past the maid's room to get to the kitchen. And here's the irritating Bart Schneider yet again, calling to apologize for using her as his shrink. And then, finally, Tom, reminding her that they have dinner reservations at Centrolire with friends who are thinking about putting their nine-room on the market. Elizabeth will talk on the phone a thousand times a day, if necessary, but she refuses to e-mail, a skill she has no interest in learning.

She takes and makes business calls until her daughters arrive within five minutes of each other, looking lovely and perfect—a summery Ralph Lauren skirt for Isabel, a gorgeously tailored short navy Escada dress with a ruffled bottom for Kate, who, she realizes, isn't her usual sparkly self. (There is no time to ask her why now, she will remember to later.) Elizabeth remains sitting while the girls gather around her. If Teddy is there and just not answering the door, she figures, the sight of the three of them will definitely tone down what she can already predict will be his exasperated response to her "meddling."

"You think he's passed out?" Kate says.

Elizabeth shrugs. "I honestly don't know," she says, and then allows herself to remember the awkward moment of her arrival at the walk-through, the heavy, stony silence, both Teddy's buyers and the seller's broker clearly frustrated and annoyed at Teddy's absence. "I'm so sorry," she'd said. "Teddy is stuck in the elevator of a new construction on Laight Street, literally—the elevator has been stuck for an hour—it's a disaster," Elizabeth said, making her entrance. Everyone laughed, and continued on the walk-through with her.

"Maybe Teddy's up there with a few of his girlfriends," Isabel says cynically now.

Elizabeth turns to Sergei. "Okay, we're ready. Do you want to get the porter?"

The porter turns out to be the super's son, a kid of around eighteen with a long, sensitive face and steel-rimmed glasses. He looks nervous, and he clutches the spare key as though it's a delicate instrument.

"Well, thank goodness you're both here," Elizabeth says. By the time they reach the twenty-second floor, she feels less tense and more resolved to delve into the mystery of why this broker of hers has gone missing.

As they exit the elevator, she notices a tall celadon vase that Teddy, after securing permission from the other resident on his floor, has positioned on a stand next to the elevator. She's remembering the day, several years ago, when he bought the vase. They picked it up at an antiques dealer near Union Square and went to lunch with a group of brokers at Il Cantinori, then attended an open house at a twenty-one-foot-wide town house on West 10th. And now a particular conversation she and Teddy had that day comes back to her. They'd been in a cab, crossing the park in the other direction, heading toward the east side. It was one of those gorgeous April days like today, and she remembers savoring the spectacular sight of the cherry blossoms (her favorite week of the year, when they bloom as a giant kiss to the city, she always thinks. Every year during that week, she and the girls would take a horse and buggy through the park, and afterward, skip in their pale pink crocodile Manolos—always their season debut in honor of the cherry blossoms—to the Plaza Hotel, where they drank tea and champagne and nibbled on scones at the Palm Court). On this day, as they went through the park, she and Teddy discussed their lunch.

"That lunch was great fun. I almost fell off my chair when you told the Lance Roberts story," Teddy said.

"I didn't think everybody would find it so funny," Elizabeth said. "You, especially."

Teddy looked bewildered. "Why, because I'm the one who punched Roberts?"

"I think 'decked' is the word here."

"Well, that jerk deserved it."

"I know he deserved it," Elizabeth said.

Teddy fell curiously quiet for a moment. "Well," he said at last, "I needed to pull him off that buyer. I was afraid Roberts was going to strangle him."

"Yes, you had to," Elizabeth said. "There was no other choice."

Again there was a strange silence, and at last Teddy said, "But there was something else . . ." His voice trailed off.

"What?" Elizabeth pressed him.

Teddy grimaced, and his momentary lopsided expression lent a goofiness to his handsome face. He said, "I also didn't like the way Lance Roberts was looking at you."

"Oh, come *on*!" Elizabeth said. "Don't be ridiculous."

"He was ogling you."

Flattery was nice, no doubt about it, but she distrusted it. "Oh, please, Teddy."

"You're a beautiful woman," he said.

There was an uncomfortable silence, and Elizabeth thought to herself that Teddy couldn't possibly be making a pass at her. The idea of it made her slightly uneasy, though she never minded a little flirting.

"A lot of guys act like animals. I don't know why women put up with it," he said.

"It's the way some men are, Teddy," Elizabeth said pointedly. "*You* of all people should know that."

He nodded but apparently chose to ignore her inference. "The stories that some of the women I've dated have told me about what some of these guys do . . ."

"Come on, Teddy, you've screwed plenty of women, both literally and emotionally," Elizabeth reminded him, starting to feel annoyed at his blindness to his own failings.

"Yeah, I've *left* women, but that doesn't mean I treated them badly."

"Oh, pleeease," she said. "Leaving them *is* treating them badly."

"Well," he said, and had to pause. "I just keep getting to the same point with every woman I date, and . . . I just can't go any further. Whether or not you believe it, I do treat them incredibly well. At least in the beginning. I buy them gifts, I take them to the opera, the theater, out to dinner, and it all seems so promising . . . and then something in me, well . . . it just freezes."

Oh, Teddy, you are so screwed up, Elizabeth wanted to say, but obviously she could not. They were passing the northern extremity of the Metropolitan Museum, and the glass enclosure of the Temple of Dendur and its reminder of thousands of years of antiquity. She watched Teddy gazing at the temple, his face slack and forlorn. "I still love Vanessa," he admitted at last. "And it isn't because she was my wife and is the mother of my kids. I just still *love* her and . . . what I did, it was the only time in my life I behaved really badly. And it was the only time in my life when behaving well really counted."

Elizabeth looked down at the tips of her Manolos and said absolutely nothing, knowing that Teddy was probably well aware that she'd always sympathized with the ex-wife he'd been unfaithful to.

She turns now to the super's son, who suddenly strikes her as barely pubescent, and hears herself say, "Do me a favor, please, and just give me the key. And do you mind leaving us?" The boy obeys. She waits until she sees the elevator doors opening and engulfing him, and as soon as they close, she turns to Isabel and Kate. "Are we ready?"

"Not really," Isabel says. "To tell you the truth, I'd rather be at Bergdorf's."

This provokes nervous laughter from her sister and her mother. "Let's just get this over with, girls," Elizabeth says.

They approach Teddy's door, and she knocks crisply. Then remembers there's a buzzer, and presses that, too.

There's no answer. She buzzes again. But then she hears something inside, almost like . . . she can't quite place it, it's like a rattling of bamboo poles, but that's not it, not exactly. Turning to her daughters, Elizabeth says, "You hear that sound?"

"Yeah," Kate says. "Weird."

And then without really knowing she's doing it, Elizabeth puts the key in the door. Before opening it to Teddy's perfectly appointed apartment, the gilt frames of the paintings, the porcelain objects, the walls covered in honey-colored rice wallpaper, much of the furniture brightly painted in an offbeat Venetian style, she imagines Teddy himself lying on his living room sofa and a matrix of deep red meandering lines staining the sofa. Soaked in his blood, the sofa itself would look like a veiny network of the inside of a body. Teddy's eyes would be fully open, lighter and more opaque than their usual deep blue, and they'd have a faraway glint of some radically different place.

Oh, come on, she tells herself, *don't let your imagination run wild like that.*

At last she opens the door. She calls out to him. She looks at the sofa, relieved to see that he's not lying on it. Without a further word, the Chases check the apartment for signs of its owner. The rooms are spotlessly clean and look as though no one has been there for a while.

They ride the elevator down to the lobby without saying a word. Then, almost as if he knows they've just left his apartment, Teddy calls Elizabeth's cell as she and her daughters are walking out of the building.

"Where have you been?" Elizabeth practically yells.

There's a short silence. "Oh, God," is all Teddy says.

"Are you drunk?"

"No, just . . . incredibly sleepy."

Elizabeth makes eye contact with Kate and Isabel. "Teddy, where are you? You missed your walk-through and have been out of it for a day."

He groans. "I know."

"I had to go into your apartment—I'm so sorry. But I was quite panicked."

"Thank you, Elizabeth. I'm . . . I was . . . sleeping."

"What do you mean, you were sleeping?"

"Well . . . actually, I'm not home. I mean, I'm in a cab on my way home."

"I know you're not home, Teddy. The girls and I just came looking for you at your apartment."

"Are you serious?" Teddy says. "You went to my apartment? I'm so—"

"Can you please just tell me what's going on?"

He briefly explains that last night he'd gone to the apartment of a woman he'd been dating—gone there with the sole purpose of breaking up with her. He'd had a drink, and the next thing he knew, he was waking up at one in the afternoon. Completely alone.

"That's very weird. Do you think she might have drugged you?" Elizabeth says.

"Slipped me one of those blackout drugs, you mean? I can't say for sure, but I think it's very possible. I'm completely confused. I've never slept like that before."

"Well, I'd suggest you get yourself together and come to the office. Are you going to press charges against her?"

"I'm feeling okay. I'm not going to press any charges," Teddy says. "I can't take the chance that something like this could get into the press." He's referring to his high-profile life, which has been the subject of articles in all the major New York papers. "I just need to get home, take a shower, and change my clothes," he continues. "I'll see you soon, Elizabeth. And again, I'm really sorry. And thank you for handling the walk-through."

"Unbelievable!" Elizabeth exclaims to Kate and Isabel when she gets off the phone.

"He thinks he was drugged?" Isabel says.

"Well, maybe he needs to use better judgment about the kinds of women he sleeps with," Elizabeth says.

"Totally!" both of her daughters say in unison.

Elizabeth hears the phone ringing as she's entering her own apartment. "Can you get that?" she yells to Tom. Her three treasured Maltese are at the door, jumping up on her and demanding attention. She hears Tom picking up the phone and listens to see who it is.

"She just walked in. Can you give her a minute?" she hears him saying.

"Who is it, Tom?"

"Somebody from Friends of Finn calling about the Humane Society gala at the Pierre," he says, referring to the animal protection organization to which the whole family is very committed.

"Tell them I'll call back in ten minutes."

Elizabeth picks up Roxy, the most frantic of her Maltese, and, followed closely by the others, carries her just a few yards down the long hallway lined with nineteenth-century paintings of spaniels and hunting dogs to the library with its enormous flat-screen TV, where the whole family likes to gather to watch old movies together. The DVD of *Bringing Up Baby*—the romantic comedy that Elizabeth and Tom and the girls are planning to watch later that night—is already in the player. A colorful framed poster for the 1938 movie hangs on the wall in the library; it shows the cartoon figures of Katharine Hepburn and Cary Grant hovering over a leopard seated upright in a high chair. Elizabeth exhales an exhausted breath, sits down in her favorite buttery leather club chair, and kisses Roxy. Lola and Dolly paw her frantically, and she picks them up.

Tom comes into the room with a wary look on his face, his finely brushed silver hair lustrous, his face tanned from their previous weekend in Boca Raton, where they recently purchased a home at One Thousand Ocean from Jamie Telchin, head of the ownership group behind the luxury new condominiums adjacent to the Boca Beach Club. The Chases have been going to Boca Raton since Kate was in the eighth grade, and every time their car from the airport pulled up the long winding driveway to the sprawling pink Cloisters of the Boca Raton Hotel and Resort, their hearts fluttered. Years later, much to their delight, a condo was built at the very tip of the beach, nestled in the corner of the ocean and the Intracoastal Waterway, where the Chase family sat to sun themselves for fifteen years. They bought residence 307 (because both three and seven were lucky numbers for them), a four-bedroom that hangs over the ocean like an awning, with a private infinity pool and outdoor kitchen on the terrace and a two-car private garage.

Tom's khaki pants and bone-white, button-down oxford shirt show off his tan now—he looks just like the young Robert Evans, Elizabeth thinks, particularly at this moment. "So what's going on with Teddy?" he asks her.

"You won't believe it. He was drugged . . . apparently by one of his girlfriends he'd just broken up with."

"I don't believe it. It sounds too ridiculous," Tom says.

"I actually think he's telling the truth, Tom. I don't think he took drugs, I think something happened. Come on, you know how Teddy is. He'd never jeopardize something as important as a walk-through before a closing."

"I guess you're right," Tom agrees. "He certainly seems to have an obsession with money."

Elizabeth stands up, holding Roxy, puts the other two down, and lets the dog rest her head on her shoulder. "I've got to call Friends of Finn back."

"They said something about the gala."

"I know. They want me to find out if the girls would be interested in being on the committee," Elizabeth says, and then, with another sigh, hands Roxy over to Tom so that she can see about getting the dogs' dinner ready.

CHAPTER**FOUR**

Kate

Have It All

Candela white-glove building, Park Avenue 90s, 8 rooms, two bedrooms plus library, 3-and-a-half baths, grand entrance gallery, huge chef's EIK, elegant finishes throughout. $6.5 million.

It's the one-week anniversary of her breakup with Scott, and the curtain has just fallen on the American Ballet Theatre's production of *The Sleeping Beauty* at Lincoln Center. Kate claps vigorously as Princess Aurora and Prince Désiré take their well-deserved bows, but already she is dreading the dinner to follow at Shun Lee West. Not that she doesn't like Chinese food—she loves it, in fact, especially Shun Lee's wonton soup (no one makes it like they do anymore), their crispy shredded beef, their prawns with garlic and scallions, a small portion of which will ornament her plate an hour from now as her date, Charlie Marcus, sits beside her on a leather banquette and struggles to use his chopsticks correctly.

Charlie places his small, clammy hand over hers for an instant now just before the two of them rise from their very pricey orchestra seats and move toward the aisle and then to the exit of the auditorium. Kate doesn't know what she was thinking when, in a moment of weakness (and perhaps desperation), she agreed to go on a date with Charlie—a neighbor whom she kept running into when she went to pick up her morning coffee at Juliano's until finally he summoned the courage to ask her out. Sorry to say, Charlie Marcus is, frankly, what she and Isabel like to refer to as "drippy." And drippy, in this case, means very decent looks (except for his thinning hair) but no sparkle, no smile, and the unfortunate habit of chattering incessantly about pretentious trivia that makes Kate just glaze over.

"So," Charlie is saying a little while later as the maître d' at Shun Lee West summons a waiter to seat them, "did you know that Tchaikovsky first staged *The Sleeping Beauty* as a tribute to France's Louis the Fourteenth?" He pronounces this "Loo-iss" rather than "Loo-ee," Kate notes with annoyance, and she shakes her head at him. Isn't there anything he can do right? Apparently not—in a few minutes, when their dumplings in hot sauce arrive, he clenches his chopsticks in his fist like a weapon. Never mind that this Charlie Marcus has a B.A. from Dartmouth and a law degree from Harvard, he's a drip, plain and simple. Kate gazes longingly at her phone next to her place setting, dying to call Isabel to tell her about this awful date of hers, and willing her phone to ring with some make-believe emergency she must tend to. Looking at Charlie Marcus, his thin dark hair barely concealing his scalp, his girlish hands splitting a dumpling apart, scooping out the pork filling, and pushing it to the rim of his plate, well, she misses Scott so keenly at this moment, she can't quite believe how much it hurts. *Oh, Scott.*

What a jerk he's been! She knows the best thing she can possibly do is turn her thoughts elsewhere, in this case to the banal droning of Charlie Marcus.

"Loo-iss the Fourteenth's reign began in 1643, when he was just four years old, and lasted seventy-two years, the longest reign, I believe, of any monarch. Any *European* monarch," he corrects himself. "And he was succeeded at his death by his great-grandson, who was five years old at the time. Isn't that incredible?" Charlie says, helping himself to another dumpling.

"Fascinating," Kate agrees. From a large table composed of a half dozen tables-for-two pushed together, a roar of laughter rises, and a crowd of men her age in sport coats and ties raise their glasses to toast someone named Kelly.

It occurs to her that maybe if she weren't so in love with Scott, she might be able to give Charlie a chance; he is, after all, an extremely smart, accomplished young man, and yes, she concedes, nice-looking.

"Did I mention that when I was in law school, I took an adult ed cooking class where I learned how to debone a chicken?" he says. "First you remove the heart, liver, and neck, and then . . ."

Kate shudders. She wants to thank Charlie Marcus for the ballet, for the dumplings in hot sauce, then tell him she has a horrific headache and must get home immediately. But her mother and father have brought her up to treat people with decency, to always show that you have a good heart. And so, instead, she chokes back a gag, asks Charlie to stop talking about a dead chicken, and then pretends to listen carefully as he goes on and on and on about another cooking class he took, this one called "The Possibilities of Polenta."

Later, before dessert arrives, she goes to the ladies' room and calls Isabel, who, she knows, is spending the night at Michael's. Kate's so tempted to tell her sister where she is and why—that Scott broke up with her last week and that she can't wait for this horrible date to be over. But as her sister's phone is ringing, Kate realizes she can't bear to hear Isabel's sigh, and then for her to say that Scott is unbelievably immature, and totally undependable, and that he will continue to disappoint Kate and break her heart. And so Kate says, when she hears Isabel's lively voice on the other end, that she has another call and will call her later.

Under the awning in front of her building, Charlie Marcus tries to put his tongue into her mouth; failing that, he tries her ear. "Please, don't!" Kate tells him, pushing him away gently. She sweetens her voice. "Thank you so much for tonight," she says, "but I'm just not ready for that."

And then she flees, past the doorman and into the elevator, wiping her ear with her fingertip and fighting back the urge, growing ever stronger, to call or e-mail Scott.

On her way into her bedroom, she stops to get a sour apple lollipop from the apothecary jar. Then she grabs a second. Candy is always a temporary antidote to an unfortunate situation, in this instance, an exceptionally disappointing date. She's shocked that Charlie Marcus read her so wrong. The drip actually tried to kiss her—did he really think she'd given him any sign at all that she'd kiss him back? Oh, it was all so awful, she thinks.

Lounging on a mound of pillows in her bed, she watches an episode of *Glee* on TIVO; she loves those scenes with sweet Mr. Schuester and the divinely nasty Sue Sylvester. Watching them now, she remembers Matthew Morrison, the actor who plays Mr. Schue, singing "Younger Than Springtime" in *South Pacific*, a terrific production that she and her family saw at Lincoln Center several years ago. Her parents had taken her and her brother and sister to the theater for as long as she can remember, and, too, as children and teenagers they were treated to movies at the Paris Theater and under the stars at Bryant Park on Mondays in the summer, and to cabaret shows at the Carlyle and the Regency, where they'd seen all the greats, like Bobby Short, Eartha Kitt, and most recently Steve Tyrell. So many memories of her family, all five of them together. She doesn't think anyone in the family would argue with her if she were to say that those were the best days of their lives, days like no other, Kate thinks.

■ ■ ■

Allison Silverman-Cole is one of Kate's favorite clients, a speech pathologist with a successful solo practice, a wealthy girl lovely as could be, and a pleasure to do business with, except for one little issue—she's highly allergic to avocados and a host of other things, including dust and paint. Kate and Allison had playdates together as far back as the 1980s, and though Allison attended Fieldston while Kate was at Horace Mann, they traveled in the same social circles all through high school, and never lost touch. Kate even remembers Allison's fifth birthday party, when a clown and a scary-looking mime were hired to entertain the tiny guests; the mime so terrified Kate with his powdered white face and bloodred lips that her father had to be summoned to bring her home in the middle of the party. To this day, mimes and clowns still give her the shudders.

Just before she calls Allison to confirm their appointment to attend an open house at 1220 Park, Kate phones the listing broker from Stribling to ask a very important question. "Madylin?" she says into her cell as she hops into a cab. "Just checking to make sure the seller didn't make a salad earlier in the day at the apartment. But if she did, do you happen to know if she sliced up an avocado in it?"

"Is this a joke?" Madylin says. "What kind of a question is that?"

"It sounds ridiculous, but my client has severe food allergies," Kate says. "An avocado could send her into anaphylactic shock."

Madylin sighs. "Is this that client who's allergic to every damn thing under the sun? Like I don't have enough to worry about without having to know whether my client sliced up an avocado. And BTW, there's going to be a nice catered lunch from Yura at the open house, no salad, no avocados, just sandwiches. So give me a break, Kate, will you?"

"Can you please call the seller? I'd really appreciate it. She's seriously allergic."

Accompanying Allison Silverman-Cole to the open house is a friend of hers, a grim-looking woman in a tennis dress and sneakers, an iced hazelnut coffee from Dunkin' Donuts in a see-through plastic cup in her hand. Allison herself is wearing a jacket and an unbecoming pair of skin-tight jeggings (the hybrid jean and legging that started as a trend with the tween market and moved its way up) that cruelly emphasize her hips; oddly, a pale blue paper surgical mask is covering her mouth. She has gotten stranger as the years have passed, Kate thinks.

"Hiii!" Kate says, and gives Allison an air kiss, knowing how she feels about germs. "Everything okay?" She gestures toward the surgical mask, and notes that Allison's friend is noisily sipping her coffee from a straw, barely giving Kate herself a glance.

"Just a precaution," Allison says from behind her mask.

"I know you told me there haven't been any avocados sliced up here in the past few hours, but just in case."

"Of course," Kate says. "Oh, hi, I'm Kate," she says to Allison's friend.

"Jessica Prettyman," the woman says. She takes one final, extra-loud sip of her coffee and hands the cup to Allison. "Is there a bathroom here I can use?"

It's always a little awkward when a client needs to use a bathroom; why couldn't Jessica Prettyman, who isn't even a client, have used the restroom at Dunkin' Donuts instead? The three women have walked from the entrance gallery into the living room now, with its soaring ceiling and lovely view of the Central Park Reservoir—Kate's favorite view in all of the city. And from another window that offers a southern view, you can see all the way down to the Chrysler Building. Pointing this out to Allison and Jessica, and then leaving them behind for a minute or two, Kate makes her way into the kitchen, where brokers from other firms—ten people, mostly women—are clustered around a table loaded with pinwheel sandwiches and bottles of Diet Coke, seltzer, and club soda, courtesy (coincidentally, because it was not a Chase Residential listing) of the Chase dream team from MetLife mortgage bankers Mark Wenitzky, Bryan Siegel, and Andrew Texeira, whom the girls call Sexy Texy, thanks to a hot fling he had with their friend Robin Dolch in college at the University of Virginia. (A few years later, Andrew did Robin's mortgage for an apartment she bought through Kate and Isabel after two years of searching for one with hallways. Robin had lived in postwar rentals with popcorn ceilings year after year while waiting for a prewar with just the right number of hallways. According to Robin, a good hallway separating the entrance from the living room, the living room from the bedrooms, was all that mattered. The girls had lovingly nicknamed her "The Girl Who Had to Have Hallways.") In a small room off to the side, Kate catches a glimpse of a dark-haired, uniformed housekeeper sitting on a cot and watching *The Price Is Right* on a small TV set positioned on a ladder-back chair.

Seeing Kate peeking in, the woman says, "Hi there" with a lovely Jamaican lilt, and smiles sweetly.

"Hi. Is there a bathroom my client can use, by any chance?" Kate asks. She'd rather ask the housekeeper than the brokers; it seems less embarrassing, she supposes.

"Bathroom in the library," the housekeeper says, smiling, and looks back at the TV. There's a cereal-size glass bowl of SpaghettiOs in her lap.

As they tour the apartment a few minutes later, Kate pointing out the magnificent living room, the oversize windows, the beautiful marble spa baths, the chef's eat-in kitchen, she senses an undercurrent of dissatisfaction, most of it coming from Jessica Prettyman, who just can't keep her big mouth shut. Why Jessica Prettyman is so concerned with whether or not Allison might prefer a regular stove to a cooktop, or whether the whirlpool in the master bath is something Allison and her husband—a successful Broadway producer who's worked with Julie Taymor and Mel Brooks—will ever make good use of is beyond Kate.

Kate continues, "The building was designed by Rosario Candela—who's considered one of America's most important architects—and that makes it terrific for resale; he's one of a small handful of architects who is always listed alongside an apartment as a 'merit.' And from how many prewars on the Upper East Side can you see the Chrysler Building? The views are gorgeous."

The grim look on Jessica's face turns grimmer. "Gorgeous? Well, not if you're an acrophobe, like I am."

"Excuse me?" Kate says.

"I suffer from mild to moderate acrophobia," Jessica says. "Fear of heights?"

"That's why she came with me today," Allison explains. "To test herself, to see if she could come all the way up to the sixteenth floor without getting nauseated and dizzy."

Suddenly, Kate wonders, could Allison—straitlaced, hypochondriac Allison Silverman-Cole—be having a wild affair with Jessica Prettyman?

Nodding her head, Jessica says, "Sometimes it gets so bad that it's even too scary for me to stand on a chair to change a lightbulb."

"Poor thing," murmurs Allison. Or at least Kate *thinks* that's what she said; it's a little hard to understand her through her surgical mask.

"What I do is, I take a deep breath to slow my heart rate, then climb down from the chair and run for my bottle of Xanax," Jessica says.

It's never ideal when a client brings friends to look at an

apartment; generally, their presence can only lead to trouble. Too many opinions, too many complaints, a lot of it coming from, she often suspects, jealous friends who would kill for the apartments Kate's clients can afford. She wishes Jessica Prettyman would get back to her tennis game and leave Allison to make up her own mind.

"Xanax," Jessica repeats, "is the best of the benzodiazepines. Calms you in an instant and doesn't leave a hangover."

Just then Kate's cell rings, and Kate excuses herself for an instant, her face burning as she sees who's calling. "Scott," she says in a whispery voice, her heart racing.

"Kate," he says slowly, and then pauses.

"Sorry, I can't talk now, I am in the middle of a showing," she tells him reluctantly, much as she might want to speak to him. And so she hangs up without another word and wills herself to concentrate, instead, on Allison.

Just hearing the sound of Scott's voice for that single moment has her feeling completely shaky, but she pulls herself together and makes her way back to Allison, who's back in the living room without Jessica Prettyman. Oh, that ridiculous surgical mask, Kate thinks, hoping that if Allison ever gets to a co-op board meeting, the mask will be left at home!

"Where's your friend Jessica?" she asks.

"Oh, in one of the bathrooms, throwing up," Allison says. "The view wasn't good for her acrophobia—a wave of nausea came over her and she ran . . ."

Oh dear, Kate thinks, to have brought a client with a

friend who is throwing up in the middle of an open house—humiliating! "Oh, no, maybe she should leave?" Kate says, and then, when Allison ignores her, "So what do you think?"

"I feel so bad for her," Allison says. "It's crippling, this acrophobia of hers."

"I know," says Kate, "But you're not an acrophobic, thankfully, and you always said you wanted a view like this."

"Jessica thinks—"

Kate just has to interrupt her. "Is Jessica living here with you?" she teases, then says, "It's what you and Chip think. Why don't you bring him to see it?"

Looking stricken, Allison doesn't turn around to face Kate; instead, she continues to stare through the window. "Because I'm planning on leaving him," she says, and whisks the surgical mask from her face. "He's been a total prick, and I guarantee you he's going to be even more of a prick when my attorney gets through with him."

Kate is shocked; she had no idea that their three-year marriage was in trouble. "Oh no, what happened?" she says. "You seemed so happy." You just never know, she thinks to herself.

Allison sighs. "I was on the Internet a few weeks ago, reading my e-mail, and then I had to check something about our American Express bill, so I needed to take a quick look at Chip's e-mail. I signed on to his screen name, and what I found queued up there in his new mail was something with the subject line 'Hey Babe'—followed by three exclamation points. I don't know, I never open his e-mails, ever, but this time I just had to. And there it was, right there on the screen—it was as obvious as could be that there was something going on between Chip and this person named, get this, Honey Baer."

"Her last name was B-E-A-R? Are you serious? With a first name Honey? Is she a porn star?" Kate says. "That can't be her real name."

"Oh, but it is," Allison says. "B-A-E-R. Chip was at work, but I called him anyway, this just couldn't wait till he came home. When I confronted him about the e-mail, he had the *nerve* to start yelling about the violation of his privacy. I mean, is he kidding me? How outrageous is that? Then he denied the whole thing, but I wore him down until he finally confessed. He just said that he and this Honey, who works in his office in human resources, had unexpectedly fallen into something and that he was sorry, but he and I were done . . ." Allison says, her voice choking up a little.

Something in the hopeless romantic in Kate makes her very upset about poor Allison and this Honey Baer. She remembers Allison and Chip's wedding in the New York Botanical Garden, the two of them married by a very talkative rabbi and a nervous-looking priest, Allison in cream satin Vera Wang, the six bridesmaids in ice-blue cocktail dresses, the reception in the Garden Terrace Room with its lovely hand-painted murals, Kate already fantasizing—three years ago—about a wedding of her own, though she and Scott had been having their usual problems at the time. *Scott Scott Scott.*

Kate hears herself sigh. "I'm so sorry," she says. "You must want to kill Chip."

Allison's eyes harden. "I want to *screw* him," she confides. "Leave him with nothing. And then live happily ever after in an apartment just like this one."

Jessica Prettyman is coming toward them now, wiping her mouth with the back of her hand. "Anybody have any breath mints?" she asks. "I'm still not feeling too great, but I have to say the marble in the master bath is gorgeous."

"It is beautiful," Kate says, again, thinking, is Jessica Prettyman Allison Silverman-Cole's rebound?

"Even so, I could *never* live here," Jessica says. "Not unless I could figure out a way to overcome my acrophobia."

"But I *don't* have to overcome acrophobia, Jessica," Allison says. "I love it here. Let's see what happens." She hugs Kate and says good-bye, promising to let her know if and when she's ready to return for a second look.

Kate stands out in front of 1220 Park now, looking around for a cab, breathing into her cell, her heart racing, as she returns Scott's call. "You called?" she says, trying to sound no-nonsense and businesslike. *Oh, how I've missed the sound of your voice these past eight days,* is what she'd like to say. *That deep hoarse voice of yours.*

"How are *you* doing?" Scott says.

"Good, very busy . . ." And that's about all he's going to get from her today. There's a bit of frost in her voice, and she hopes he hears it. Cool as a cuke, she hears her mom telling her. "Okay, anything else? I have to run," she says.

"I," Scott begins, "I, well, no, not really. Just checking in to see if everything's, you know . . . okay."

She feels herself collapse with disappointment; she had so hoped he would break down and tell her how much he misses her and what a mistake he made. She contemplates hanging up on him, cutting him off this instant now that she knows he's calling for a reason that has nothing much, really, to do with her and her broken heart. "I actually went on a date last week," she says instead.

"Uh-huh, okay . . ."

"Yeah, he's very smart, really nice, and he graduated from Harvard Law a couple of years ago," she says, wanting, foolishly, she knows, to hurt Scott just a little. "And he's a balletomane and an amazing chef."

"Really? Well, I know what a chef is, but what the fuck is a balletomane?"

"A devotee of the ballet," Kate says, laughing. "But are you sure you know what a chef is?" she teases him. Oh, what is she doing? Flirting with him? She can't control herself!

"Whatever," Scott says. "Sounds like this date of yours went really well." It seems he's about to say something further, but there's only silence.

"Really well," Kate lies. A woman with a toddler in a stroller stops at the awning in front of 1220 Park. She lifts the little boy, a platinum blond, out of the stroller, and the moment she sets him down on the pavement, he makes a mad dash down the block. "Cooper Kleier!" the woman yells, dropping her diaper bag and running after him. "Cooper—

freeze!" Kate sees the adorable little boy mimic "freeze" and then keep running. He reminds her of her brother Jonathan at that age.

Watching the way the little boy shrieks with glee, racing down Park Avenue, Kate finds herself imagining her own life—who knows how far into the future—with Scott and a child, theirs with dark hair and Scott's dimples. It's what she wants for herself, she knows, smiling at the blond baby boy now as he waves good-bye to her and disappears into 1220 with his mother. Kate's thirtieth birthday is only months away; just contemplating this undeniable fact makes her a little anxious. She thinks of her friends, and how, one by one, they've gotten engaged and married over the past few years, all those weddings she's gone to, not to mention engagement parties, bridal showers, and nearly a dozen bachelorette parties, many of them held at the luxurious Mayflower Inn and Spa in Washington, Connecticut, where the owner actually knows her by name because she's been there so often. (And where Kate and her mother and sister had a magical girls' weekend with Carolyn Klemm, the biggest broker in Connecticut, who famously told them over their margaritas on the rocks when they lamented that their cells and BlackBerries had no service that "sometimes you just have to write yourself out of the script.") The husbands of these friends of hers are nice enough, she thinks—young men working in banking, in finance, in their fathers' marketing firms, men so different from Scott and his friends, almost all of them moving from one unconventional job to the next, from one girlfriend to the next, none of them even considering the possibility of settling down in any way at all. But there's not one of those husbands she would take—no matter the size of his bank account or apartment—over Scott, working now at a new magazine called *Texture*, making no money, working insane hours laboring over articles about music, design, and technology—copyediting and proofreading through the night to meet deadlines. . . . But how long can she wait for him? Who's going to get him to see that there might actually be something desirable about living well, as his parents do, in a grown-up home and eating at proper restaurants? Maybe when he turns thirty-five he will grow up and realize that he needs Kate in his life, that she can make it even better. But who could wait three years? Oh, how much and how deeply she could love him, if only he would let her!

"So, Kate," he's saying now, "gotta go, okay? Got a big deadline coming up. I'm just . . . just glad you're okay, going out on dates with, um, balletomanes, and enjoying yourself."

"You're such an idiot, Scott," she hears herself say.

"What?"

"I've got a client waiting for me," Kate says, lying to Scott for the second time today, as she steps into the street to flag down a cab. "You've gotta go, I've gotta go."

"Did you just call me an idiot?"

Kate is silent.

"Can you at least explain why?"

"I'm sure you can figure that out for yourself," Kate says.

"Listen, I don't understand why you're mad all of a sudden."

"Oh, you're a bright guy, Scott," Kate says, and hangs up, though what she'd really like to do, of course, is stay on forever, or at least long enough just to hear him say, "I was wrong. I love you."

When she gets back to her office in midtown, Kate finds Lorelei Lyne sitting beside her desk, about to light up a cigarette and looking, Kate thinks, pretty horrific; there are smudges of mascara under her pink-rimmed eyes, and her bra strap is visible, peeking out from her sleeveless, see-through shirt.

"What's wrong?" Kate says immediately, and then whispers, "Are you crazy? You can't smoke in here, it's not the 1990s!" Lorelei, she thinks, is clearly unraveling.

"Oh, for God's sake, you'd think I was a crack addict or something!" Lorelei says, and wipes what looks like a tear from her badly Botoxed eye, arched up in a semipermanent triangle of surprise. "It's only a damn cigarette!"

Reaching toward her, Kate takes the Marlboro from between Lorelei's twitchy fingers and drops it into the wastepaper basket under her desk.

"I did it," Lorelei whispers. "And God, it turned out really, really bad."

Getting up now, Kate rushes to close the door to her office. "Don't tell me," she says. "How could you be such an *idiot*? Oh, Lorelei, what were you thinking?"

"I know, I know, I can't believe I did it, either," Lorelei

says, running her fingers through her brittle black hair. "He was in St. Barts for a week, and then last night he called and told me to meet him at his office so he could show me some stuff about his financials. I knew what that meant, but I went, all gussied up and all, and I just kept thinking, while I was down there on my knees last night looking out his windows with the lights of the whole city in front of me, that this wasn't just anyone, this was Rodney Greenstein, one of the most powerful men in the entire city. And somehow at that moment, I felt better about having his big disgusting dick in my mouth. Almost excited . . . Oh, Kate, I'm so ashamed." She pauses, then continues, tears now leaking from her heavily mascaraed eyes. "Today I got an e-mail from one of his assistants—not from him, but from his third assistant!" she says, outraged. "She thanked me for my help, and said that he'd decided not to buy the apartment after all." Sobbing, Lorelei says, "Give me back my cigarette, will you please, Kate. Look at me!"

"Oh, God, Lorelei," Kate says.

"Oh, it was that damn commission, the biggest I'll ever see, singing to me like one of those Greek sirens. How could I walk away from that?" Lorelei says.

Without a word, Kate leans over her and slides Lorelei's errant bra strap back under her shirt. "Let's not share this with anyone," Kate says.

"Not even with your mom or Isabel?"

Kate puts the tips of her thumb and index finger together and makes a gesture as if zipping her mouth shut.

"Well, of course Mom and Isabel," she says. "But no one else."

At that moment, Teddy Wingo glides into the office dressed in an exquisite tan Prada suit and a robin's-egg-blue tie with pale pink elephants, one of the many in his delicious parade of Easter-egg-colored Hermès ties, his thick, longish dirty blond hair gleaming. As is customary, he pokes his head into Kate's office and gives the two brokers a big, smiling hello. Kate thinks to herself at that moment how attractive he is, but in a Jeff Bridges in *Jagged Edge* sort of way. Lorelei glances at him. "I'm mortified," she murmurs.

You should be, Kate thinks, and then, Poor Lorelei.

"What's going on?" Teddy looks from one woman to the other. There's a trace of sympathy in his voice. "Are you okay?"

"Oh, nothing much going on," Kate manages to say. "Just a really impossible client."

"Looks more like boys behaving badly again!" he says, an amused smile on his face.

"You'd know all about that, wouldn't you?" Lorelei says, standing up straight, sticking her cleavage out.

Oh, God, Kate thinks, is she flirting with Teddy?

Ignoring her, Teddy turns to Kate and says, "Are you showing my listing tomorrow in the Apthorp?"

"Yes—at two thirty."

Teddy consults his BlackBerry. "Okay, perfect, I just scheduled a three forty-five." He squints at Kate. "So this client of yours is that English mystery writer?"

"Yes, looking for a pied-à-terre."

"Well, tell him that the apartment is right down the hall from where Joseph Heller used to live. . . . Anyway—I've got a mound of paperwork. I'm off, girls," he says, continuing along to his office. "Looking forward to tomorrow, Kate." And Teddy winks, smiles a big, big smile, and saunters out of her office.

A month from now, when Rodney Greenstein buys a co-op from another broker, he will come crawling back to Elizabeth and Chase Residential, knowing he'll never get past the board without her help, and offering her $200,000 if she'll assist him with his board package for the deal he excluded her from. When he is finished begging her, Elizabeth will tell him "go fuck yourself" and hang up the phone. Two months later, Rodney Greenstein will indeed be turned down by the board. And that, Elizabeth will tell Lorelei, is Rodney Greenstein's happy ending.

CHAPTER FIVE

Isabel

Magnificent Limestone Town House

80s East off Fifth, 25-foot-wide 6-story single-family town house; 6 bedrooms, 7 baths, beautifully landscaped 50-foot garden with terraces off master suite. Must see. $22.5 million.

At ten o'clock the following Friday morning, Isabel leans back in the limo idling in front of Barney's on Madison Avenue. Her new client, Delphine Homan von Herenberg, has instructed the driver to wait for what sounds to Isabel something like "a teenzy, tinzy leetle minute" while she rushes inside to retrieve some expensive bauble or other from a saleswoman who she swears is waiting just inside the luxury department store's front doors. Isabel can't quite place Delphine's accent, which seems to hover somewhere between French, German, and, at certain moments, Italian. But that makes sense, since Isabel has been told that her client is part German, part French, and spent considerable time in Rome when she was growing up. In addition to all that, Delphine is a bona fide countess, thanks to her husband, Count Homan von Herenberg, and the count's pockets seem to be exceedingly large and deep. The countess has come to Isabel through the courtesy of Mimi Ross, whose West End Avenue classic six Isabel sold for $2.5 million last year. Mimi met the countess at a dinner party in East Hampton, and when she learned that her new acquaintance was interested in buying in Manhattan, she recommended Isabel. Isabel makes a note to herself to send Mimi a big box of Swiss chocolates—champagne truffles, she decides—from Teuscher this week.

"Zhere! Zat vasn't too bad, vas it?" Isabel hears, and watches as Delphine scrambles back into the limo, the discreet black shopping bag with its silvery letters bobbing on her arm. "Would you like to see?" Delphine pushes her hair—pale blond and falling almost to her waist—out of her face as she opens the shopping bag to give Isabel a glimpse. Inside is a dense profusion of leather and suede, both in the same deep shade of scarlet; the Valentino handbag, which Isabel can see more clearly when Delphine extracts it, is a giant, intricately petaled flower, hanging down from a pair of scarlet handles.

"It's gorgeous," Isabel says.

The driver moves back into the stream of traffic making its way up Madison. They are headed to 1 East 82nd Street, just off Fifth Avenue, where Isabel is going to show

Delphine not an apartment but a six-story, twenty-five-foot-wide town house, with a newly restored limestone facade, a state-of-the-art underground wine cellar, and an enormous garden designed by one of Tokyo's leading landscape architects. It's an exceptional listing owned by a wealthy Arab businessman, and it requires an exceptional buyer; Isabel hopes the count and countess might just be the ones.

"Is that the house?" Delphine asks, pointing out the window as the driver turns adroitly onto the side street.

"No, the one next door," Isabel corrects. "Number one."

"My lucky number!" says Delphine, actually clapping her hands together in delight. Although she must be in her late thirties, more than a decade older than Isabel, she has the gestures and mannerisms of a delightful little girl. Isabel is absolutely enchanted with the countess—her only concern is why she's so adamant that her husband, the count, not accompany them on any of the showings.

"I hate to bother him," Delphine had explained earlier. "He's just so busy. And he's mostly in Europe for his business."

How busy could a person be? But Delphine has insisted that Franz—or Fritzie, as she likes to call him—has left the details of this purchase entirely up to her. "He loves to indulge me," Delphine said with a breathy little laugh, a laugh that sounded to Isabel like that of a thirteen-year-old. "What can I say?"

■ ■ ■

The limo pulls up to the curb, and the two women get out. Delphine pushes back her hair—again—and adjusts the supple, whisper-thin fawn suede jacket—perfect for spring, Isabel thinks—that she wears over a pair of matching suede pants; on her feet are a pair of glossy and elaborate black cowboy boots that remind Isabel of the matching Billy Martin cowboy boots she and Kate had in every color in their early teens. Her long, slender fingers glitter with diamonds, and diamonds sparkle at her ears as well. She leans over to say a few words to the limo driver, who nods before driving off. Then she turns back to Isabel, her face lit by a wide, innocent smile.

"I'm ready!" she says, and follows Isabel into the house, the heels of her cowboy boots tapping as she walks.

Isabel introduces Delphine to the exclusive broker Jed Garfield—a young man in a navy suit and a white shirt, no tie—and Delphine squeals, "That smell! Vat is that delightful smell?"

"They're flowers from Plaza Florist," Jed says. It's an explosion of white freesia, roses, and gardenias selected and arranged by the stager Jed had hired; the scent, as they walk in, is certainly intoxicating. The black-and-white marble floor, laid in a pattern of diamonds, not squares, shines like a mirror. Overhead, a six-armed crystal chandelier glitters as brightly as Delphine's jewels. And this is just the entrance gallery.

Delphine oohs and ahhs her way through the house, exclaiming over the garden with its burbling fountain and prettily arranged slate pathways and the double-size parlor that could easily be used as a ballroom. Isabel imagines that Delphine is one of the few women left in this world who is divine enough to host her own ball. She swoons over each bathroom—where the stager has filled a massive covered glass jar with hyacinth and pink oval bars of soap, and made sure there is another, smaller bouquet on the bathroom vanity. And then there are the his-and-hers walk-in closets, the kitchen with its glazed terra-cotta tiles, collected and shipped from a Tuscan farmhouse of a previous century. "Fritzie will love these!" Delphine says, kneeling down to run her bejeweled fingers over the floor. "He can truly appreciate history!"

"Then he'll love this house," Isabel assures her as they descend the stairs that lead to the wine cellar. Forty minutes later, Isabel and Delphine emerge with Jed onto the street again, where the driver has been waiting.

"What a pleasure!" Delphine says. "This house is like a little palace. I can't wait to tell Fritzie about it." Jed smiles, and then Delphine leans over and, European style, plants two light kisses on either of Isabel's cheeks. Despite her initial wariness, Isabel is charmed by the gesture. Occasionally a client treats her with such barely veiled contempt that it makes her blood boil. But not the countess. No, she has manners, lovely manners, in fact. And yet there is about her just an ever-so-slight air of gracious condescension, that of a sophisticated, discerning buyer toward a person trying to *purvey* something to her.

"Please just wait one leetle second," Delphine says to Isabel after Jed leaves.

Isabel waits patiently by the curb as the countess slides into the limo, and watches as her new client slips her hand inside the Barneys shopping bag. When Delphine pulls her hand out again, she's holding a small package swathed in tissue paper and tied with a silver ribbon. "For you," Delphine says, handing the package to Isabel.

"For me?" Isabel is surprised. She is accustomed to buying gifts for her clients. Buying gifts is just one of the ingredients in the Chases' real estate "rules"; they love to send a beautiful bouquet from the right florist or the right wine from Sherry-Lehmann. And when an apartment closes, she has often been rewarded—by a stack of Ippolita bangles or a gift certificate to Jimmy Choo—by a client who is rapturously happy with his or her new home. But getting a gift so early in the process is a new experience for Isabel.

"I hope you like it," the countess says. The driver makes no move to leave; clearly, Delphine is waiting for Isabel to unwrap her gift.

Isabel unties the ribbon and pulls the tissue paper aside. In her hands she holds a bottle of perfume made by Clive Christian. She's familiar with the British furniture designer and has read about his new line of scent in *Town & Country*; at over $865 for a 1.7-ounce bottle, it is said to be the most expensive perfume in the world.

Isabel opens the box, uncaps the elegant bottle, and

sniffs delicately. A subtle mix of . . . what? Rose? Maybe gardenia? Isabel isn't sure, but she knows that she loves it.

"Thank you," she says with great sincerity. "So much."

"No, it is I who must thank *you*," the countess says in her slightly elusive accent. "You have shown me a great treasure." She signals the driver, and they're off.

Isabel muses over this gift on her way back to the office. Her family has certainly had its share of super-rich clients, to say nothing of celebrities. She can remember the time, more than fifteen years ago, when Christie Brinkley accompanied Elizabeth after a showing to pick up Isabel and Kate at dance class at Helen Butleroff; she was so glamorous that even Isabel's ten-year-old self couldn't take her eyes off her. When it came time to show her own apartment on West 67th Street, Elizabeth said that, fittingly perhaps, the only thing to be found in Christie's fridge was a bottle of champagne. Isabel remembers, too, the time her mother was showing apartments to John Travolta, with Isabel and Kate tagging along after school. John was so patient and sweet with them; he even let them climb all over him in the back of his limo while Elizabeth took pictures. Later, when they opened up the camera and realized there'd been no film in it, John messengered over a box of personally autographed photos.

Turning her thoughts back to Delphine, Isabel just knows there's something different about her, though what it is she cannot readily pinpoint.

Back at the office, she puts the perfume on her desk like a trophy. Violeta has turned the radio on to their favorite

1980s station, and hearing Madonna's "Material Girl" makes Isabel smile. (She and Kate love the "Material Girl" video where Madonna imitates Marilyn Monroe singing "Diamonds Are a Girl's Best Friend," from the movie *Gentlemen Prefer Blondes*, another Chase family favorite.) Isabel decides she will tell both her sister and mother about Delphine and the showing later; right now her mother is on the phone, and Kate is out somewhere. Isabel has plenty to do anyway, including scheduling a vet's appointment for Dixie (vaccination and check-up) and sending a quick follow-up e-mail to the countess as well as another to Kimby Bennett. As she types, her phone rings nonstop: two more clients trying to set up appointments, a frazzled seller worrying about an upcoming open house, another client, offer accepted and fretting about whether his financials are going to work with a dreaded Fifth Avenue co-op board. And then her friend Nancy Scarlata, an obsessive reader of Page Six, who always seems to get to it before Isabel. "Here's the latest," Nancy reports gleefully.

> We hear that Elizabeth Chase and her real estate cutie daughters Kate and Isabel just sold a two-bedroom condo to actors Amy Poehler and Will Arnett.

Then Kate calls, followed by her mother, both of whom are, of course, so excited to hear that they are on the *New York Post's* coveted Page Six again.

Isabel turns back to her work, taking a moment to grab

a handful of Gummi Bears from the jar she keeps on her desk. She and Kate adore candy, all of it from Dylan's Candy Bar—gummy anything, sour balls, licorice, both red and black—and they keep an enormous jar of it in between their desks. Elizabeth, though, is not one for just any candy—only the occasional black licorice twist and anything incredibly sour. She is totally a chocolate addict, and she always says to the girls, "You're lucky I don't like that kind of candy or I'd make you throw that jar away, because I'd be two hundred pounds!" As Isabel pops a few gummy dots into her mouth now, she thinks about the Bennetts. Although they acted as if they never wanted to see her again, she is not so easily deterred. Elizabeth has taught both of her daughters a thing or two about the value of persistence. "Never let a client slip away," she's said. "Send an e-mail, pick up the phone. Send flowers if you feel you need to."

Isabel remembers a story her mother told her: years ago, when Elizabeth heard that Warren Beatty was in town and looking at real estate, she devised a plan to get him as a client. She'd had a crush on him since grade school, when she fell in love with him in *Splendor in the Grass*, and so she wrote a number of identical, beautifully handwritten notes explaining why she would be the perfect broker for him, and because she didn't know which hotel he was staying at, she left those notes at the Plaza, the Carlyle, the Ritz-Carlton, and several other exclusive New York hotels. She virtually papered the city with notes. Remarkably, not only did she hit the right hotel, but Warren Beatty was so impressed by her note that he called her, and after nearly two years of working with her, he and Diane Keaton actually bought an apartment through Elizabeth, though, in the end, after they'd split up, it was Diane who wound up with the co-op. Even all these years later, Elizabeth still has the tiny tape she extracted from the answering machine, containing Warren's messages; she keeps it in her jewelry box.

So Isabel knows all about the importance of being persistent. She sends the necessary e-mails, and then checks her book for her next appointment, which, as it turns out, is across town, on Riverside Drive at a beautiful, amenity-filled new condominium called the Aldyn. She glances at her watch. No time for lunch today. She grabs a Ronnybrook peach yogurt from the office refrigerator and heads across the park in a cab. She doesn't, after all, want to be late; the client she's meeting is a busy, imperious investment banker. Newly divorced, he seems to have a chip on his shoulder about women in general, and Isabel doesn't want to do anything to offend him.

When she arrives at the showing, an ultramodern luxury building with a pool and a spectacular roof deck, her client, Clive Brooks, is already waiting. Isabel can sense the tension in his body and in his face, and she can also see that Dee Bradley, the heavily made-up fiftysomething broker representing the sponsor, is rattled by Clive's attitude. Isabel is determined to get past his annoyance. "Clive!" she says. "Good to see you, I love your tie." Clive is a meticulous dresser, extremely tan, with big black-rimmed glasses and a nervous sort of fidget. He is a very small man, but seems to make up for his lack of stature with attitude.

"I'm not sure about this building," he says, ignoring her hello and compliment. "It looks too big. Impersonal, even." Clive shoves his glasses up on his nose. Dee wilts a bit.

"It *is* big," Isabel agrees. "But it's also very sophisticated, and a great social building. They host pool and roof deck parties, and there are film showings in the entertainment center."

"Entertainment center?" says Clive. "I didn't know they had one."

"Yes, they sponsor mini film festivals twice a month. My sister and I love old movies, and if we lived here, we'd go to all of them!"

"That *is* a nice amenity," Clive says, and Isabel can see he's loosening up a bit. And after she shows him the thirtieth-floor apartment—oversize living/dining area, partial views of the Hudson, two bedrooms, two full baths tiled in pale green Italian glass—Clive seems to be a different man.

"I have to say you changed my mind," Clive confesses later as the elevator whisks them down again. "I wasn't prepared to like it this much. To be honest, I was all set to hate it. But now . . ." He trails off, pushing his glasses back up his nose.

"See, you never know!" Isabel says.

"You're right, I made a hasty judgment," Clive says. "I mean, I'm not ready to make an offer, but this place is definitely an apartment I'll consider. It seems like a good building for me, with my situation as you know it."

"I agree," says Isabel. "Which is exactly why I brought you here. You have my cell phone number for when you're ready for another look."

Dee nods a grateful smile before saying good-bye.

By the end of the day, Isabel is thoroughly exhausted. An irate seller called to complain about the asking price set for her apartment; another broker canceled a showing for an apartment that Isabel's client was dying to see. But she has no time to relax at home; in fact, she's not even going home. Instead, she's meeting Michael, her boyfriend, at LaGuardia, straight from the office, which she hates doing, so that they can take off on a much-needed weekend getaway to Palm Beach. Michael is an up-and-coming actor, and although his work is of an entirely different sort than her own, he applies himself to it with the same fierce and determined desire to succeed. And succeed he has, already having played very small roles on *30 Rock*, *Law & Order SVU*, *Damages*, and, when he was first starting out, the last season of *Sex and the City*. Just recently, through a friend of a friend who told him about an audition in L.A., he was able to get a tiny part as a waiter on *Brothers & Sisters*, one of Isabel and Kate's favorite shows.

Her bags are already packed with her Lily Pulitzer flowered dresses and skirts—those cheery colors and crazy prints always make her smile—and sitting in her parents' office, Isabel needs only to grab her luggage and find a taxi.

Between rush-hour traffic and an accident on the Grand Central Parkway, Isabel's nerves are completely on edge by the time she arrives at the JetBlue terminal, but her anxiety fades as soon as she gets through security and sees Michael and the boyish grin he's beaming directly at her.

"Finally!" he says, scooping her up in his arms; easy enough for him since he's 6'1" to her 5'3". (Kate is just under 5'2"—both girls are small, but have huge personalities that make everyone who meets them think they are much taller.) "I was getting worried," Michael says. That is so like him, Isabel thinks. He has this sweetness about him, and it's as if he wants to take care of everyone; in college he had a handful of dogs living with him at all times, ones he'd found hiding in the streets of West Philadelphia, or abandoned by some of the students he tutored. He couldn't say no. And the fact that he is *truly* gorgeous, with beautifully sculpted cheekbones, aquamarine eyes, and thick, dirty blond hair that reaches almost to his shoulders, doesn't hurt either. He takes her breath away.

"Sorry—the traffic, the day . . . oh, I'm happy to be here," Isabel says.

"I'm so happy just to see you," he says, kissing her. "The flight's about to board. We should head over to the gate."

"I need to stop for a few magazines—I forgot to pack them," Isabel says.

"Got them," Michael says, and holds out a plastic bag. Inside are copies of *People* and *Us Weekly*, a package of nuts and raisins, and a bag of M&M's, Isabel's favorite. "Airplane care package, courtesy of yours truly." He smiles again, but this time more shyly, more sweetly. It's that sweetness that gets her every time. Oh, was she lucky when Kate's boyfriend Scott introduced her to Michael, who was a few years younger than Scott and in the same fraternity. *Lucky, lucky, lucky.* And she knows Michael thinks he's lucky as well. An only child from a small town outside of Oklahoma City, Michael admires Isabel's sophistication and her fierce attachment to her family. "I envy you your childhood," he's said more than once.

There's a slight delay before takeoff, and the plane sits on the runway for a while. Isabel sighs, but she is merely annoyed, not anxious. Both her mother and sister are terrified of flying, take at least one Ativan before they even get on the security line, and have dozens of rituals—always sitting on the left side of the plane, knocking three times with their left hand, saying "toy toy toy" and touching red before they step onto the plane, and always wearing the same clothes on every plane trip (Kate's rule). They also check the weather up and down the coast for a week before flying, and once delayed a trip to Boca so many times because of a potential hurricane, they ultimately ran out of days to go and canceled the whole trip. For Isabel, though, boarding a jumbo jet is just another version of stepping into a taxi.

As soon as she thinks of her mother and sister, she pulls out her phone. Since the flight is stalled on the runway, she might as well call one of them. She's just about to dial Kate when Michael leans over and places his hand over hers, effectively arresting the gesture.

"Who are you calling?" he asks. "No, let me guess. Your mom."

"Actually, no, my sister first."

"I was close, no surprise." He continues to hold her hand.

"And is that a problem?" Isabel feels the tiniest prickle of annoyance with him; this is not the first time he's alluded to the fact that she calls her mother and sister so often. Nor is it the first time that he's expressed a mild displeasure with it.

"Kind of, now that you mention it," he says.

"Michael," Isabel begins mildly, extricating her hand from his grasp. "I'm not going through this again. You know how close I am with my family, especially my mom and sister." Michael, still looking a bit sullen, nods. "So I'm never going to stop talking to them as much as I do. I'm just not."

"It's not just a lot—you talk to them all the time!" Michael protests.

"Not *all* the time," Isabel says suggestively, trying to be nicer, and laces her fingers through his. But this time, he's not holding her back from anything; the gesture is reciprocal. "Besides, aren't you crazy about my family, too? Haven't you always said that you envy how close we are?"

"That's true," Michael says. "I guess."

"There's room for everyone," she says.

"I don't know, I guess so . . ." Michael doesn't sound so sullen now.

"I know you understand," Isabel tells him, and then leans over to give him a quick but somehow sexy kiss. Michael has a very short temper, meaning he gets upset and an instant later he is like a puppy dog. He smiles and picks up his latest script—he's recently landed a small role in an off-Broadway play, his first such role ever—leaving her to place her call to Kate without further interruption while they're still on the runway. She loves Michael; no, she *is completely in love with* Michael. But his failure to fully understand her attachment to her family has got to change.

Once they are up in the air, Isabel opens the bag of nuts and raisins and has just opened *People* when the southern-accented baritone of the pilot intrudes on her plan. "Ladies and gentlemen, this is your captain, and ah have an important announcement for y'all," he begins. Isabel looks up from the glossy pages of the magazine, a slight wave of fear going through her. She hopes nothing is seriously wrong. The truth is, she tends to tense up quickly, while Michael is a rock; he rarely gets upset over things. But when Isabel looks, Michael is gone; she never even noticed that he got up.

"This is kind of an unusual announcement," the captain continues, "and, in fact, ah need the help of one of our passengers to make it." There is a hiccup of static and some muffled voices from the cockpit. The magazine slips, unheeded, from Isabel's lap, and her fingers tensely grip the armrests.

"Isabel?" says a voice over the loudspeaker.

She instantly recognizes Michael's rich, resonant, born-to-be-an-actor voice. But what's he doing in the cockpit with the pilot? She realizes this is nonsense, that her imagination is running away from her (*terrorists? hijackers?*); she knows she's being ridiculous, but she's gripped by anxiety nonetheless.

"Isabel, please listen," Michael says. "Will you marry me? I'll be back in my seat in a minute—please don't say no to me."

Michael is proposing to her on an airplane? This is so Michael, she thinks—very movie star! And crazy, impulsive, over-the-top, and totally romantic! And now Michael is back at her seat, kneeling down on one knee in the narrow aisle, extending a small navy blue box tied with a white satin ribbon.

"So will you marry me, Isabel?" he asks softly.

Isabel takes the box from him, her hands trembly. She undoes the ribbon and lifts the cover. Inside sits a large round diamond, wrapped in pavé diamonds and sitting on a pavé diamond band.

"Yes," she says in a tiny voice. "Of course!" she says loudly, delightedly; in an instant the other passengers have burst into applause, and Michael is looking both relieved and ecstatic. A pair of flight attendants appear with two big bottles of Möet & Chandon and two crystal champagne flutes, and the festive sounds of corks being popped can be heard amid the wild clapping. There, a mile above the earth and surrounded by a crowd of strangers, Isabel and Michael kiss. Even though he sometimes has to fly out to L.A. for work, he promises Isabel that he will never, ever ask her to leave New York—or her family. And given their little moment of tension earlier in the flight, this seems to her an especially important declaration—a must, in fact!

When the commotion dies down, and Isabel and Michael are snuggling in their seats, he does make one request.

"Just for the weekend, let it be our secret, okay?" he says. "Even though you adore your family—and so do I—let's not tell them just yet, okay?"

And so, even though Isabel's dying to call her sister and brother and parents the instant the plane touches down in Palm Beach, she agrees to Michael's request. After all, it was almost as sweet and romantic as the proposal itself, and she doesn't want to do anything to spoil it.

But later she finds this is too big a secret to keep to herself, and so, feeling only the slightest twinge of guilt, she waits until Michael is taking a long, hot shower to call first her parents, and then her sister and brother. If he's going to be her husband, he'll have to understand—and accept—her relationship with her family, and that's that.

Her mother is thrilled, of course, and her father sounds like he is crying. Kate shrieks "Oh, my God!" into the phone. "I can't wait to plan a wedding. I can't believe you are engaged!"

The water is still running in the shower, so Isabel figures she has time to make one last call, and she does—to Jonathan. He's as thrilled as the rest of the family and the most surprised, she thinks, and Isabel knows that if she could see him, he'd have an enormous innocent grin on his face, shocked that his big sister is old enough to get married. He's an angel, her brother. Just sweetness and goodness through and through.

"Michael is going to be the best husband," Jonathan is saying. "I've seen you two guys together, and I can just tell."

Michael steps out of the shower while Isabel is on the phone with her brother. Her fiancé (oh, the fun of that word!) has a fluffy white hotel towel wrapped around his waist and a slight scowl on his handsome features. Isabel quickly says good-bye to Jonathan and braces herself.

"I thought you weren't going to tell your family," he says, sounding a little petulant. "I thought this weekend was going to be just us."

"I know," Isabel says. "But I just couldn't—I'm so excited, I had to, I'm sorry, but I had to—" She tries to kiss him, but he pulls away.

"So this is what it's going to be like when we're married, huh? Your family will always come first?" He sits down on the bed where Isabel is stretched out.

"Michael," Isabel says, willing her voice to remain calm and free of exasperation, "isn't it as obvious as can be that the same devotion and loyalty I feel for my family, I have for you—please understand that it's a good way to be."

"Yeah, yeah, I get that," he says, and Isabel can see that he's softening.

"Oh, you should," she murmurs. "You really should. Because I never disappoint the people I feel that way about," she continues, leaning over and giving the towel a little tug. "I am yours one hundred percent . . ." Her voice trails off, and Michael smiles, offering no objection at all as she tugs again at his towel.

They spend the rest of their weekend enjoying the Ritz-Carlton in Palm Beach, where their spacious room overlooks the ocean. The bedsheets are 400-thread-count percale, the pillows white goose down, the TV a 32-inch flat screen. The weather is gorgeous both days. Neither one of them has much inclination to go into town, preferring instead to lounge around the hotel and wander lazily down the beach. But they do make a quick stop at Rapunzel's Closet, where Isabel buys some darling little T's, and sparkly collars for all the dogs in their family.

The rest of the time, she and Michael dine at the restaurants in the hotel, and when they want a bit more privacy, they order room service, enjoying their $20 sirloin burgers with jalapeños and caramelized onions, and they eat gazing out at the view or happily at each other.

The only time they're apart for more than ten minutes is when Isabel slips into the Eau Spa by Cornelia on the hotel's first floor, where she has a manicure, so that her fingers will be gorgeous for the ring. The ring! She and Kate have been talking rings ever since they were teenagers, weighing the differences between emerald and cushion, oval and round. She takes a picture of the ring—so pretty on her delicate finger, and set off exquisitely by the pale, angel-skin pink she's chosen as a color for her nail polish (Vanity Fair mixed with Waltz, by Essie)—and sends it to Kate, who responds with an e-mail that says, "OMG!!!!!!!!!!"

Isabel smiles when she sees it. She can imagine the Page Six item now:

> We hear that Michael Prescott has just announced his engagement to his adorable, bouncy blond girlfriend Isabel Chase. Will lucky Isabel be a June bride?

Isabel and her family all read Richard Johnson's Page Six as soon as they get up. They call it their "gossip gospel," and it's a vital source of information about their clients. Weddings, divorces, babies on the way—all these key life events have a big impact on who is buying, who is selling, and why. But the Chase family is also successful enough in its own right to make it into those same pages themselves, and their own accomplishments and celebrations occasionally appear in the column; Isabel hopes her engagement will be boldface!

The weekend passes in a romantic haze, and not until Sunday night, when Isabel is back home in Manhattan, does she sense that something is going on with her sister. Kate throws her arms around her the moment Isabel walks through the door of their apartment, and sounds happy for her, but even then, Isabel, who knows her sister so well, can detect a certain tension, and an accompanying sorrow whose source she can't quite pinpoint or name. It's only when she sits face-to-face with her sister and says, "You *have* to tell me what's going on, Kate," that she learns the whole story about Scott and the break he is once again taking from the relationship—a break that apparently was so mortifying to Kate she just couldn't bring herself to discuss it with Isabel or their mother when it first happened that Sunday night exactly two weeks ago.

"Two weeks? I can't believe you waited this long to tell me!" Isabel says. "And you know, I wondered why Scott wasn't around, but when I asked you a couple of times, you seemed so evasive I just didn't want to keep asking. But how could you have kept it from me? Don't we always tell each other *everything*?"

"I don't know," Kate says, "it's just so horribly embarrassing every time it happens. And each time he takes one of those breaks of his, you and Mom keep telling me that I shouldn't take him back the next time he shows up again. And I couldn't bear to hear it yet again from you guys, and I didn't realize it's been two weeks. I just couldn't say the words, I guess."

"Oh, what's wrong with Scott?" Isabel says. She wants to cry for her, she seems so fragile, her tiny hands rubbing Dixie's pink stomach.

"He's an idiot, I guess," says Kate. She gets up from their purple velvet Shabby Chic sofa and walks into her bedroom with Dixie, then closes the door quietly behind her. Isabel sits there for a moment until a wave of exhaustion comes over her, and she falls asleep on the sofa with a chewed-up issue of *Vogue*.

The next morning she feels hungover, despite the fact that she hasn't touched a drop of anything more potent than seltzer. But it's Kate's unhappiness that's making her feel queasy, she's sure of it. Kate is her older sister; she was supposed to become engaged first. So Michael's proposal, thrilling and wonderful as it is, has inverted the natural order of things. Plus, the timing couldn't be any worse: Why couldn't Scott have chosen some other moment to take a break? She has the fleeting thought that she could ask Michael to talk to him; the two were in the same fraternity at Penn, after all, and have been friends ever since. But men, or at least the ones *she* knows, are generally not inclined to have long, heartfelt conversations about their love lives, like girls do, and so this idea probably isn't a very good one, she realizes.

These are the thoughts that tumble through her head as Isabel gets dressed and ready for work. She keeps waiting for Kate to emerge from her bedroom; unless one of them has a really early showing, they almost always take a taxi to the office together, and pick up their parents along the way. But today the door remains shut, and there's no sign of her sister. Finally Isabel knocks on the closed door, and when there's no answer, she steps inside. The room is empty, except for Dixie curled up on Kate's ruffled white duvet cover. Unlike Isabel, who is very neat, Kate always leaves her room in a state of disarray. The bed looks as if it has exploded, the bevy of crisp pink-and-white-checked throw pillows tossed every which way, magazines opened and strewn all over the floor. On one night table is a cluster of silver-framed photographs from every stage of their growing up—Isabel and Kate dressed in matching nighties and ribbons in their hair on Christmas morning; Jonathan in footie pajamas snuggled in Kate's lap as she reads him a Dr. Seuss book; more than a decade later, there's Jonathan in his Horace Mann Lions number 32 football uniform; Jonathan and Jen, his high school sweetheart, posed in front of the Chases' building on Park Avenue on prom night; Jonathan, Isabel, Kate, and their mother in Jonathan's black Mercedes SUV on freshmen parents' weekend at Emory. Next to all the photographs are the wrappers from a dozen sour balls, an empty seltzer bottle, a tub of L'Occitane shea butter foot cream, a crystal lamp with a white silk shade, and a William Yeoward bud vase that contains a cluster of pink peonies.

The closet doors are flung open to reveal the riot of pretty shirts, skirts, and dresses stuffed inside. Shoes are piled in a cheery heap; this is completely different from the strict order that governs Isabel's own closet. Her eyes stray to the dresser, where there are yet more framed photos and a collection of antique perfume bottles from shops in London, from a trip Kate took there one Fourth of July with her friend Sam Siegal. Seeing them reminds her that she hasn't told her sister about Delphine's gift of the perfume; she hasn't yet had the chance.

Deflated, Isabel leaves the room. When she checks her phone, there's an e-mail from Kate that reads: *Couldn't sleep, left early. See u @ the office xoxo.* So there really is nothing for Isabel to do but give Dixie a kiss on her damp black nose and then get a taxi to the office herself.

In the cab, she calls her mother, and they go over the

showings for the day, as well as which sellers need to be called, which buyers they need to prepare for co-op board interviews, which listings need updating. Then she e-mails Mary Beth Flynn, a broker, to confirm a meeting later that week, to be followed by cucumber martinis at Jean Georges at the Mark. She loves Mary Beth, who is as much a friend as a broker she works with. As soon as she is finished, her phone rings, and she sees a text from Michael: *Agent called—just landed Verizon commercial! Love ya.* Isabel smiles at the message, as if it were Michael's gorgeous face. Commercials, of course, are the first step in a young actor's career; how many actors did commercials both before and after they became major stars? And a Verizon commercial would be huge—and noticed—which has to be good for Michael's visibility. *Fabulous!* Isabel e-mails back. *Love you.*

At the office, things are already popping. Her mother is deep in negotiations for a ten-room exclusive at 1120 Park; there's a bidding war, and Elizabeth needs to advise her client, the seller, on how to maximize the interest without losing anyone. In the middle of one heated call she actually puts her hand over the phone and yells, "Isabel, get John Poirier on the phone, Dad's BlackBerry isn't working." John is their IT consultant, who lives in Ohio and comes to the office once a month. He is gorgeous, sweet, and shy. In his early thirties, he looks like Michael Vartan in *Never Been Kissed.*

Isabel is half listening now while she goes over her own day in her head. Her phone rings three times while she's doing this, but she presses ignore—they can wait, at least for a few minutes, while she figures out her day.

Fifteen minutes later, Elizabeth gets off the phone and walks into Isabel's office. She loves Michael, and she and Isabel's father were clearly thrilled when he asked her to marry him (though of course they already knew, because he'd asked their permission first).

"Still floating?" Elizabeth asks. She seems to regard her younger daughter with her unique blend of fierce maternal love and objective, practical assessment.

Isabel stretches her fingers, looks at her engagement ring, and then looks at her mother. "Floating, but I don't know . . ." Neither she nor her mother mentions Kate's name, nor the fact that Scott just seems to keep breaking up with her for no reason. Sometimes, Isabel thinks, she'd like to just strangle him. Her mind flashes back to Michael. Maybe his proposal will push Scott along? Maybe she'll bring up the subject with Michael after all.

"You know, Isabel, every one of us is thrilled for you," she hears her mother say.

"I know," Isabel says, and nods. "So where's Kate?" she asks. "She's out?"

"Early showing," Elizabeth says. "Four East 70th Street. The garden apartment right across from the Frick."

"Mmm," Isabel says, remembering the apartment with the French doors leading out into the garden.

"And don't even doubt for one second that she's happy for you," her mother says.

"I know, but I still feel, I don't know, guilty, and—"

"Isabel, that's ridiculous—Kate would be shocked to hear you say that," Elizabeth says.

Isabel looks at her mother. "I guess," she says, and "Right." Before she can say anything else, her cell phone buzzes, and she quickly reaches for it. She sees it's the countess, with whom she has an appointment this morning; they made it before they went their separate ways on Friday.

"Gut morning to you," Delphine says. "I am running just a *teensy*, tinesy bit late today. Will that be all right?"

Teensy, tinesy, teenzy, tinezy. Whatever.

"Of course," says Isabel, sitting up straighter in her chair. "What time do you think you'll be here?"

"Ten thirty," says Delphine. "I'll have my driver pick you up in front of your office."

"Ten thirty is fine," says Isabel.

"Perfect!" Delphine says, and then adds, "Ciao, ciao!" before she clicks off.

"The countess?" asks Elizabeth. Isabel nods and pulls out her show sheet for today's apartment. "By the way, where does she actually live?"

"She's been staying at the Dartley," Isabel says. "She says it's very elegant, of course! But sort of small, and so she doesn't like to entertain guests."

Elizabeth nods, then gets up and gives her daughter a quick kiss on the cheek before hurrying back to her own office.

Half an hour later, Isabel is slipping into the white limo

next to Delphine (Isabel has a giggle to herself every time she gets into Delphine's limo—no one in New York uses a limo anymore, it is all about the Escalade or Navigator or even chauffeured Benzes). Today the countess wears a long silk Chloe paisley skirt. The jewel-like colors of the fabric—red, blue, green, gold—swirl gracefully around her ankles, which are in what Isabel quickly realizes are her signature black lizard cowboy boots. Over the skirt, Delphine is wearing an exquisitely tailored short black jacket; a thick, braided gold collar encircles her delicate neck. Once again, her flaxen hair is worn long, loose, and straight; her fingers and ears sparkle with enormous diamonds.

"Today we are going downtown, *ja*?" she asks. Although Delphine had said she "adored" the town house, she wants to see a number of different properties in different neighborhoods before she commits.

"We are," Isabel says. "And I think you're going to love it." She leans back as the limo makes it down to Tribeca, where there is a sumptuous, completely renovated loft that she is showing Delphine. Even though this apartment has nothing in common with the Upper East Side town house Isabel showed her last week, she knows that the countess is looking for something distinctive and exceptional, and Isabel is determined to prove that she can find her the best, the most desirable, one-of-a-kind properties.

"Wait until you see this," she tells Delphine when they're in the elevator heading up.

The loft in the Zinc Condominium at 475 Greenwich

Street, which belongs to a very important Hollywood mogul who uses it only when he's in town, occupies the entire tenth floor of the building. It's flooded with the most incredible morning light. The effect is magnified by the twelve-foot ceilings and the enormous wall of floor-to-ceiling windows. There are four bedrooms and three full baths, plus a powder room. There's a separate laundry room (a huge luxury in New York) with a big sink and a brand-new Miele washer and dryer, and, on the north side of the apartment, an enormous terrace that offers an expansive view of the city. Although Isabel has told her client about all of this, she hasn't disclosed the most exceptional—jaw-dropping, really—feature of the apartment. And Nickie Monroe from Sotheby's, the exclusive's broker—an elegant redhead with distinctive turquoise-framed glasses—has kept her secret. Isabel waits, and when she hears Delphine say, "Mon Dieu!" she's sure that her quasi-royal client has found it. "It" is a 700-gallon aquarium with, Isabel knows, a six-figure price tag, custom designed by one of the city's premier experts and filled with a dazzling assortment of catfish, tangs, pink damsels, and, tucked in a far corner underneath some coral rock, a two-foot eel. To some, this would be beautiful but ridiculous—another "built-in" to have to get rid of. But Isabel knows Delphine will love it with a capital *L*.

"*Incroyable*!" Delphine says as she circles the tank, drawing her elegant hands up to her chin. "I have never, ever, seen such a thing in a private home!" She brings her face right up to the glass, clearly transfixed.

Her last words are more than a little gratifying to Isabel,

who knows that the aquarium elevates the loft to a new level of luxury. Never mind the thousand-dollar monthly maintenance fees for the aquarium alone; the countess and her "independently wealthy" (as she'd described him) husband can more than afford them, she has made clear.

Together, Isabel, Delphine, and Nickie tour the kitchen—very modern and minimalist, all brushed steel with a black-and-gray terrazzo floor—and the bedrooms, which have enormous walk-in closets. But they keep returning to the fish, whose metallic beauty seems to mesmerize Delphine. "I have to tell Fritzie!" Delphine says, and then whips out her iPhone to text him.

She gushes jubilantly about the apartment on the way down in the elevator. "Are there many more apartments like this for sale?" she asks innocently.

Isabel smiles. "No, this is completely and totally unique, a one-of-a-kind, as Mom would say."

"Ah, your mother," the countess says. "I've seen her photo in the *New York Times*. She's a very beautiful woman, a classically beautiful woman, really." She turns to Isabel. "Of course you are also beautiful as well. You've inherited your mother's looks. I must say, she seems remarkable."

"Thank you so much! Kate and I are lucky enough to look like her, only I'm blond, of course."

"What is *her* apartment like?" Delphine asks.

"Well, it's actually the apartment I grew up in," Isabel explains. "I love it—all antiques, big, and very classic, on Park Avenue."

"I'm sure in impeccably good taste."

When Isabel says good-bye to the countess a half hour later, she isn't altogether surprised to be handed yet another little package. "You didn't have to do this," she protests; she's really falling in love with this unusual European woman, who is now looking at her with the beaming trust of a small child.

"Just open it," the countess instructs.

Isabel finds, inside the peach-colored tissue paper and sky-blue ribbon, a box filled with an assortment of sugar cookies, each shaped and decorated like the most fanciful of hats, complete with bows, feathers, and lace. She thanks the countess, already imagining how crazy Kate and her mother will be about these little cookies when they see them; sugar cookies are her mother's and sister's favorite. They're obsessed with them! Isabel thinks, smiling to herself. Her mother in particular can't control herself around them; her love for those sugar cookies is, unfortunately, at odds with her constant dieting. She can go up and down five pounds in a week, or even after one salty Nobu dinner. Whereas for Isabel, self-control comes more naturally. Kate and her mom always tease Isabel that she can eat just one M&M—while *they* would eat the whole bag.

"It's nothing," Delphine says. "A little trifle, really." Her smile widens. "Enjoy! I look forward to our next meeting. *A bientôt, oui?*"

"*A bientôt,*" Isabel echoes, remembering the phrase for "see you soon" from her French classes in middle school. She waits as the limo swings into the stream of traffic before getting her own taxi back to the office.

When she walks in, her mother is there, but still no sign of Kate. Isabel tells her all about Delphine, with details of all her clothes and jewelry.

"She seems to love you, Mom," Isabel says. "She's seen and read about you in the *Times*."

"That reminds me, I have to give Diane Cardwell a call. She wants a quote from me for the *Times*." Then her eyes fall on Isabel's ring. "*And* I need to look at this ring again." Elizabeth gently grabs her daughter's hand. "One more look before I get back to work. Maybe I should reset mine? I love pavé," she says. Elizabeth has a classic pear-shaped diamond with two exquisite baguettes on the side, but the Chase family loves sparkle, and nothing is more sparkly than pavé.

Isabel holds out her hand. The ring sits regally on her finger, she thinks.

John Mehigan, a broker in their office, walks in at that moment. He is dashing, about five foot nine, salt-and-pepper hair, piercing blue eyes, and an Irish accent the girls adore. "Eeeeee-lizabeth," he says, "can I borrow you for a moment?" He smells of cigars, minty gum, and Purell. "I'm having a problem with a bloody board package." *Bloody* is John's favorite word.

Elizabeth laughs. "Are you here for a little bit? I'll come in in about ten minutes."

"Okay, Eeee-lizabeth," he says. "I'll be bloody waiting." John scurries out, flashing a glimpse of his signature hot pink socks as he goes.

"Hi, girls."

Looking up, Isabel sees Kate. "Hi," she says to her sister, and looks at her lovely, smoky eyes. Kate and their mother love makeup; Isabel wears only mascara and lipstick, a more natural look. Years ago, with Isabel looking on in fascination, Kate used to study and practice on the sketched face from Boyd's makeup emporium on Madison Avenue that Elizabeth kept taped to the mirror. But despite her makeup and her adorable pink-and-turquoise floral Rachel Riley dress, Kate looks a little wilted and sad.

"How was the showing?" Elizabeth asks.

"Terrific. They're making an offer," Kate says. "They" are Don and Justine Prince, an exceedingly difficult couple who seem to agree on just about nothing. If Justine thinks an apartment is charming, Don finds it suffocatingly small; if she loves the views, he hates the layout. "I'd rather drink paint," he's said on more than one occasion, "than live in this apartment." On and on it goes. They have been looking for how long—a year? Or is it longer? So for them to make an offer is a miracle.

"Fabulous!" Isabel says.

"Well, let's see what happens—they could change their minds."

"Isabel's right, though, Kate," Elizabeth points out. "Just getting those two to make an offer is no small thing."

"I guess," Kate says vaguely. She sets her white Chanel

surf bag down on Isabel's desk. The bag is identical to the one that both Isabel and Elizabeth carry.

Isabel suddenly gives Kate a hug.

Kate hugs her back, though not very enthusiastically, and says, "You don't have to do that, Isabel. Honestly, I'm perfectly fine."

Stung, Isabel stares at her sister. "I'm sorry," she says at last. But Kate is already reaching for her purse and walking away. Isabel is teary-eyed as she watches her go. To think that what should be the happiest time of her life might be marred even in the slightest by her sister's distress is just too much.

Leaving her office, she walks briskly toward the ladies' room. There, with the door tightly closed and the faucet turned on and running at full blast, Isabel cries.

But she doesn't even have the luxury of a good long cry because she has to pull herself together—she and Kate have to be at the NBC studio at 30 Rock in midtown for a satellite shoot for *Access Hollywood*; they do segments on celebrity real estate from time to time, and today just happens to be one of those times. Damn! Isabel loves doing these segments, as does Kate, but she wishes it were not today of all days. Still, she knows what she has to do, and so she blots her tears, quickly brushes her hair, and splashes cold water on her face—good thing she and Kate will be getting their hair and makeup done at the Valery Joseph salon on Madison before the shoot. Then she walks out of the bathroom in search of her sister.

"Oh, there you are!" Kate calls out to her. "The car's downstairs already. We've got to go." They say good-bye to their mother and get into the elevator; outside, they get in the black Escalade. "Christine's called me twice," Isabel says once they're on their way. "She wants to know where we are. The producers are getting anxious." Christine Fahey, a senior producer for the show whom the Chases first met when they were handling a fading musician's town house (a musician who successfully begged them to try to get *Access Hollywood* to do a tour of it in hopes that this would help generate interest); since then, Christine calls them whenever the show needs a real estate expert, and they have become close family friends.

"We're not even late yet," Kate says.

Isabel agrees.

They make a quick stop for hair and makeup, and then it's on to NBC, where Christine is awaiting their arrival. "Hurry!" she urges, kissing them each hello and telling them how gorgeous they look. "You haven't got much time." Isabel and Kate scramble to get ready; they're there to talk about which New York City neighborhoods are hot for celebrities these days, as well as what amenities the stars are seeking. And they dish a little by sharing who's buying, who's selling, and most importantly—*why*.

After they're finished, they're back in the SUV once more, collapsing into giggles about how the producers were screaming for their presence on the set while Kate was touching up her petal-pink Chanel lipstick in the ladies' room.

They're still laughing when Elizabeth calls to find out how the shoot went. "Fabulous!" Isabel says, and proceeds to fill her mother in. "Billy Bush said we're hotter than the Manhattan real estate market!" Then she clicks off and smiles at her sister happily. She feels so lucky to work with her family. They are all so lucky, she thinks.

CHAPTER SIX

Elizabeth

Modern Apartment in the Sky

3 bedroom, 2 bath cathedral of steel and glass, gourmet EIK, cloud-gazing skylights. $2.95 million.

Elizabeth, along with her friend Monique Lazard and Kate and Isabel, are lunching at Sette Mezzo at a front table by the window. The Chases are frequent and favored customers of the clubby Upper East Side eatery, and are always greeted with hugs and double kisses by Oriente, one of the owners. He seats them at this coveted table so they can view the fabulous clientele, which today happens to include Catherine Zeta-Jones and Michael Douglas. Monique, a first cousin of the Lazards, as in Lazard Frères, met Elizabeth when they were both MSWs working in social services, Monique trying to escape the wealthy clutches of her family, whose only ambition was for her to marry well, and Elizabeth pursuing a fleetingly youthful notion that social work was her true calling. Monique had been married briefly in the late 1980s to a rich diplomat from Spain, and she left the marriage with nothing except her original apartment at 1010 Fifth and a Judith Leiber pineapple clutch. (Monique, who simply loves hot weather, collected pineapples, as they reminded her of romantic nights on faraway islands.)

Elizabeth was a graduate student in social work at Columbia University, working for Mayor Lindsay. There is a photo of them together, the mayor giving her a Social Worker of the Year award, sitting on the Chases' piano, Elizabeth—hair middle-parted and down to her waist, brilliantly tan in a very Jackie Kennedy lemon shift dress—gazing up at him with such infatuation that Kate used to tell her blond little sister that the mayor must be her father. Of course this was not true, but it was fun to torture her little sister sometimes. When Elizabeth was held up with a gun a few years later by her favorite social work client, Tom told her, "This is it, Elizabeth." So Elizabeth became, quite briefly, a lady of leisure before following her destiny into real estate.

Monique has a considerable personal fortune and is on the board of the American Ballet Theatre; over the years, she's sent Chase Residential many of her wealthy contributors, who buy and sell fabulous trophy properties in Manhattan. Elizabeth invites Monique out to lunch at least once every couple of months, and always insists on paying.

Monique enjoys catching up with Elizabeth's girls, particularly weighing in on their love lives. Excited at the news of Isabel's engagement, she goes on for a few moments about possible wedding venues—the Plaza, the Metropolitan Club, the Maidstone Club in East Hampton—until Elizabeth gives her a look. Monique nods her head ever so slightly, as if to acknowledge the delicacy of the situation, one daughter newly single and the other newly engaged. "Okay, girls, I think it's time for some champagne," she says, just as the waiter arrives with a bottle of Cristal (which she'd obviously prearranged, Elizabeth understands). "This is my treat," Monique tells Elizabeth. "So don't you dare try to pick up the tab today."

"I wouldn't dream of it," Elizabeth says, laughing.

The Chases have their favorite dishes. For Kate and Isabel, it's *pollo patanato,* chicken with a thin potato crust. Elizabeth absolutely adores food, and is in a constant state of dieting; although she can certainly appreciate a good spoonful of caviar, she always says the one thing she can't resist is a plate of crispy French fries with the perfect amount of salt and a basket of warm bread with soft, salted butter. And then, of course, there's the chocolate—specifically, rich milk chocolate. Today, at Oriente's urging, she's dining on tagliatelle with white truffles. Monique, picking at her penne Sette Mezzo, addresses Kate, saying, "Listen, sweetheart, I was so sorry to hear from your mom about you and Scott. But I'm sorry—what an ass."

Kate is visibly withering in her chair, reluctant, Elizabeth knows, to discuss the tender subject of her relationship with Scott but also not wanting to offend Monique or make her think she's not close enough to the family to discuss such things. Elizabeth recalls, all too well, how utterly devastated Kate sounded two weeks ago when she shared with Elizabeth the latest chapter of Scott's breakups. The news was delivered to Elizabeth over the phone late one night last month, their final conversation for the day just as Elizabeth was getting into bed. Elizabeth couldn't sleep all night after hanging up with her firstborn; she lay, with all three girls on her—Roxy on her head, Lola on one side, and Dolly tucked at her hip—thinking of how hard it was to see her daughter's heart broken yet again.

"How about we change the subject?" Elizabeth suggests now, and both her daughters look relieved.

"Okay, but let me just say one more thing," Monique says. "Next time Scott calls you, Kate, I don't think you should answer or return his call. You need to just plain ignore him for a while." She dips a piece of sourdough bread in olive oil.

Elizabeth doesn't try to silence her friend—she does, in fact, agree with her completely.

This sort of girl talk is something that Kate, Isabel, and Elizabeth prefer to share mostly with each other. They are so alike in their thoughts that people often call them "Chase in Stereo," because they all talk over each other and say the same things, like, "We hate the color brown."

Luckily, Monique is also obsessed with Teddy Wingo, whom she finds irresistibly attractive as well as fascinating in his moving target of a love life, and so the conversation turns quickly to him. Elizabeth confides, "Teddy was supposed to show up at a walk-through a few weeks ago and didn't. He made some kind of weird excuse about a soon-to-be-ex-girlfriend drugging him."

"She *drugged* him?" Monique says, taking a sip of champagne, leaving a perfect imprint of her lipstick on the glass, and then leaning in like she was about to be told the city's biggest secret. No one loves a secret more than Monique.

Aware of the complicit looks on the faces of her daughters, Elizabeth smiles. "Oh, who knows? We don't necessarily believe his story—it sounds a bit ludicrous—and I have to say he's not always reliable about showing up when and where he's supposed to, though, in spite of that, he's extremely successful," she says.

"He's a *really* big producer, right?" Monique says.

Isabel says, "Let's put it this way, if he were to leave us, we would make less money, but have a lot less aggravation. He's extremely high-maintenance and very demanding."

"But he has so much cachet," Monique says, stroking the three Hermès enameled bangles on her deeply tanned arm. "That's why I always thought he was such a good fit for Chase Residential."

Elizabeth, Kate, and Isabel shrug simultaneously, and Kate says, "And that's exactly why Mom always indulges him."

"Yes," Isabel goes on, "he's incredibly polished. But he can also be very cutthroat—"

"It's a little unnerving," Elizabeth agrees. "It's one of the reasons you want him with you, not against you. And he does get great listings. Oh, he had the most charming ten-room at 149 East 73rd, with Juliet balconies off nearly every window—I sold it to a twenty-nine-year-old couple for just under five million."

"I bet the client's mommy and daddy paid," Monique says.

"Oh no, the husband makes more than three million a year, just a couple of years out of Harvard Business School," Elizabeth tells her.

"He's a wolf," Kate says, "but people adore Teddy."

"Oh, I'm tired of talking about Teddy," Elizabeth says. "So, did you want to see our new gem on Fifth Avenue?" she asks Monique as she finishes her champagne.

"You mean the penthouse? I think that would be nice to take a look at, after a bit of shopping, perhaps?"

"We can't," Isabel says—the listing is actually hers. "I got a call from the owner just as Kate and I were coming in. There is a leak from the terrace. She's frantic. The place is a mess. She asked me not to schedule any showings until it's fixed."

Monique runs her fingers through her helmet of bleached platinum hair—such an unnatural color, Elizabeth thinks to herself—and says, "Well, the pictures of it look wonderful, and just remember, my friends the Campbells from Toronto might very well be interested. Courtney just adores terraces."

Isabel nods her head. "Call me in a few days, it should be okay, I hope."

"Just let me know."

Elizabeth finds herself staring at Monique's diamond and wondering if her friend actually dares to wear that rock when she goes to work. Elizabeth and her daughters are known for dressing exquisitely, but Monique is in a different category altogether, with all her custom-made clothing and collection of $3,000-a-pair crocodile Manolos in every color of the rainbow.

"Why don't you and Tom come out to East Hampton this weekend?" Monique is saying. "Just relax, walk on the beach, it's supposed to be beautiful."

Elizabeth smiles and says, "You know me, Monique—I don't need to relax, I need to work. That's my relaxation."

Kate and Isabel laugh. Elizabeth avoids the Hamptons if she can help it—if she's going away, even for a weekend, she doesn't want to be somewhere she's likely to run into half her clients. It's too much of a social scene, and she and her family much prefer their very low-key gem, Atlantic Beach. Atlantic Beach is like the 1950s; the Atlantic Ocean on one side, sprinkled with beach clubs straight out of *The Flamingo Kid*, the bay on the other side, and two blocks of houses in between. The Chases have been going out there for years; Elizabeth used to take a cabana with the children and two girlfriends and drive out weekdays even when the Chase family had a house in Southampton. A few years later, they sold the Hamptons house and bought one in Atlantic Beach, three houses from the ocean, on a block that has the entrance to the divine boardwalk, where Kate, Isabel, and Jonathan spent summers riding bikes as children and holding hands with dates as teenagers. The girls never went to camp, not for one day, not even day camp. They moved out to the beach on Memorial Day every year, with the car packed so high with suitcases that their feet were in the air, and returned on Labor Day. Elizabeth once asked them, "Do you want to go to sleepaway camp? They'll throw you in the freezing lake at six a.m." Terrified, Kate and Isabel said, "No, Mommy," and that was the end of the camp conversation. Their summers in Atlantic Beach were just heaven. It's still their favorite place to go all these years later, only they no longer move out for whole summers, where they would always wait for Tom to come over the bridge so they could light the barbeque and put his wine on the table.

They still go every weekend in the summer, and they absolutely adore their neighbors out there; on one side, a famous hedge fund icon and his wife, who owns a fabulously cool designer boutique called Edit, in a beautiful town house on Lexington Avenue (coincidentally, the family of five also live in the Chases' Park Avenue building in the city), and right across the street Doug and Susie, who live out there year-round (and will call Tom at 2:00 a.m. if the alarm at the Chase house goes off), and whose three adorable teenage sons shovel the snow in the driveway when there's a storm.

"I'm going to stay in the city this weekend," Elizabeth says, "but thank you so much, I promise we'll come another time."

As Monique shakes her head and tilts it back slightly,

Elizabeth sees her plastic surgery scars and thinks, Oh, I hope I never go there! Then the four of them get up to leave.

The girls extend an invitation to Monique to come shopping with them, and are secretly happy when she says she needs to get back to her apartment at 1088 Park, where she lives with her bichon frisés Sunny and Snowy and her daughter, who is taking a year off after graduating from Oxford. Not that they don't adore Monique—they do—they just always prefer it to be the three of them.

As soon as Monique leaves, Elizabeth and her daughters stroll toward Madison Avenue, delighting in the balmy May air that makes them feel full of excitement that winter is far gone. Spring is the Chase ladies' absolute favorite time of year. Elizabeth is completely compulsive about answering her cell phone, so having a two-hour lunch or going shopping never gets in the way of negotiating a deal. Once, in the midst of having root canal in Dr. Zane's office next to the Regency Hotel, she actually answered Kate's call and spoke to her for at least three minutes before saying, "Is it anything important? I'm in the middle of having root canal." Another time, she negotiated a $30 million deal at 1030 Fifth Avenue while shopping for monogrammed Ralph Lauren towels with their personal shopper, Karen Lomerson, at Bloomingdale's. (They met Karen at the Ralph Lauren Black Label department on the third floor and have since used her everywhere in the store—whenever they emerge off the escalator, she plucks them like flowers and sings, "Ladies, I have the three silver sweaters you wanted!" or "Ladies, we are in presale today for forty percent off!")

Elizabeth does call to check her office voice mail—by habit, she does this every half an hour or so when she isn't there—as they walk down Madison. Today there are five messages, three from Violeta confirming appointments, one from her vet, Amy Attas, about blood work for Lola, and one, of course, from Bart Schneider. Glancing at her daughters, who are listening to their messages and e-mailing, she decides to give Bart five minutes of her time. She's relieved when a woman answers his cell phone, thinking that he's obviously too busy to talk. But after the woman says hello, she asks, "Is this Elizabeth?"

"It is."

"Bart's with some European clients, but he told me to call him to the phone if it was you on the line."

"Please don't interrupt him," Elizabeth says. "He can call me back."

"No, he needs to talk to you. Please hang on for another moment."

A frantic-sounding Bart Schneider is soon telling her that he's been unable to sleep, racked once again over choosing between three radically different apartments. To make matters worse, nobody in his life has a strong opinion about any of them, each of the properties possessing its own virtues: a town house, a penthouse, and a duplex. But Elizabeth has told him this numerous times already, and it has done little to relieve his anxiety.

"I'm with my daughters," she explains now. "We're on our way to a showing, Bart. Can we maybe speak later? I just wanted to check in."

"I just need to hear your voice," Bart says. "The sound of it's really soothing. I wish you worked for me. I'd probably sell ten times the amount of art I normally do."

"Why don't we speak about this when we see each other Thursday?" she suggests. The two will be going out yet again to look for apartments.

"Okay. I just need to sit with it all a little more."

He is perhaps her most time-consuming and irritating client, but he means well, she reminds herself. And Bart Schneider was recommended to her by a very important friend, and she would never abandon a referral like that. It is what the Chase family business was built on—"friends and family," they like to call it.

Her phone beeps with another call coming in from one of her close friends, a broker at Sotheby's from whom she's expecting an offer on a duplex at 155 East 72nd just off Lexington Avenue.

"Bart, I have to jump," she tells him. "I have a possible bid, and the other broker is on the line."

"Okay, talk soon," he says, sounding let down.

"Hi, darling, what do you have for me?" Elizabeth says to her friend Roger Erickson, one of the only men whom she calls "darling." The Chase ladies don't believe in calling the men in their lives names like "honey," "darling," or "sweetie"—they think there is something reminiscent of *The Stepford Wives* about it—knives in their apron pockets poised to stab their husbands. "I hope you're calling with good news," Elizabeth says.

"Yes, they're putting in an offer of $2.8 million, non-contingent, and financing between thirty and forty percent," Roger says. The full ask on Elizabeth's listing is $3.2 million.

"Okay, Roger, but that better be opening," she says in the singsongy voice they use when they speak to each other. "Can you put it in writing for me and e-mail it to the girls?" Elizabeth is legendary for not owning a computer or a BlackBerry—ironic, the girls often muse, as Elizabeth's first job was as a computer programmer for IBM. She has never sent an e-mail in her life; Kate and Isabel do it all for her.

"Yes, I'll send over the offer with all their financials when we hang up," Roger says. "And one more thing, they want to close in about three months. Their lease expires, and they can't renew it."

"Okay, let me run. I'll speak to the seller and get back to you." They make a big kissing sound and hang up.

The three Chases are now on Fifth, chatting about clients, and what might be the first weekend they are all free to sleep at the beach. The girls love to shop. On rainy weekends they can spend an entire day between Saks, Bloomies, and Bergdorf's, buying, returning, and sometimes just looking—there is something about being in a department store in particular that they just love. No matter the weather or your mood, the lights, the shoes, the music just lift you, they think. Today, they stop at the window of Bergdorf's to gaze at a pair of five-inch purple platform Louboutins in glass—"To die for," they all say at the same time.

Then Kate looks at her watch. "Mom, what time is your showing at 52 East 4th?" she says. 52 East 4th is the luxury steel-and-glass new construction whose apartment listings Teddy has supposedly been trying to maneuver away from LEX, the much larger agency that rivals Chase Residential but is totally different—whereas Chase is owned and run by New Yorkers, LEX is owned by a corporate conglomerate in the Midwest whose name Elizabeth conveniently can't recall when anyone asks her. LEX's top brokers have to go through ten layers of management before being able to take a reduced commission, or sign an exclusive. Chase brokers simply have to call Tom or Elizabeth.

"Not until four o'clock," Elizabeth says, and glances at her gold Cartier Panther watch, a gift from Tom for her fortieth birthday.

"We thought we'd come with you," Kate says. "We want to preview the building for a few clients."

"Okay, so we have almost two hours," Elizabeth says. "Let's skip Bergdorf's and go back to the office. I have some phone calls I need to return, and Dan Wollman needs to speak to me."

When they get off the elevator, they can hear Teddy from the landing. He is sitting at his immaculately organized desk, the phone cradled to his ear, gesturing wildly. "Your client has got to be more flexible about showing the town house, Leslie. I know she says she's super busy, but she has to leave when I show it. She just can't be there. If you want my opinion, I think it's a case of one celebrity giving attitude to another—a big-deal newscaster thumbing her nose at a major ABC TV star. Really, it's rude and counterproductive. Does she want to sell or not? I hated canceling my client, who rearranged his entire schedule for the showing. . . . Okay, fine, please get back to me with some alternatives."

Teddy puts down the phone and smiles adorably at Elizabeth.

Looking at him now, his face flushed with the emotion of his conversation with the other broker, Elizabeth finds herself thinking of that weird day, three weeks ago, when Teddy was apparently drugged by an irate about-to-be-ex-girlfriend. He's never mentioned a peep since then about the incident, and thankfully everything seems back to normal.

He quickly explains now that a famous newscaster who has her West Village town house for sale is scheduling showings and refusing to leave while prospective buyers are there. It makes everyone completely uncomfortable. Rolling his eyes, he says to Elizabeth, "I love celebrities as much as anyone, but they sure can be prima donnas sometimes." As if she doesn't know. She's thinking now of a member of an iconic girls' group, who, while looking at a quadruplex at the Beresford on Central Park West long ago, tossed her floor-length mink to seven-year-old Kate to carry—a coat so heavy it almost knocked her little girl over! And then there was the movie star who wanted park views from his bed, so he insisted on lying down in the master bedroom of each property he looked at, testing to make sure he could see the park. Not that any seller wouldn't be thrilled to find him in his or her bed! Elizabeth always said, giggling. And she will never forget the crowd-pleasing Academy Award–winning actor and client whom she brought to one of her own listings, a co-op owned by her friend Dominique—an exceptionally stunning divorcée in a low-cut black dress who was clearly hot to trot the moment the actor showed up on her doorstep with Elizabeth. The Academy Award winner took one look at Dominique and invited her to join him as he went from one showing to the next with Elizabeth. "Just let me grab my coat," she told him, and when Elizabeth tried to phone her for three days in a row after that, there was no answer. Dominique and the Academy Award winner had, she later learned, checked into a hotel for "an unforgettable three days and nights" of a word Elizabeth wouldn't repeat.

Sitting once again at her desk in her glassed-in office, Elizabeth informs the sellers (both of them oral surgeons with offices in midtown) of the 72nd Street duplex that they have a $2.8 million offer on their $3.2 million apartment.

"Uh-huh," Lara Kennish says, clearly disappointed.

"I'll have to talk to Edward about it and see if he thinks we should even counter."

"I strongly recommend that you do," Elizabeth says. "It's our first offer, and they *will* come up."

"Well, fine, but there's something I need to tell you. If we're actually able to make a deal with these people, we won't be able to close for at least seven or eight months. And that's because I promised my daughter last week that she'd have the apartment to come home to from college until next Christmas. I just never thought it would sell so quickly. And also, the whirlpool bath isn't really working. I had an estimate for repairing it and was told that putting in a new system would cost several thousand dollars. We don't want to spend the money on fixing it, so you're going to have to inform the buyers that they'll be responsible for getting it taken care of. Also, the thing in the dishwasher where you put the soap won't stay closed, and the stove has a missing knob that I can't replace. So the buyers will have to take care of that as well."

Oh, please, Elizabeth thinks to herself, looking for a nail file in her drawer.

"Lara," she says, "very few people will agree to an eight-month closing. These people are in a rental that they can't renew, and they want to close in about three months, which is what is normal in a co-op. Perhaps we can push it to four, but I can't imagine that anyone buying your apartment will want an eight-month closing. Can't you tell your daughter you'll have a fabulous new home for her to be in before Christmas?"

"Well, our board is very difficult, it may take them a very long time to approve them, and I may just—"

"Lara," Elizabeth says before she can continue, "why don't you just speak to Edward and get me a counter, and then we can negotiate the closing. I'm sure for the right price we can make it work, okay?"

Lara falters for a moment and then says, "The buyers need to know that they might have to get a new dishwasher."

Elizabeth sighs. "Why don't you discuss the offer with Edward, and I'll give you a call this evening, okay? Let's not worry about the dishwasher now."

When she hangs up, she calls Roger.

"Hi," he says. "I'm walking into Michael's for lunch with two clients, so I only have a second. Did you get them?"

"I talked to the wife, and she wants more time before closing—don't ask how long, I'm working on them. She's going to speak with her husband, but the close date will become a matter of price. They're going to have to come up significantly, especially if they want them out in three months or so."

"Give me a hint?" Roger says.

"It's going to have to end up with a three in front of it, certainly."

"I know. They'll come up," Roger promises.

"Good," Elizabeth says. "You're my favorite broker to do a deal with," she adds. And with that, they hang up.

At 3:30 her Mercedes S550 arrives, driven by Dave, the family's favorite driver at Chauffeurs Unlimited, a company the Chases use to drive their car; he's a gangly twenty-three-year-old graduate of Swarthmore who's trying to figure out what to do with his life.

"Hello, ladies," he says as they all climb into the car. Elizabeth finds him charming and unassuming; he reminds her a little of Jonathan.

"So what do you think, FDR Drive?" Elizabeth says.

"You bet," Dave says.

At ten minutes to four, Elizabeth and her daughters are standing in front of a steel-and-glass structure just off the Bowery. Because the neighborhood is still a bit iffy, the building, despite being exquisite to the eye, still has half its apartments remaining to be sold. But then again, the slowed economy has something to do with the slowdown of sales as well. Since it's a buyers' market lately, a more established location that guarantees a stronger possibility of resale has become even more vital than space and comfort.

Elizabeth's clients are a young couple living in what they'd described to her as a cookie-cutter two-bedroom in a postwar building on the Upper West Side. They're looking for something larger and more interesting: the husband is a hedge fund manager, and the wife a graphic designer. They are the sort of people who claim to be less conscious of neighborhood ("We make a location," they said, "the location doesn't make us") and more interested in space and character, particularly the wife, who works from home. They've told Elizabeth that they want to see *everything everywhere* before they make up their minds.

Soon Elizabeth and her daughters and the listing broker, Christopher McKinnon, a tall, lanky, slightly sweaty dark-haired thirty-five-year-old man who happens to be one of Teddy's principal rivals from LEX, are standing in the lobby, waiting to go up to one of the most desirable three-bedroom apartments in the building. Even the lobby feels like a glass pyramid: floor-to-ceiling window, an enormous skylight where you can actually watch the clouds moving.

Christopher turns to Elizabeth. "If you like, I'll just give you the keys and let you show, since you know the apartment so well. And I'll be on my cell if you want me to come up and answer any questions."

Elizabeth thinks, just for a moment, that she notes something odd in his manner, but then perhaps it's just that she's never particularly liked him. Kate and Isabel excuse themselves to look at some of the building's other model apartments, as they have so many downtown clients and always love to tell someone, "I know a building and you will love it," or "No, that's not for you—it's beautiful but so cold."

Elizabeth's clients the Wolcotts arrive at precisely four o'clock. Todd Wolcott, short and stocky, is wearing a dark Valentino suit that makes him look thinner than he actually is. Naomi, his wife, is elegantly dressed in a black jacket and skintight black jeggings. They get in the elevator and go up to the fourteenth floor, where the elevator opens directly into the living room.

"I love all this glass," Naomi is saying.

"Definitely! I get a good feeling here," Todd says, and his excitement is palpable. Then again, the Wolcotts have gotten excited over many other apartments she's shown them and ultimately decided for one reason or another that they weren't for them. Some clients fall in love at first sight, then "out of sight, out of mind." The Wolcotts are, unfortunately, such clients.

"You can see the bridges from every room," Elizabeth tells them, pointing out the Brooklyn and Williamsburg and Manhattan bridges from the master bedroom windows. "And you can imagine the views at night when you see all the magnificent lights of the city," she adds.

"Love the skylight in the bedroom," Todd says a few minutes later. "And that no one else is above you here."

"Well, the bathrooms are disappointing," Naomi says, "quite simple, and not in a good way. The finishes don't seem very high-end, though I guess that's easy to change."

"The kitchen is amazing," says Elizabeth. "Let's go see that." And she shows them the enormous open kitchen, all top appliances, limestone counters. Happily, the Wolcotts agree.

The two additional beds are off the living room—not ideal for a family, but perfectly suitable for the Wolcotts, who need an office and an "extra room" (it seems that these days everyone in New York needs an extra room). Naomi is already determining which of the two will be hers—she wants the one with the most morning light, since that is when she does most of her work.

The three stand together in the eighteen-by-eighteen-foot living room with its fourteen-foot ceilings, and there is a moment of contemplation.

Todd is the first to speak. "It's a great apartment. It's almost exactly what we want, but you know . . . I know the neighborhood is up and coming, but it's not there yet. And that makes me a little nervous."

Elizabeth pauses, and then says, "I know that location isn't a priority for you, and the truth is, there's generally better value to be had in a neighborhood that hasn't yet arrived. This apartment in Tribeca or SoHo would be about ten to twenty percent more expensive."

"I know, I just thought neighborhood wouldn't make a difference if we were really wowed—" Todd says.

"We *are* pretty wowed," his wife corrects him, sweetly but firmly.

Now is Elizabeth's moment. "Well, here's the thing. I used to not get the East Village. I had a friend who bought an apartment on 3rd Street . . . for virtually nothing. A big one-bedroom. I told her the neighborhood would *eventually* come up. At the time, I thought: five years, maximum. But I was wrong. She held on to it for six and then sold it for what she paid for it. But two years after that, the apartment tripled in value."

"Yes, but now that the bubble's burst—" Todd says.

"Well, I wouldn't exactly call it a bubble," Elizabeth points out. "The market has already rebounded a lot, and the truth is, the lower end was hit the hardest—the two-

and-a-half-million-dollar-and-up apartments are still pretty strong." She pauses and puts her bag down on the oak floors. "Plus, this neighborhood has already changed a lot—Dean & DeLuca is two blocks away, Whole Foods is opening up a few blocks farther. Three years from now, this area will be a different place and a different price."

The Wolcotts exchange a glance. Todd shrugs and says, "You're right." He gazes at his wife, who nods her head. "We'll think about it seriously and let you know."

"Of course," Elizabeth says, and presses the elevator button. Soon the couple is gone.

As she walks toward the girls, who are on their BlackBerries on a sofa in the lobby, Christopher McKinnon reappears. "How did it go?" he asks Elizabeth. "What did your clients think?"

"They love it," she says. "Their only issue, which I'm sure you've heard before, is the neighborhood."

"Well, you should know that I have another very interested party, and the apartment may be gone in a day or so."

"I'll be sure to let the Wolcotts know," Elizabeth says, and nods her head toward the door to motion the girls to get up.

Christopher offers a smug, ingratiating smile. "Always a pleasure to see you and your gorgeous daughters, Elizabeth," he says. "I'd love to do a deal with you."

"Well, thank you, Christopher," Elizabeth says, and the three Chase ladies click-clack off in their four-inch heels.

■ ■ ■

"We haven't all been together downtown in a while," Isabel says. "So let's go to Balthazar for a snack."

"Yes!" Kate says, "French fries and bloodys!"

"Just what I need after that lunch!" says Elizabeth. "My fingers are already so blown up, I won't be able to get my rings off tonight!"

"Oh, we'll split one order," says Kate, "and you can skip dinner." They see Dave stopped at a red light and walk toward the black Benz.

"Dave, a quick stop before we go back uptown," Elizabeth says. "We're going to 80 Spring Street."

The three Chase ladies sit down at a burgundy banquette by the bar. Isabel and Kate get up to use the ladies' room, and Elizabeth takes a moment to check her messages at the office. As she is dialing the number on her purple cell phone, she hears a male voice that she knows as well as her own heartbeat. Jonathan saunters through the door, in a Ralph Lauren navy blazer and faded jeans (always too big—"It's the look, Mom," he tells her every time she points it out); as usual, there's a baseball cap on his head—this time a Superman one—and ear buds in place with the latest iPod dangling out of his back pocket as he listens to hip-hop. He always has the air of looking slightly, adorably disheveled, as if you've caught him off-guard, but he is completely prepared. He drops his worn black bag with his laptop, the only thing he carries, at his feet, which are in one of the dozens of pairs of sneakers he owns—like his mother and sisters, Jonathan is a shoe collector. This particular pair is a navy suede Nike with a white swoosh, totally classic.

The unexpected sight of her rangy, darkly handsome son fills Elizabeth with utter happiness.

"Oh, my God, Jonathan, what are *you* doing here?" she says.

"I had to fly in for the afternoon for a meeting with HBO. I didn't tell you because I wanted to surprise you," Jonathan says, pulling the iPod earphones out of his ears as his sisters walk back in. "Kate and Isabel told me you'd all be down here. So after my meeting was over, I just hopped on the subway, and here I am!" He grins and gives his mother and sisters a hug. No one hugs like Jonathan, they always say—he gives enormous, larger-than-life teddy bear hugs.

Elizabeth laughs, now knowing the real reason why Kate and Isabel wanted to tag along: to see their mother's rapturous surprise when Jonathan unexpectedly walked through the door. As close as she is with her daughters, there is something different about her relationship with her son, the baby of the family, something that makes her the absolute happiest when she sees it's Jonathan calling on her phone, or Jonathan who wants to go to dinner with the family, Jonathan who wants her to come shopping with him for a new Polo button-down for a date.

Waving a manila folder, Jonathan says, "Hey, guess what, I got a commitment. It looks like all I have to write is a few more episodes, and HBO might—if I'm *really* lucky—actually develop my series!" He grins sheepishly, his ruddy cheeks glistening.

There is a moment of stunned silence, and then the

family begins clapping. With the encouragement of Isabel's good friend from Penn, Maria Slavit, whom Jonathan had interned with at HBO the previous summer, he's been working till 4:00 a.m. every night at school on an *Entourage*-like comedy about New York college students in Atlanta missing the comforts of home—like good bagels and good pizza, and food that is delivered in fifteen minutes—aptly titled *From New York*.

"It's just an agreement to develop my idea. But it's pretty amazing, right?"

"HBO!!" Elizabeth insists.

"It's cool," he says, smiling, "I know. Can you imagine, my writing may be on HBO one day."

An hour later, after a few orders of French fries and a cheeseburger for Jonathan, who hadn't eaten lunch, they are all outside waiting for Dave to pull up. "Are you girls coming home with me?" Elizabeth asks, but they tell her they are going to look at a loft on Spring Street and that they will see her later at her apartment for "movie night."

"Jonathan, are you staying?" they ask.

"I wish I could, but I have to go back to study—I have my econ final and a paper due for creative writing on Friday."

The girls think back to the first parents' visiting weekend at Emory, when Jonathan was a freshman. They had flown down to Atlanta for the weekend, and stayed at the Ritz-Carlton in Buckhead, which was just divine. Jonathan drove them around in his black SUV Benz—his Horace Mann graduation gift—and they listened to Billy Joel nonstop with the windows wide open. They remember seeing his freshman dorm room—huge! terraces!—in a *Melrose Place*-type development with a swimming pool, nothing like where Kate and Isabel had lived in West Philadelphia. And Jonathan's adorable roommate Corey Cohen, the two of them with their *Sopranos* and *Curb Your Enthusiasm* posters scattered among half-finished bottles of Grey Goose and Gatorade. It was one of those magical weekends that they knew they would remember their whole lives.

Dave honks and snaps them back to New York City. "Love you, Jonathan," they say together, "speak to you later," and each of them puts an arm up for a taxi.

Then Dave takes Elizabeth and Jonathan uptown. He will drop Elizabeth and then take Jonathan to LaGuardia.

As Elizabeth gets out in front of their home, Jonathan opens up the window and screams, "Love you, Mom!! I'll be back before you know it."

Elizabeth has several phone calls to make once she gets home, one to the broker whose clients outbid their competitors for her listing on the East 93rd Street town house, about to have a building inspection, but somehow she's feeling exhausted and just wants to sit on the sofa with the girls—Lola, Dolly, and Roxy—thinking about how wonderful it was to be surprised by Jonathan today. She calls Tom to see where he is; it's almost six o'clock, and he's usually home by now.

"I'm just leaving Williams-Sonoma," he says. "I got a new frozen margarita maker." Tom is always buying something new, whether he needs it or not. The slickest kitchen appliances, the newest TVs—he just bought a 3-D TV for the library that cost over $3,000, and he needed to pay their AV team, Prestige Sound and Video, a father/son team named Garrey and Lonny from the Five Towns, a hundred dollars an hour to come over and set it up. He is constantly updating everything in their home and giving the old to either one of their children or to their adored housekeeper/dogsitter/personal assistant, Cecilia, who has been with the Chase family for over fifteen years.

"Can you believe it about HBO?" Tom says. "I mean, we don't know what will happen, but just for Jonathan to even have had that meeting, to have the interest—how many twenty-one-year-olds can say that HBO is interested in their series?"

"It *is* unbelievable," says Elizabeth. "Oh, I hope they buy it!"

Her cell phone rings, and she sees it's Monique. "Hello," she says, "one second, I'm just hanging up with Tom." Odd that she'd be calling. If anything, Elizabeth should be calling to thank *her* for lunch.

"Tom, it's Monique," she says. "See you at home."

"Hi—can you talk?" says Monique.

"Of course," Elizabeth says, kicking off her Choos.

"Well, I just got off the phone with my friend Marilyn, whose daughter was recently hired to work for LEX Realty," Monique says. "And she told me something that was really weird."

"Does it have to do with us?"

"Well, it seems to. But let me tell you."

"Okay." Elizabeth starts to feel slightly apprehensive; Monique is hardly an alarmist.

Monique goes on. "So, *entre nous*, you know I sort of have a thing for Teddy Wingo."

"I know, Monique."

"So I was talking about our lunch today, and maybe I shouldn't have, but I mentioned the fact that Teddy had missed an important appointment."

"Doesn't matter," Elizabeth says, although she would have preferred that Monique had kept quiet about this.

"And there was a strange silence on the other end of the line. And then Marilyn said, 'Actually, I don't envy Elizabeth Chase having to deal with the likes of *him*.' So of course I asked her what she meant, and at first she tried to steer me to another subject. But I wouldn't let her, and finally she just came right out and said, 'According to my daughter, he's not to be trusted.' And I said, 'How would *you* know?' And she said this: 'Monique, this can't come from me. You absolutely have to promise.' And I promised. And then she said, 'I know for a fact.' And I said, 'You're still being vague,' and she said, 'I've already said too much.' And then she absolutely refused to say more. She made me promise I wouldn't identify her, but, well, my loyalty is obviously to you, Elizabeth."

"I don't suppose you can tell me who the daughter is."

"I'm already breaking a confidence. But—"

"It's all right. But why would this woman say anything to you at all?"

"Because her daughter went out on a few dates with Teddy. And it didn't end well."

"Uh-huh," Elizabeth says. "But in that case she and her mother have reason to hate him. They could be making this all up."

"Marilyn's not a petty person. She was warning me, knowing that I would warn *you*," Monique says. "But here's the thing. I know this girl has had a problem with drugs. She's not exactly what I'd call stable. And therefore is probably kind of a loose cannon. I'm just wondering if she might be the one Teddy was breaking up with and who, you know . . . slipped him that really strong sedative."

Monique must have won the game Clue all the time as a child, Elizabeth thinks to herself. She takes in everything Monique has just said and doesn't immediately respond.

"You there?" Monique says.

"I'm here. I don't even know what to say."

"Well, let me know what you find out. And if I find out anything more, I'll call you."

"Thanks so much, Monique."

Elizabeth hangs up and looks into the entrance gallery. The girls, mid phone call, had jumped down from her lap one by one, and Lola and Dolly are now wrestling with a stuffed lavender penguin that one of them has pulled from a nest of dog toys. Elizabeth gets up, walks into the kitchen, and pours herself a glass of Lillet, and then opens the freezer to drop in some frozen berries. Then she gets out the eggs and turns on the stove to make the girls their scrambled-egg dinner.

Just as she's finishing the eggs and ladling them into three identical blue bowls that she bought in a market in Provence, Tom walks quietly into the kitchen; he's wearing his Topsiders, jeans, and an Emory University T-shirt. He sits down at the rectangular country farm table around which they've built banquettes and where the family eats instead of the formal dining room, which they use no more than twice a year.

Elizabeth turns to Tom. "Amy's coming tomorrow to give them their shots," she says.

Dr. Amy Attas is the founder of CityPets, a veterinary house call service, and Elizabeth always feels reassured knowing that she will come to their apartment to treat the dogs whenever necessary. Dr. Attas was, in fact, the one who prolonged the Chases' beloved Fluffy's life by four years by doing her chemotherapy in the Chases' apartment. Though some of her friends thought it extravagant, there was nothing Elizabeth wouldn't do for her dogs.

Returning to the sink and washing the frying pan, she says, "So I got a weird call from Monique," and then relays the rest of the conversation. She sets the pan in the stainless steel drainer and turns to face Tom.

"So what do you want to do?" Tom says.

"I guess we have to start watching Teddy carefully, seeing what he's up to."

Nervously running his fingers through his hair, Tom says, "I've always wanted to get rid of him. Actually, I wish he'd go somewhere else."

"Yes, but don't forget, it's because of him that we're getting the business from Luxury Estates. I wouldn't even consider confronting him about anything until that deal is done."

They're speaking of a program that the venerable auction house Barrington's created called Luxury Estates, in which they select one real estate brokerage company from each major city in America and do an all-out marketing campaign for the company's properties. They offer this as a way of helping to promote estate and heirloom auctions held in major cities like New York, Boston, Chicago, and Los Angeles, events that comprise a substantial percentage of their business. Teddy, who has contacts everywhere, cultivated an "in" at Barrington's. With some finessing, he was able to get what they were aiming for in a marketing campaign. The major real estate brokerage companies in New York City spent thousands of dollars on proposals, and all but Chase Residential and LEX were eliminated.

A month ago Teddy received the unofficial assurance that Chase Residential was to be chosen by Barrington's as its real estate company from New York City. Not only would this mean a priceless amount of free publicity but, more importantly, all the other companies selected around the country would be referring their clients directly to Chase Residential and vice versa. It would be huge for the

Chase business, particularly since so many wealthy Americans were—because of the weak dollar against the euro—opting to buy in New York City rather than in France or Italy or Spain.

"But the Luxury Estates program isn't going to be announced for a while, is it?" Tom asks.

"Maybe not until Christmas."

"So what are we going to do until then? Teddy might be seriously compromising us—we have no idea."

"We'll just have to watch him," Elizabeth says. "And try to find out just how true this is. I still distrust it, only because we're dealing with a woman Teddy probably was awful to."

"We should get the password to his e-mail account," Tom says suddenly.

They both simultaneously think of Jonathan, who's a computer whiz and might be able to hack into Teddy's e-mail.

"I don't know, Tom," Elizabeth says. "Should we really do that? If he ever found out . . . let me marinate on this, as Jonathan says."

"Okay, but let's not forget that Teddy can pretty much go anywhere," Tom says. "Any other company would be thrilled to have him work for them."

"Maybe he already *is* working for them—"

"—And we just don't know it," Tom says, finishing her sentence.

Elizabeth goes and sits down next to Tom, and as soon

as she does, Dolly, Lola, and Roxy gather around her legs, waiting for her to pick them up.

"I've trusted Teddy with so much," she admits to her husband, picking a frozen blackberry out of the Lillet. She folds her hands on the table. "But now that I think about it, he's always sort of vague with me."

Tom shakes his head and says, "All right, the girls are coming over tonight—are we going to tell them?"

"Of course we're going to tell them," Elizabeth says, and leaves the room, Roxy, Lola, and Dolly trailing behind her.

CHAPTER SEVEN

Kate

Heaven on Earth

Fifth Avenue/70s. 8 rooms. Sprawling, sunny 3 bedroom, 3-and-a-half baths with 11-foot ceilings and spectacular wraparound terraces. White-glove full-service cooperative. $8.5 million.

Hey you!" Alexa says cheerfully. "No more turn-downs from nasty bitch co-op boards, right?"

"Hope not." Kate smiles, and waits to be introduced to the little man accompanying Alexa.

"Oh, and this is Mr. Butterworth."

Mr. Butterworth pulls the ascot from around his neck, wipes his forehead with it, then arranges it under his chin again. He takes a mini bow and says to Kate, "Delighted to meet you, pretty girl."

Who *is* this man? she wonders. Why can't any of her clients show up alone or with their spouses or parents? Why do they have to complicate things by bringing along their friends and neighbors?

"Oh, and BTW, Mr. Butterworth's my psychic," Alexa says.

Oh, my God, Kate thinks. "Really! How interesting! How long have you two known each other?" she asks as they ride up in the mahogany-paneled elevator.

"Umm, sometimes it kind of seems like forever," Alexa says. "I wouldn't dream of making a move without consulting with him first. He told me that the last co-op, the nasty one that turned us down, probably wasn't going to work out, but I just didn't want to believe him, I guess. But I won't make that mistake again, and that's why this time around I figured I'd bring him along to actually see the apartment."

"Not to be boastful, but I do know whereof I speak, darlin'," Mr. Butterworth says. "Perhaps your friend Kate here would be interested in having me take a peek at *her* future sometime."

It isn't a bad idea—maybe he can tell her whether Scott is ever going to just give in and let himself be in love with her, because this is truly what she feels in her heart, the reason she keeps giving him one more chance, the reason Kate hates every date she ever goes on. She is just so sure Scott will come back to her. Kate has always been an utterly hopeless romantic in the weeping, perfect-movie-ending kind of way. In her high school yearbook, in the dedication page to her boyfriend Jimmy, she quoted "You're in my heart, you're in my soul. You'll be my breath should I grow old, you are my lover, you're my best friend, you're in my soul." At the time, she thought that life would not exist past Jimmy. Isabel and Jonathan, who each also had their first loves at age fifteen, both used the same quotation; Isabel with Essene, and Jonathan with Jen.

"I charge two-fifty for forty-five minutes, but frankly I'm worth every penny," he adds.

"Oh, he is!" Alexa agrees enthusiastically.

Kirk Henckels, one of the top brokers from Stribling and a close friend of Elizabeth's, greets them at the door, and then takes Kate aside to whisper that a broker from Corcoran is just finishing up a showing with his clients, and that he'll be out the door in a couple of minutes. "I'm so sorry," he says. "They're taking a little longer than expected," he explains.

"That's okay," Kate says graciously, and then suggests, since the other buyers are in the living room, that they start in the kitchen. She shows Alexa and her psychic the $6,000 Sub-Zero refrigerator, the marble center island (Alexa loves an island!), the gleaming utility room with a stainless steel washer and dryer.

"Nice," Mr. Butterworth says approvingly, and Alexa smiles.

The sweeping thirty-two-foot entrance gallery is filled with Warhol, Picasso, and Milton Avery, and Kate knows they're all originals, worth many millions. She thinks of Mr. Yates's wonderful AP art history class she took at Horace

Mann, and the endless memorizing she had to do, always staying up all night before exams (a last-minute Lucy, Kate was, always printing papers on her way out the door to class a few years later in college—always marveling at how she managed to meet every deadline) and assigning each artist to a friend of hers so she would remember him. She wonders briefly now why she didn't go on to law school after graduation or pursue a doctorate in English literature. But joining the family business was always her destiny, and after seven years in real estate, she can't imagine or want a different life for herself. There is nothing like working with your family, she always thinks.

Mr. Butterworth suddenly looks uneasy, and he grasps both of Alexa's hands in his own as he says, "I have to tell you that I'm feeling the presence of a ghost within these walls. Nothing to be afraid of, darlin', but I thought it prudent to mention nonetheless."

"Wait, hold on, what do you mean?" Alexa says, her voice rising five octaves in a high-pitched squeal. "I just don't—"

"Should we go see the spectacular wraparound terrace?" Kate interrupts, seeing that Alexa is about to have a total meltdown.

"But what do you mean by 'nothing to be afraid of'?" Alexa says loudly, her voice shriller and shriller as she clutches her purple ostrich Birkin like a life vest. "You're telling me there's a ghost in this apartment, and I'm supposed to be fine with that?"

The broker from Corcoran appears now with a youngish couple dressed in jeans and T-shirts. "Would you mind keeping your voice down?" he tells Alexa, and ushers his clients toward the front door. He's a man in his thirties in a navy blue Barbour coat and tasseled loafers; his name is Eric Austin, and Kate doesn't much like him. She's watched him over the past couple of years and finds him slick. And then there's the condescending way he's speaking to her client.

"I *do* mind," Alexa says. "If Mr. Butterworth feels the presence of a ghost in this apartment, I have every right to be upset, don't you think?"

"Who's Mr. Butterworth?" the broker says, and then recognizes Kate. "How's it going, Kate?" he says. "I know the Langfelders and I were supposed to be out of here a few minutes ago, but well, I'm sorry."

"I'm Mrs. Walden's psychic," Mr. Butterworth offers. "May I give you my business card?"

"Thanks, not interested in you and your ghost stories." Then he whispers, "You better keep your mouth shut—my client loves this apartment."

"It would be highly unethical of me to keep to myself what I've seen here," Mr. Butterworth announces. "And of course when it comes to ghosts, I say live and let live, darlin'."

" 'Live and let live'—that's a good one," Eric Austin says. He and the Langfelders make their way from the door back toward the center of the entrance gallery.

"Actually . . . I'm very interested in the paranormal,"

Daniel Langfelder says. "I think the idea of a ghost inhabiting the apartment is really pretty cool."

"Well, then, my boy, what all of you need to know is that the ghost I'm seeing is one hundred percent real," Mr. Butterworth says. "He tells me his name is Everett Shea Crawford Junior, and that he died in the master bedroom on March 15, 1938, after a long battle with . . . with . . ." Squeezing his eyes shut tightly, the psychic cants his head toward the ceiling. "With, I think he's saying . . . syphilis!" he says triumphantly, waving his ascot like a flag. "Which he contracted from a prostitute and dancer named Crystal . . . something or other." Mr. Butterworth flutters his hand in front of his face and wipes his forehead again.

A ghost with syphilis! Kate stares glumly at the herringbone floor. Her hopes for selling the apartment fade and then disappear completely. She can just picture Alexa going home and posting on Facebook this delightful piece of information about a ghost with a sexually transmitted disease.

"Fascinating!" Daniel Langfelder is saying. "I'd be thrilled to live in an apartment that comes with a piece of history like that."

"Uh, right, fascinating," Eric agrees.

Daniel Langfelder's wife, a dark-haired woman with a tortoiseshell headband in her hair, is staring at them both. "Have you two lost your minds?" she says. "Over my dead body will I let you buy this apartment for us, Dan. Let's get out of here. *Now.*"

"Oh, Amanda, why are you always so narrow-minded?" he says as he and his wife and broker head back toward the front door.

As soon as the door shuts behind them, Mr. Butterworth lets out a little whoop of pleasure. "I *knew* the wife wouldn't go for it!"

"I'll never go for it, either," Alexa says. "Never."

"Never say never," Mr. Butterworth advises. "Because, guess what, darlin', the ghost didn't die from an STD, he died of a broken heart following the death of his wife, whom he'd been happily married to for over half a century. There's a love story for you right there."

"Wait, you lied to them?" Alexa says.

"Well, I prefer to say I rearranged the facts, darlin'. But only because I knew, the moment we set foot in here, that this was meant to be *your* apartment, a home where you and Bobby and your sweet little angel Chloe would be truly happy."

"Ha," Kate says, her smile matching Alexa's, "but I had that very same feeling. Now let's go fall in love with the three enormous bedrooms—Alexa, the master suite has its own dressing room! And I hope you have noticed the eleven-foot ceilings. . . ." Alexa squeals and claps her hands. Kate wants to kiss Mr. Butterworth on his chubby little cheeks.

When they're done looking, Kate isn't at all surprised to hear Mr. Butterworth's prediction: this time, the interview with the co-op board will be a piece of pecan pie for Alexa and her husband.

And they'll just have to take Butterworth's word for

it—after all, who knows better than a psychic when it comes to the vagaries of co-op boards?

On her way to her parents' apartment for dinner that night, Kate runs into the family dermatologist, a striking thirty-five-year-old in a Prada suit whose younger sister, Annie, was a high school classmate of hers. Dr. Paul Frank stops her on the street with a big kiss hello and asks, laughingly, "How is that lollipop treating you?" Kate takes the lollipop out of her mouth—wishing she wasn't sucking on it right now—and smiles. "Mom and the family all good?" he continues.

"They're great," she says. "Actually, Mom may need to come see you soon for a little Botox." She smiles, remembering the last time she and her mother went to Dr. Frank's office, a few months ago; even while getting her injection, her insanely busy mother continued to take calls on her cell phone. Paul Frank had to virtually chase her around his office as she paced on the phone, thumbing through the pages of her Day-at-a-Glance, begging her to sit in his chair and stop talking or he'd stick the needle in her lip by accident.

Paul is staring at her intently now, and Kate's starting to feel self-conscious; does she have crow's-feet? Or under-eye circles that need fillers, like all her friends get? He's so good-looking she feels her cheeks start to turn red. Why does this always happen to her? she thinks. She can't control the flush of her cheeks.

Offering his diagnosis after a moment, Paul tells her, "You're way too pretty to not be married, Kate."

"Oh, thank you," she says, blushing even more, not knowing what else to say. She was excited to see him on TV not long ago, talking on *Good Morning America* about Botox helping to ease his patients' migraines, and she remembers his funny response when Barbara Walters asked if he used the stuff himself: "Well, I look pretty good for sixty, don't I?" She looks out toward the median that divides Park Avenue and at the beautiful purple tulips and hydrangeas that bloom there.

"Are you seeing anyone?" Paul is saying. "Because if you're not, I'm wondering whether you'd be interested in going out with my cousin Jeff. He's an architect, a Yale grad, a really great guy, everyone says he looks like Robert Pattinson. What do you think?"

As gorgeous as you? she'd like to ask. But instead she smiles and says, "Oh, I don't really like blind dates, but how could I say no to a cousin of yours?"

"I think he's on Facebook. Jeff Matthau. Check him out for yourself and then give my office a call, okay?" Paul says kindly.

Paul Frank is gorgeous and sweet. And so cute—darkly handsome like Dermot Mulroney in *My Best Friend's Wedding.* "Thanks so much," she tells him. And then, even though she's going to be seeing Isabel in less than five minutes, Kate calls to tell her about Paul Frank and his cousin.

"Too bad we're not on Facebook," Isabel says. "If we

were, I could look at him right now. Although the thought of you with someone else is so weird—I just keep picturing you with Scott."

And at that moment, as happy as Kate is for her engaged sister, she wonders how it came about that Isabel became engaged first. As the big sister, Kate had done everything first. Every major event in their life—whether walking and talking, attending Horace Mann nursery school, getting their first bras or manicures, having their first kisses—Kate had gone first. So Isabel's getting engaged first completely goes against the natural order of things. It isn't that Kate is jealous; it was just so unexpected that Isabel would do anything before her, let alone get married. Kate, the English major, received her first A+ for a paper she wrote in the seventh grade titled "The Unwelcome Gift." It was about the birth of her sister, and the story began with the moment her mother's water broke all over the green shag carpet during their Sunday night Chinese dinner. Isabel, with her roly-poly legs and cheeks (infancy seeming to be the only time in a girl's life where chubby is more coveted than skinny) was a sheer delight to everyone who saw her, including Kate. Kate was in love with her, helping her mother change diapers and shaking a rattle when Isabel was in the cradle, her "little babysitter," Elizabeth called her.

But there was another side. Kate also loved to pinch the baby. The more Kate pinched, the more Isabel wanted to be held by her. The more Kate dressed her in her doll's outfits—crinkly, ruffly, totally uncomfortable crinolines and ruffles and petticoats, propping her up in their parents' green-and-white-flowered bed, Isabel's head lolling forward—the more Isabel squealed and gurgled with glee. So Elizabeth, sensing an undercurrent of something other than pure glee in Kate, created the "Yaya and Tralala" stories that she would tell Kate at bedtime in her lavender bed with the big white eyelet canopy, in her bedroom with the *Wizard of Oz* yellow-brick-road wallpaper. These were stories where the older sister—a dark-haired, brown-eyed, scrawny little girl (Elizabeth always attributed Kate's smallness to a terrible cold she developed at two months old)—was named Yaya (a whine), and the angelic younger sister, a blond, blue-eyed, and perfectly rosy-cheeked baby, was called Tralala (a singsong). Elizabeth figured these sort of make-believe stories would help Kate adjust to no longer being an only child.

"I know," Kate says to Isabel now, with a teeny-tiny lump in her throat at the thought that she could be anything other than purely joyful at her sister's good fortune.

There's a vase of lovely pink peonies and periwinkle hydrangeas in the entrance gallery of her parents' apartment, Kate sees when she arrives. And then she sees that Isabel is sitting there in the library, Dolly in her lap, Roxy and Lola on the floor at her feet. All three pure white dogs are in a state of total glee at the sight of Kate, scratching at her bare legs; it's almost as if there's something important they'd like to tell her, if only they could speak.

"Come and sit with me, girls," she says, and lifts one and then the other onto the sofa.

"So how'd everything go with Alexa and the three-bedroom on Fifth?" Isabel says.

"Oh, what a story!" Kate says, then tells her all about Mr. Butterworth. On the coffee table in front of them is a tray of crackers, an aged Gouda, Gruyère, and a sinfully delicious triple-crème St. André, and her sister's half-filled glass of virgin Bloody Mary. Kate takes a big sip, and remembers all those after-school snacks exactly like this one, from the time she was in second grade. Oh, how the Chase children loved their childhood, how excited the girls were when it was announced over the loudspeaker at Horace Mann, Kate in the middle of reading *Ramona the Pest* with Mrs. Wendy Steinthal, "Will Kate and Isabel Chase please come to the principal's office" to get the news that their baby brother had been born! Every Friday she and her sister went to Helen Butleroff's School of Dance close to home on 84th Street, where Helen, a former Rockette, taught them tap, jazz, and ballet. And after dance class, their parents would pick them up and drive them to midtown in one Mercedes and then another, as years passed (for Tom was always replacing his cars with the latest models), to the Palm on Second and 45th, where she and Isabel stubbornly and routinely refused to eat steak and, instead, would order the same spaghetti marinara week after week, the four of them sitting in "their" booth by the bar, where their parents drank Bloody Bull shots and dined on roast beef and lobster, creamed spinach and hash browns, the floor under their feet sprinkled with sawdust, all of it presided over by the lovable manager, Al, who is still there today. (These days the Chases sit at a table in the front, next to the caricature of Tom and the family that has been painted on the wall.) She remembers, too, the Chinese food she and Isabel loved at those restaurants, now long shuttered, with names like King Dragon and City Luck, Jonathan a baby who, after every dinner, came home with a diaper full of white rice, no matter what he was wearing.

They decide to order pizza now—as always, with extra cheese—from Mimi's on Lex, where they've been ordering from before Jonathan was even born. And when it arrives, their mother has a salad ready for them with Good Seasons dressing and a pitcher of fresh-brewed iced tea. Over dinner in the kitchen, they discuss work until, very casually, Isabel says, "I've been thinking of black for the bridesmaids' dresses."

There are, Kate notices, a couple of dark green specks of oregano at the corner of Isabel's mouth, and Kate leans over and brushes them away with her napkin. She remembers how, as the older sister, she would always look out for Isabel, and later Jonathan, trying never to sound too bossy but probably failing at that, she thinks now. It was her job to protect them, she thought; even though when their parents went out in the evening and left them with a sitter (which was very infrequently), it was Kate who asked Isabel to wait up for their parents with her in their parents' bed (whenever they did go out, Kate always slept in her parents' bed) because she was scared and missed them. She would hold her little sister's and brother's hands as they crossed the streets of the city, their mother beside them as they walked home from playdates after school. A lifetime ago, it seems.

"Black is always a sexy color," Kate says. "And it looks good on everyone."

"You know, Meme used to say black was only for old people. She never wanted your mom or Aunt Bobby to wear it," their father says.

"We love it when you talk about fashion," Isabel teases him.

"I just don't see black for a summer wedding, sorry, girls," Elizabeth says, and that ends the conversation. "Are we going to watch *Gone with the Wind* tonight or no?" she says plaintively a moment later. She seems distracted, so unlike the way she usually is when Kate and Isabel are over for dinner—usually she's bustling about, slipping in and out of her seat to get the phone, or more lemon for their iced tea.

This is all about Teddy; Kate is sure of it. Her mother has always been on top of everything, but the possibility of Teddy trying to sabotage the family business is extremely disturbing. She's managing, though, working even harder than usual, and that's always been her mother's way, a sort of purposeful state of denial.

In a few minutes they move to the library, the three women on the sofa, Tom in his club chair with his feet up. *Gone with the Wind* is in the Blu-ray player; Kate and Isabel have probably seen the four-hour film a dozen times since childhood, once even at the Sony theater on Broadway and 68th—it ended at 1:00 a.m. and even had an intermission, "like the good old days," their father said. "This is the way movies should be shown." The Chases love the film more every time they see it.

"You should be kissed, and often, by someone who knows how," Kate hears Clark Gable advise Vivien Leigh, and she savors, if only for a moment, the thrill of longing for Scott that goes right through her.

CHAPTER EIGHT

Isabel

High Drama over Park

CPW/70s. 10-room penthouse duplex in the fabled San Remo. 4 bedrooms, 4 baths, sunroom, and wood-paneled library. Central Park views throughout. $10.5 million.

The bridal salon on the seventh floor of Bergdorf's is an enchanted little paradise. Isabel delights in the dove-gray carpeting, the armchairs upholstered in cream silk, the three-tiered tray offering petit fours and chocolates, the rods of sumptuous bridal gowns in every subtle shade of white, ivory, cream, and champagne. As she moves around the small space, she flicks the hangers—first an exquisite, simple silk slip, then an elaborately beaded and lace-trimmed gown, a full, bell-like tulle skirt that is straight out of Cinderella. This extravagant dress would have danced its way through the lavish court of Versailles a few centuries back, she thinks.

Isabel didn't plan on coming here; she never goes shopping—especially for a wedding dress!—on her own. The Chase girls barely commit to buying an umbrella without their mother's opinion. But the client Kate's taking to a luxury high-rise on Third Avenue is running late, and the potential seller whose 72nd Street apartment she's scheduled to see needs a bit longer to get the apartment in shape, so Isabel finds herself with a little time to play. Since she needs a new lipstick, she pops into Bergdorf's, and once she's bought the lipstick and a box of Santa Maria Novella bath salts, on impulse, she gets on the escalator up to the bridal salon.

"May I help you?"

Isabel turns to see a pretty woman with shoulder-length dark hair advancing toward her. She's wearing a flame-colored sheath dress and four-inch black patent leather pumps. Isabel recognizes Christian Louboutin's trademark poppy red on the soles when the woman takes another step.

"I'm just looking," Isabel says. She doesn't want to do this without her mother and Kate, but she can't resist a little peek.

"Okay, I'm here," the woman says. Her voice is low and melodic; Isabel is instantly drawn to it. "Just let me know if I can help in any way."

Isabel nods politely and continues her study of the room. She glances up at the Venetian glass chandelier and looks longingly at the chocolates on the stand.

The lovely saleswoman reappears, and hands her a card. "When you're ready, you can schedule an appointment," she says.

Isabel looks down at what is printed on the card. "Beth," she reads. "Thank you." She permits herself a last look around the bridal salon.

"You're welcome," Beth says.

"Isabel!" She hears a familiar, European-accented voice. It's the countess, who, when she says her name, places the emphasis on the last syllable, so it sounds like "IsaBELLE."

"Delphine, what are you doing here?"

"I've been shopping!" Delphine says with sweet delight, and holds aloft the orchid-colored Bergdorf's bag, "and I was just going to stop for a cappuccino." The countess waves her arm, indicating the restaurant that is also on Bergdorf's seventh floor. "Why don't you join me?"

Isabel hesitates for only a second and then thinks, Why not? Since her appointments have been pushed back until three, she has some time.

Being in the bridal salon made her feel so giddy, so hopeful, even though she didn't actually try on a dress, that she decides she's entitled to a little self-indulgence, and besides, the countess is a client. And so she says, "I'd love to join you."

The countess doesn't actually clap out loud, but she presses her hands together before linking arms with Isabel. They enter the restaurant, and before they can say anything, the maître d' approaches them and announces that there is a half-hour wait. "We're just here for a cappuccino. We'll take that small table by the window, *va bene*?" Delphine says, and the man gives a little bow and enthusiastically answers her in a flood of Italian. Within moments, Isabel and the countess find themselves at a table overlooking the magnificent Plaza Hotel and condominiums, and beyond that, the gorgeous green of Central Park.

"How did you know that he was Italian?" Isabel asks, amazed at how skillfully this transition was made.

"His accent in English is unmistakable," the countess says. "I come across so many like him here in the city." She smiles that girlish smile of hers, the one that Isabel finds hard to resist.

A waiter appears and Delphine says to Isabel, "Latté, cappuccino?"

Delphine's long, straight blond hair falls in her face as she dips into her handbag, seeming to look for something momentarily. There is nothing girlish about the massive gold and aquamarine ring—the stone nearly as large and rectangular as a domino—that rests on her slim finger, or the heavy pearl drops that dangle from her ears. Over her shoulders, Delphine has artfully tossed a snowy white silk shawl; her skirt is a rich silk paisley in delicate shades of yellow, turquoise, ivory, and black. Isabel knows that if she looks down, she'll see the countess's shiny black cowboy boots on her feet.

The countess seems to find what she's been looking for, and with what Isabel could swear is a twinkle in her eye says, "So what brings you to the seventh floor of Bergdorf's? Everything really good is down below!"

At that moment, the man who seated them appears

holding Isabel's cell phone. Why does he have it? She must have dropped it somewhere; she hadn't even realized it was gone.

"I believe this is yours," he says. "Beth in the bridal salon just brought it by. I recognized her description."

"Oh, thank you so much," says Isabel, gratefully accepting the phone. Oh, she can imagine if she had lost it—a disaster! "Please thank Beth, too."

The man nods and walks away. Isabel glances over at the countess, who has said nothing. But her eyes, Isabel sees, are bright with curiosity.

"The bridal salon!" Delphine coos. "Are you engaged?"

Isabel puts her hand on the table to show her client the beautiful diamond.

"Well, I must be very unobservant because I didn't even notice the ring. What wonderful news! When did this happen?"

Isabel tells Delphine about the proposal.

"This Michael, he sounds so romantic. And an actor! On television as well as on the stage! How glamorous! You must let me know when he is appearing in something. Fritzie and I adore the theater. So . . . why don't you look as happy as I think you should?"

Isabel hesitates. And then the cappuccinos arrive; as she takes a sip, she says, "It's just that my older sister's boyfriend broke up with her right before my boyfriend proposed to me, and I guess I just wish the timing had all been different."

The countess shakes her head. "With love there always

seems to come a payment of one sort or another. Your sister will find someone else, I'm sure of it."

"Well, she's been totally in love with him for years, despite the fact that he keeps breaking up with her. He always comes back, though."

"I admire her for this," Delphine says. "I was, you might say, addicted to Fritzie, who had to disentangle himself from his former wife to marry me. How long have your parents been married?" she asks.

"Forever," Isabel says with pride.

"My goodness, really?" the countess says, but her tone, Isabel can't help noticing, is slightly skeptical. "It's so hard these days to find marriages that last a lifetime. You don't know how lucky you are that your parents have remained together." She smiles. "It gives your own marriage a much greater chance."

"I think so. I hope so," Isabel says, just for a moment imagining herself growing old (gracefully, of course!) with Michael and having a marriage just like her parents'. She can see them living in the same apartment building on Park Avenue, in a lovely classic nine with a private elevator landing, raising her children with all that she and Kate and Jonathan had growing up.

"I know only a few couples who have stayed together for a lifetime, but all of them have had affairs," Delphine remarks, looking down at her bejeweled hands. "However, they are Europeans. Whereas your parents are Americans. Do you think they have been faithful to each other all these years?" she says, gazing up at Isabel now.

Isabel can't quite believe that Delphine has the nerve to ask such a thing. Before she has a chance to respond in any sort of measured way, Delphine says, "Forgive me, don't even tell me. How impertinent I've been! I don't know what has gotten into me. Tell me instead, did you find your wedding dress yet?" she asks as she daintily sips the last drops of her cappuccino. "No, of course you didn't!" she says, answering her own question. "Finding the right dress takes time. It's a whole process. But a lovely one, I should think. I never had the pleasure." The countess looks down and sighs. She sets her cappuccino cup down with a tiny clatter.

Still irritated by Delphine's inappropriate question, Isabel says, "You mean you didn't pick out a dress for yourself when you married the count?" How can this be?

"No," the countess says. She leans back in her chair and carefully rearranges herself. "We eloped."

"Well, that must have been romantic," Isabel says.

"Not entirely," says the countess. "Fritzie has a grown daughter from a previous marriage. She doesn't like me, and that's an understatement. Believe me when I tell you that she was not at all happy—and this, too, is an understatement—that her beloved father was taking me as his wife." The expression on her face darkens; it's as though a momentary shadow has fallen across her sunny disposition.

"Oh, sorry," says Isabel. "That's . . . sad."

"Most unfortunate," Delphine says before signaling to the waiter and taking the check. "Another cappuccino, please," she says to him before turning back to Isabel. She's smiling at

her now; she's once again become the charming, girlish client Isabel has enjoyed working with these past weeks.

Poised in front of the doors to Bergdorf's, they spend a few minutes discussing the next apartment that the countess wants to see. Because she's now expressed an interest in the west side as well, Isabel is considering two possibilities—a penthouse in the storied San Remo on Central Park West and a Riverside Drive gem with unobstructed views of the Hudson River from six of its ten vast rooms.

"Next week, then?" Isabel says as she sees the white limo pulling up.

"Any day but Thursday," Delphine says. "Let's say Friday. Friday would be perfect. I'll call to set the time." And with a quick double peck on each side of Isabel's face, she slips into the waiting limo and drives away.

Isabel's eager to get back to the office to tell her sister and mother all about her conversation with the countess.

As if Elizabeth knew Isabel was thinking of her, her phone rings. "Oh, hi, Mom," she says, and then listens as Elizabeth explains a complicated situation with a seller who has now decided to pull his apartment from the market. "Uh-huh," Isabel repeats a couple of times, nodding vigorously even though of course her mother can't see her. But Elizabeth's phone calls, like Elizabeth herself, are always so filled with energy, it's impossible not to be infected with her larger-than-life spirit.

After she says good-bye to her mother, her phone rings again. Kate? No, it's her friend Nancy Scarlata. "Isaboo, you ready for this?" Nancy says, her voice percolating with excitement. Nancy is the only person Elizabeth allows to shorten her daughter's name; Elizabeth is not one for nicknames.

"What?" Isabel says, stepping aside on Fifth Avenue to avoid a crowd of French-speaking tourists walking three abreast.

"You made Page Six—again!" says Nancy, clearly delighted. "Let me read it to you!" she says, and Isabel hears her flipping the pages of her *New York Post* like a detective hot to trot on a murder mystery.

"OMG! *Now*, please!" Isabel says.

> We hear that dashing young actor Michael Prescott has proposed to the blond and beautiful Isabel Chase, of the high-end real estate firm Chase Residential. Isabel and her brunette look-alike sister, Kate, are the celeb real estate experts for NBC's "Access Hollywood."

"OMG, I love it!" Isabel squeals.

"Hold on one sec," says Nancy. She says something in her rapid-fire style to someone else; Nancy is a high-powered book editor responsible for several notable best sellers, and she's as busy as Isabel. "Listen, I've got to go," she says, returning to Isabel. "Want to meet for drinks one night next week? At the Carlyle? Although I'm too fat to go out, really." Nancy is all of a size four or six, on a bad day. Tall, nearly 5'7", with long, thick black hair, long gorgeous legs, beautiful tanned skin, and big brown eyes, Nancy is extremely pretty, but doesn't realize it. Her only flaw is that she is sometimes so insecure in her looks that she moves around like a pony, one who grew too big too fast and isn't quite sure how to walk yet.

"Next week is perfect," Isabel says. "Love you, and you are never fat!" And then she phones her parents and e-mails her brother and sister to let them know the exciting news about Page Six!

Back at the office, Isabel waves to Kate, who is on her cell and office phone at the same time. Isabel slips into her chair, turns to her laptop, and pulls up the listing for the San Remo penthouse. Ten rooms, ten-foot ceilings, all original details—a dream! The penthouse looks out over Central Park. This could be the one for the countess, she decides!

Just then she hears laughter booming from Teddy's office, and she can make out bits of his manic conversation—about a certain boutique hotel in the French Riviera whose owner is a prep school friend of his. "Trust me on this one, Diane," he's saying. "This is the place to stay. It's so . . . well, discreet, and they have a great staff just waiting for you to ask them for something."

Isabel wonders vaguely which Diane this could be. A girl he is dating? Or perhaps, by the way Teddy is going on, one of his celebrity clients? Diane Sawyer? Diane Lane? Just at that moment, he breezes by Isabel's office on the way to confer with Elizabeth in hers, impeccably dressed in a slim-fit charcoal gray Ralph Lauren suit and cotton candy pink Hermès tie with baby blue dolphins. Isabel can see her mother's stiff, slightly bristling response to Teddy's sudden appearance in her office. They exchange a few words, then he walks out the door, presumably going to an appointment. The truth is, Isabel hates the fact that they just can't get rid of Teddy. She allows herself to fantasize that, maybe a year or so from now, they'll be done with him. Of course, without Teddy in the office, it will be a lot quieter and, arguably, a bit duller. She knows her sister would agree with her, though, that on a day-to-day basis sometimes that charm of his is just too much.

A couple of hours later, after she's returned dozens of calls and e-mails, and just as she's attaching the listing in an e-mail to Delphine, Violeta approaches, carrying a silver box tied with a silver ribbon.

"This *just* came for you," she says, handing the box to Isabel.

"Really? From who?" Isabel gazes at the expertly tied bow.

"It was brought by messenger," Violeta explains. "There's a card."

Isabel opens the envelope, and there, in lavish script, is a short message that reads:

> I asked you far too many personal questions. And I talked too much about myself

today. I didn't mean to cloud your happiness, even for an instant. Please accept this little antique tea schedule. This is what ladies used to write their tea engagements on with a certain kind of pencil that can easily be erased. I think it should be yours.

As ever, D.

Isabel sets aside the note and opens the box. Nestled beneath the tissue paper is a small, delicate ivory fan with seven wide blades. It is simple and beautiful, and she imagines herself as a nineteenth-century woman of stature, writing her weekly engagements on each blade and then erasing them at the end of each meeting. Oh, to have lived back then, she thinks.

Kate, curious, walks over to her now. "What's that?" she asks, looking at the delicate ivory object in Isabel's hands.

"It was apparently used to keep track of ladies coming to tea." They hear the sound of jingling bracelets and know their mother is steps away. Elizabeth's jewelry, at least the sound of it, always precedes her.

"Where did you get that?" Elizabeth says, putting her red Birkin on Isabel's desk.

"Delphine, of course."

"What a client to have!" Elizabeth says.

"Have you shown her the duplex in the San Remo yet?" Kate says, smiling. "I feel like that is *so* her kind of apartment, just from the gifts she gives you!"

"Next week! We're going!" Isabel says, glad that Kate's sadness seems to be passing. Both girls turn to see where their mother has gone, and then realize that she is back in her office. They watch her behind the large glass window through which Elizabeth likes to observe the comings and goings of her daughters and all the other brokers. Looking more than a little displeased, she has her reading glasses on and is studying something intently; though Isabel can only guess at what her mother may be thinking, she imagines it to be some document that casts doubt on Teddy's loyalty to Chase Residential. Ever since Monique passed along information that Teddy might not have Chase Residential's best interests at heart—and who knows, he could even be selling private details about the firm's new exclusive clients and listings to other companies (in particular LEX)—Isabel has watched her mother struggle with denial and disbelief that somebody so close to her might actually betray her.

She pulls open her desk drawer now and begins going through it—so that's where her Chanel sunglasses went! After a moment, she locates the small unopened box of engraved note cards her mother ordered for each of them from Mrs. John L. Strong. Elizabeth's has a big E on the front, Kate's a K, and Isabel's an I. Each is engraved on heavy, cream-colored vellum paper, and each envelope is lined in a rich shade of amethyst. Now all she has to do is compose a note equal to both the stationery and the gift, and send it to Delphine at the Dartley.

CHAPTER NINE

Elizabeth

Luxe Lucida Condo

80s east. 3000 sf interior, 1000 sf of terraces in this high-floor 4 bedroom with south and west open city views. 40 foot living/dining. Full service Extell condo offers lap pool, spa, fitness center and more. $8.9 million.

Elizabeth has an extremely busy day ahead of her. First, a closing for a two-bedroom, two-bath apartment at 130 East 75th Street, a prewar building a few steps from Park Avenue whose co-op board was perfectly fine about her South American clients buying a seven-figure apartment for their granddaughter straight out of NYU law school. Then she has back-to-back showings for a classic-six buyer at 125 East 84th, 1111 Park, and 975 Park, all in the $2.5 to $4 million range. Then a showing at 860 United Nations Plaza. Finally, she's got to finalize the RSVPs for the party she's throwing at the Lucida that evening, a new glass Extell development on East 85th Street that is the first "green" building on the Upper East Side.

Although Elizabeth had always planned to throw a party for top brokers in the $8.9 million penthouse apartment she has listed in the building, once the family learned about Teddy's possible allegiance to LEX, they thought it best to invite all the LEX brokers. "Keep your friends close and your enemies closer," Tom always told them, citing *The Godfather: Part II.* And that would include the "daughter" of Monique's friend whose identity Kate quickly learned by making a discreet phone call to a broker friend of hers in LEX's downtown office.

The Chases are more than a little suspicious of Teddy's relationship with LEX; after carefully rummaging through his desk, they found plenty of printed matter involving LEX listings and policies, which struck them all as very odd. Just yesterday Elizabeth had called Jonathan about possibly breaking into Teddy's personal e-mail account—only Jonathan would know how to do this. Once again, the general consensus among the family was that they had to be very careful with Teddy.

She returns from the closing and her first showings a bit before two thirty; her appointment at 860 UN Plaza is at three. The apartment is a "For Sale by Owner," who has agreed to pay any selling broker a 4 percent commission, more than one might normally expect. Elizabeth had no time for lunch and eats a few pretzels instead. The client meeting her at the UN Plaza showing just happens to be Lance Roberts, the hotheaded bond trader who, when he discovered there was competition for an apartment he'd bid on, barged his way into a showing and physically attacked one of the other prospective buyers. It was Teddy who pulled him off the poor buyer, and then Teddy who punched Lance, as if to say, *Are you insane?*

Lance had been the client of Elizabeth's best broker friend, Barbara Fox, a lovely woman originally from Rocky Mount, North Carolina, someone who's always managed to retain her impeccable manners in dealing with brassy, no-nonsense New Yorkers but who got fed up with Lance Roberts and stopped returning his phone calls.

The day he finally got through to Elizabeth, he started off as pleasant as could be, thanking her profusely for returning his phone call and apologizing for his abominable behavior during the apartment showing way back when, and then got down to business.

"You may or may not know this, Elizabeth, but I've been rejected by several co-op boards," he began.

"Actually . . . I'm well aware of it, and, to be honest, not at all surprised."

"I remember Barbara telling me that the president of the co-op board at 860 UN Plaza is a good friend of yours."

"Yes, that's true," Elizabeth said.

"Well, there's an apartment for sale in the A-line that I'd like for my daughter, Kristina, who just graduated from college," Lance said.

"Wow—that's a big apartment. What a lucky girl," Elizabeth had remarked.

"As far as I'm concerned, Kristina can stay there for the rest of her life. She can get married there and raise her children in that apartment."

Elizabeth paused for a moment, imagining a conversation with her friend on the co-op board. "The board probably already knows about your . . . unfortunate behavior," she'd told Lance. "The truth is, you're notorious. Lots of brokers around town have been talking about you and your antics." She couldn't help it.

Lance Roberts remained remarkably cool despite Elizabeth's pointed words. "I was hoping that you could tell your friend on the co-op board that I've been reformed," he said.

"Oh? How so?"

"Well, believe it or not, I've taken anger management classes."

The thought of this gave her a big giggle on a very trying day. She gave in and agreed to show him the one listing.

Elizabeth slips into a light Burberry raincoat with a hood—thundershowers are predicted on this warm May afternoon, Elizabeth knows; she's obsessed with weather, and the Weather Channel is always on in the background—and reminds Violeta of her appointment with Lance. Then she takes the elevator down to the street, where Dave is waiting with the Mercedes. She's glad that Lance Roberts agreed to meet her at the eastside building; the truth is, she has no desire to ride anywhere with him. "Hi, Dave," she says as he opens the rear passenger door for her. "I forgot to ask you last week, how are your applications for grad school going?"

Dave grins ironically and waits until he's behind the wheel. "Actually, they're sitting just where they were the last time you asked about them." He puts the car in drive.

"Dave, you cannot drive people around forever—you're so brilliant, you're wasted doing this."

"I could imagine worse things."

"You went to one of the best schools in the country," Elizabeth reminds him. "And economics is a great field."

"I know, I know," Dave says as he carefully maneuvers the car into Park Avenue traffic. "I'm getting to it."

"If you haven't done those applications in six months, I'm going to have Chauffeurs Unlimited fire you," Elizabeth jokes.

Dave catches her eye in the rearview mirror. "You *are* tough, aren't you?"

Her cell rings; it's Roger Erickson, calling with what Elizabeth hopes will be a higher offer on her sellers' duplex at 155 East 72nd. Roger's clients have steadily gone up $50,000 with each negotiation—they are now at $3.05 million. Truth be told, Elizabeth thinks the sellers, the Kennishes, should take the money and run. However, the Kennishes have not taken her advice and have only come down to $3.1 million. The two parties are now $50,000 away from a deal.

"Good news or bad news?" Elizabeth says.

"Elizabeth, they'll split the difference. Can you get the

sellers to take three million seventy-five? Honestly, they're overpaying at that price—the place is a wreck parading in good condition! But they only want a prewar duplex, and these kinds of buyers are few and far between, as you know."

Elizabeth sighs. The Kennishes have been stubborn, but at least they finally agreed to a 120-day closing; however, the apartment will be sold as is, with no repairs to the whirlpool bath or the dishwasher. "I'll see what I can do, but I don't know."

"Let them know that there's another apartment the buyers are interested in; they like this far, far better, but they're at the end, and they may try and move forward on something else if they think the sellers are being that unreasonable."

There is a short silence. This is a ploy that brokers will use to inject urgency into a bidding situation. And yet Elizabeth knows Roger is telling the truth. "Listen," she says, "you and I are not going to lose this over $25,000. I'll call you back," she says, and hangs up.

She dials Edward Kennish at his dental office; she tells his receptionist it's urgent, and a few moments later Edward picks up the phone.

"The buyers have come up twenty-five thousand—they want to split the difference," Elizabeth says. "This is it for them, and honestly, Edward, you should take it. We've been on for a month now, and the best offers come at the beginning—we've had no others. You want to run the risk of sitting and eventually having to reduce the price? This is a very, very strong price, from very qualified people with a terrific broker." A good broker makes all the difference in a deal, especially in a co-op. Elizabeth will often advise her clients to go with perhaps a slightly lower price to get a deal done with a top broker. There are so many idiots out there!

"You don't have to tell *me.* You have to tell my wife," Edward says. "She obviously is having what you described as 'seller's remorse.' But okay. I accept the offer on behalf on my wife and myself."

"Edward, you need to speak with her."

"If you don't hear back from me within five minutes, go ahead and accept it."

"Are you sure?" Elizabeth says.

"Yes."

The phone rings just as she is saying good-bye to Edward. She sees that it's Kate, and when she picks up she says, "I finally might have a deal with the Kennishes, at $3.075 million."

"Fab," Kate says. "Where are you, anyway?"

"In the car with Dave. On my way to see that jerk Lance Roberts at 860 UN Plaza."

"Why are you even bothering with him? Will he even pass a co-op board?"

"He thinks that I can convince them."

"Ha!"

"He apparently has more faith in my powers than you do," Elizabeth teases, "but why that is, I haven't the faintest idea."

"Mom, he's an animal! Why are you wasting your time?"

Elizabeth contemplates this for a moment. "I don't know . . . he keeps calling me. It didn't seem like the worst idea at the time when I said yes— $2.5 million, all cash, and I know the board president. And Lance promises to behave." As Elizabeth says all this out loud, she thinks to herself, Why am I doing this? She still has a little social worker in her after all these years, she supposes—Lance claims to be reformed, and she'd like to see it.

"I'll believe that when I see it. Why don't you show the apartment to him and Bart Schneider at the same time?" Kate teases.

"Hmmm . . . interesting thought. Maybe I'll leave the two of them in a room and lock the door," Elizabeth says wickedly. "Lance would eat Bart alive!" She and Kate have a good giggle. In their business they often have to deal with rich people behaving badly, but then again, isn't that part of the fun?

"You sound back to your old self—my plucky Kate," Elizabeth says now, relieved. "Gorgeous and smart and everything going for you. That Scott is just an idiot!"

"I know," Kate says. "Love you."

Elizabeth looks at her watch. Ten minutes have gone by—does she have a deal on the Kennishes? She guesses so. . . . She will wait till she's done with Lance to call Roger, just in case. As Dave drives her down 49th Street, crosses First Avenue, and loops into the semicircular parking area in front of 860 UN Plaza, Elizabeth remembers that when Teddy learned of her recent conversation with Lance Roberts (in which she was clearly resisting doing business with Lance), Teddy offered to take him on as a client and had the audacity to suggest an 80/20 commission split in his favor. (Traditionally in the business, brokers and company owners work on a 50/50 split. And when brokers gross over a certain amount, the split goes to 60/40 in their favor.) The nerve of him!

Isabel calls and says, "I have the best story!"

"I'm meeting Lance Roberts right now, let me just see if he's here."

"Just listen for one second. It's hysterical, I promise."

"Okay, hold on." Elizabeth tells Dave to pull into one of the temporary parking spaces in front of the building's revolving doors, scans the lobby to see if Lance Roberts is there, and when she doesn't see him, takes a few steps so that she's standing out of view of the lobby at the side of the building. The one (and to be honest, the only) thing she enjoys about being in the UN Plaza area is the breeze off the East River, but only in spring and summer. In the wintertime, it's terribly windy and frigid. "Okay, quick," she tells Isabel, "Lance isn't here yet."

"Remember Cindy Kazarian, the hot young designer who's giving Juicy Couture a run for her money? I sold her that one-bedroom on East 69th?"

"Yes, how could I forget her?"

"She called me today to report that she found a five-foot-long king snake in her apartment, slithering around in one of the back closets!"

"Oh, my God!" Elizabeth gasps. "I would have run out the door!"

"Well, Cindy managed to hold it together. She said the snake was really beautiful. Lovely color bands, was how she described it. Can you imagine? And it didn't seem at all startled when she discovered it. She thinks it's been living in the wall."

"I just shuddered," Elizabeth says. "How does a snake get in the wall of a New York City apartment?"

"The previous owner."

"But hasn't Cindy owned the apartment for a couple of months now?"

"Six weeks. I guess it was in hiding. Apparently it's nocturnal. Anyway, Cindy looked it up and found out that they're gentle and curious and can live in captivity for as long as twenty years on a diet of what they call 'prekilled' mice."

Elizabeth shudders again. The Chase house is a no-kill zone—they even make Tom carry ants into the backyard at the summerhouse! The doormen in the city once caught Elizabeth, Kate, and Isabel carrying a white garbage bag with a pair of dishwashing gloves over to the center island on Park Avenue, where they deposited a tiny field mouse they'd found hiding under the refrigerator. "So what's she going to do?" she asks.

"Well, she called the previous owner and asked about the snake. He told her he'd come right over. She showed it to him, and he actually said, 'I did have a snake, but that one's not *my* snake.' "

Elizabeth bursts into laughter. "Oh, this just gets more ludicrous!"

"Anyway, one of the building porters was brave enough to nudge the snake into a garbage bag. They poked holes in it and then took a taxi to the Bronx Zoo."

Elizabeth is still laughing, but then she thinks she notices Lance Roberts sitting in one of the lobby's waiting areas.

"Speaking of lunatics, mine is here. I see Lance wandering around the lobby. I've got to run."

"I hope Lance doesn't forget what he learned in anger management," Isabel says.

"Oh, don't worry, I have on four-inch platforms today. My shoes could kill," Elizabeth jokes.

As she enters the building, all smiles, she sees Lance sitting in one of the Knoll Barcelona chair reproductions in a corner of the red-carpeted lobby. He's in the process of sending a text message, his big thumbs tapping the keyboard of his BlackBerry. Elizabeth finds herself thinking that he looks a bit like George Costanza: short and squat and balding with a bad haircut. He's one of those men who grows his remaining hair long, as though to compensate for what has been lost. "An unfortunate haircut," she'd whispered to Kate when she met Lance for the first time, Elizabeth remembers.

When Lance catches sight of her now, he jumps out of his chair and hurries over, holding his dampish hand out to shake hers. She hates a handshake—a ridiculous tradition, she thinks—and so do her girls. She offers him a polite, though unenthusiastic, shake in response and glances over at the long desk where the doorman and the concierge sit. She raises her chin toward them. "The owner is at work, so they'll have to let us in," she tells Lance. When the owner told Elizabeth a porter would be working in the apartment today, moving some boxes, she was actually relieved at the thought of not being left alone with Roberts.

A porter comes down now to escort them up. Elizabeth knows him because she has sold several apartments in the building. He's a friendly man with twinkly eyes, slightly chubby and short, with a full head of black curls and dimpled fingers that made her like him at once when she first met him. He tells her, smiling breathlessly, that he has just had his first child, a baby girl, and she was born early—at twenty-nine weeks. "She was a real fighter, my little girl, like her mother," he tells Elizabeth. "Me, when I found out she was going to be in the hospital for all that time, I cried every day. My wife told me to stop behaving like a baby, that if I wanted to bring our daughter home, I better shape up. So I did. And she's home now, and boy, she keeps me busy!" he says proudly.

Elizabeth wants to hug him. "Oh, Tony," she says, "what a happy story, and you're going to be the most wonderful father." Unfortunately, at that moment, she feels the thumping of Lance's leg; he has begun to twitch in the elevator. Thankfully, the elevator arrives at their floor just then.

Tony lets them into an apartment with such intense sunlight that solar shades are pulled down to protect the rugs and artwork. Now it is virtually pitch-black. Elizabeth presses a button, and slowly the sunshades rise and retract into recesses just above the window. The light flooding the apartment is strong but lovely. Lance drifts over to the window and gazes down at the vast, expansive, opalescent East River. For only a moment, this restless, aggressive man seems at peace. The porter, in the meantime, retreats into the depths of the apartment to begin his work.

"I have a friend who lives in this building," Lance says dreamily, still looking down at the East River. "He told me that you can throw golf balls right into the water from here."

"I don't suppose *he's* on the co-op board?" Elizabeth can't help asking.

Lance shakes his head.

Elizabeth shows him the kitchen—totally renovated, with Gaggenau appliances and marble countertops—then a perfectly nice guest room, a library with its built-in bookshelves, and the master suite. Every room in the apartment, even the master bath, has a mounted flat-screen television. Decorated tastefully in neutral tones, the space definitely has a masculine feel to it.

Elizabeth's phone rings. Bart Schneider. She presses ignore.

Lance turns to her and, looking her straight in the eye, says, "I really want to buy this apartment. I'm not going to screw around this time. But I need you to be on my side so that we can work together. Because we have a mountain to climb."

"You can say that again," Elizabeth tells him.

"I'm not an idiot. I know how I affect some people," Lance says.

"Well, knowing is one thing. Doing something about it is another."

"I told you I took that anger management class."

Oh, please, Elizabeth nearly says. "Even if you behave yourself from start to finish, Lance, I honestly don't know if your making a bid here is going to be worth it."

He looks crushed and then desperate. "There's got to be *some* high-end building in New York City who will take my money."

"Why don't you do a condo instead? They don't have boards in the same way co-ops do."

"I haven't seen a condo that I like," Lance says. "Besides, I want to buy in *this* building. My friend lives here."

"Well, then we'll try," Elizabeth tells him.

She leads him back into the living area, and they both sit down in wing chairs. "So," she says. "You should start by offering full asking price."

"Understood," Lance says, nodding his head and cracking his knuckles, a habit Elizabeth finds infuriating.

"All cash?" she continues.

"Yup."

"And you will close . . . ?"

Glancing out the window at the stunning view, Lance says, "Sixty days, ninety days, whenever they want."

"Let's say seventy-five—you have to get your board package together, and from what I'm guessing, we're going to have to do some creative things with the reference letters. Your financials won't be an issue."

"Well, fine," Lance says, "but of course I don't want to bark up a tree that's going to shake me off it." Where did he come up with that saying? Elizabeth wonders to herself. A bizarre cliché. She loathes clichés.

"I'll make a phone call to my friend the president of the co-op board and try to prescreen you. How's that?" Elizabeth says.

"That sounds fair."

"But you have to understand that my friend would never look favorably on any kind of . . . coercion on my part."

Oddly, Lance Roberts has no response to this. He stares out the window. Elizabeth hears the sound of the porter moving boxes. At last he says, "I think you have more influence than you're admitting."

The man is impossible, Elizabeth thinks. Why is she wasting her time with him? He must be desperate for this apartment. Somewhere in the apartment she hears the thud of a closet door being shut.

In a way, she almost feels sorry for him.

Her phone rings—it's Tom. And even though normally she would answer a call from the family but speak only for a second and hang up, she doesn't care what Lance Roberts thinks of her. "Please excuse me, but I've got to take this call," she tells Lance, and turns away from him.

Several hours later, after hair and makeup at Valery Joseph and a quick stop at Saks for a new lipstick, Elizabeth is joined by Tom, Kate, and Isabel at the door of her $8.9 million listing at the Lucida on the Upper East Side, greeting A-list brokers like MacRae Parker, Donna Olshan, Cathy Franklin, Sol Howard, Shaun Osher, Fred Peters, Charles Curkin, the legendary Alice Mason and her chic daughter, Dominique Richard, Robby Browne, and new "it" broker Jared Seligman, all of whom have come to view the two side-by-side penthouse units in the hopes of selling one or both of them. Because there are so many broker cocktail parties, Elizabeth wants to make this one over-the-top. The apartment has been completely staged, with exquisite contemporary pieces to mirror the all-glass building. Two long tables are covered with sushi from Nobu, and waiters in white tuxedo jackets pass all sorts of delicacies like spoonfuls of caviar, mini burgers with truffles, lobster rolls, and, for dessert, mini ice cream sandwiches, mini milkshakes, and brownies and chocolates from Maison du Chocolat on silver trays. Drinks are all-white—champagne, white wine, and sparkling water. Models wearing the perforated, lacelike spring dresses of designer Roberto Cavalli in candy colors like pink, lemon, mint, and peach are displayed throughout the apartment like mannequins. Kate and Isabel are dressed identically in short black rhinestone-studded Ungaro dresses, each wearing Art Deco pavé diamond bracelets. Elizabeth wears one of her signature vintage Chanel pins, a big enamel Maltese cross in red, blue, and yellow, right in the center of her Nina Ricci black chiffon cocktail dress. The dress was a last-minute find from Edit. Often Elizabeth or the girls will run over there if they need something quick and fabulous for an event or party. The smaller of the two units, at around 3,300 square feet, has an astonishing 1,000-square-foot terrace that boasts views of the Empire State Building. Photographs of the building's amazing amenities—the building's lap pool and sauna, Kidville playroom, video arcade, and state-of-the-art fitness center—are on display throughout like artwork. If guests want to view any of these amenities, Elizabeth has brokers ready to take them on a tour. It seems as if every top broker in New York City is in this room, including Teddy, of course, and Christopher McKinnon with his entourage from LEX. Kate and Isabel have been told to mingle, but also to keep an eye on Teddy and the LEX brokers.

Elizabeth makes sure to say hello to all her favorite real estate writers, who almost always come when she throws an event—Jhoanna Robledo from *New York Magazine*, Joey Arak from Curbed.com, Dana Jennings and Christine Haughney from the *New York Times*, Josh Barbanel and Craig Karmin from the *Wall Street Journal*. And then she moves on to Jennifer Gould Keil, who writes for the *New York Post*, Chloe Malle from the *New York Observer*, New York's most famous photographer, Patrick McMullan, and Richard Lewin, the Chases' frequent family photographer. Tomorrow morning she will be thrilled to see that the party makes Joey Arak's column on Curbed.com, and she will see photos of her and her family in the Social Diary.

She is in the midst of speaking to three brokers when she notices Teddy talking to Christopher McKinnon on the terrace. With a quick glance around the crowded room she manages to make eye contact with Kate, who makes it clear that she's already watching. Elizabeth, Kate, Isabel, and Tom have all already discreetly combed through Teddy's desk and all his files and correspondence, thinking they might find something that would support Monique's friend's insistent claim that Teddy may be selling private information about listings-in-the-works to other brokers for a kickback. But so far their only lead has come from Violeta, who, checking the caller IDs, discovered that Christopher McKinnon has been frequently calling Teddy at night when the office is officially closed. Still watching as she laughs and sips champagne with the other brokers, Elizabeth is distracted by two details: Tom approaching Teddy, and a stunning dark-haired young woman, no one she has ever seen before, staring at her.

Soon Monique arrives at the party, in head-to-toe Chanel. Elizabeth has already told her that Kate was able to find out the name of the real estate broker who allegedly drugged Teddy after he suddenly broke up with her, so Monique (never shy) discreetly points out the stunning young woman, who is now chatting with a LEX broker.

Elizabeth finally excuses herself to find Teddy, who is talking with Robby Browne, one of the top ten real estate brokers in the city, famous for arriving by bicycle at even his most expensive listings and has degrees from both Princeton and Harvard.

When Elizabeth approaches, Robby's face lights up. "Elizabeth!" he says warmly.

"Robby was telling me about the apartment he sold to one of the Rockefellers," Teddy begins. "And he—"

Just at that moment, Christopher McKinnon comes over and taps Teddy's shoulder. "Somebody wants to meet you," he says.

Elizabeth suddenly feels a nervous flutter in her stomach. It now seems obvious that something of significance is going on between Teddy and LEX.

CHAPTER TEN

Kate

Park Avenue Princess

80s east. XXX Mint 3 bedroom, two-and-a-half baths, enormous EIK with adjacent family room in full-service doorman building. $4.1 million.

Kate loves the summer. She'll take 100 degrees and humid any day over freezing. But today, sitting in the back of a poorly air-conditioned taxi in bumper-to-bumper traffic, her tanned legs sticking against the ripped black vinyl, the driver screaming in another language on the phone, the smell of his lunch (is it Indian food? onions?) permeating the backseat, she feels hot, bothered, and nauseous.

The ordinarily friendly doorman opening the door of 973 Park Avenue (deliciously air-conditioned, thank goodness, if only she had a moment to just sit on the marble bench in the lobby to cool off, but no . . .) where she and Isabel have sold a half dozen apartments over the past couple of years knows perfectly well who she is—and yet, oddly, this generally lovely middle-aged man with short silver hair ignores her.

"Thanks, Leon," she says, "Oh, I nearly stuck to the taxicab, it was so hot!" she says, trying to get him to react. He stares at her. Oh, well, Kate tells herself, it couldn't have anything to do with her. She gets into the elevator and takes it to the tenth floor, where her client, small, slender K. K. Pearlbinder, is waiting to discuss her fourish-million-dollar apartment one more time before officially putting it on the market.

K. K., the divorced stay-at-home mother of two small children, is in her thirties and on the receiving end of what was apparently a very generous settlement from her husband, an orthopedic surgeon who happens to be one of the official doctors for the Mets, and who gave her the co-op as a parting gift before exiting their marriage. It was K. K.'s mother, a friend of Elizabeth's from their childhood days in Pittsburgh, who suggested she call Kate. When she greets Kate in the doorway this morning, K. K.'s wearing denim short shorts and a skimpy white tank top, her highlighted brown hair twisted into a low ponytail. Her feet are bare, her toenails ornamented in the chicest new color—silver gray (gorgeous for a dress, hideous for the toes, the Chase girls say). K. K.'s children are nowhere in sight, nor is their nanny, but there is in fact someone else in the entrance hall—a hunky, muscular thirtysomething in sweatpants and a basketball shirt, no shoes. He looks vaguely familiar, but Kate doesn't know why.

"How are ya?" K. K. says, and as she and Kate have a seat at the kitchen table, the man nods at Kate, murmurs his name (Anthony), and then busies himself at the marble island in the center of this vast room, where he's squeezing fresh orange juice for what is apparently a late breakfast.

"So where are your little angels?" Kate asks. She has her eyes on this man she assumes must be K. K.'s boyfriend, so enthusiastically crushing one orange after another directly into one of two crystal Tiffany wineglasses arranged on the marble. She knows she's seen Anthony before, not once but numerous times, but she can't figure out where.

"Oh, Blake and Taylor are with my parents and the nanny out in Sag Harbor for a couple of days," K. K. tells her, and smiles—a smile seeming to say, What a relief, I sure need a break! "And next week they'll be back in the city at a new summer dance program for two weeks, all day—so excited."

"I actually kinda miss them," Anthony says.

"Come on, you do *not*," K. K. teases him. "Don't lie to me, babe."

Kate doesn't understand why so many people have children and never seem to want them around.

Gazing idly around the kitchen, at the chandelier dripping glass overhead, at the beautiful zebra wood cabinets and the stainless steel Wolf stove that looks as if it's never been used (and probably hasn't been), Kate catches a glimpse of a man's brimmed gray cap sitting next to a crystal bowl of bananas, and then it hits her, in that instant, where she's seen Anthony before. The cap isn't just an ordinary cap, it's a doorman's cap, and the reason she hadn't been able to place this man named Anthony is because she's never seen him without his uniform on! Oh, the scandal! K. K. Pearlbinder, Upper East Side mom and owner of a multimillion-dollar Park Avenue apartment, is sleeping with—in love with, too?—her doorman. The very man who's paid to open the door for her as she approaches the building, to smile at her politely in the lobby, to address her as "Mrs. Pearlbinder," to rush out to her taxi in the rain with an umbrella and carry her packages to the elevator.

"OJ?" Anthony is saying.

"Sorry?" Kate says.

"Fresh-squeezed," Anthony says, and offers her a crystal wineglass after wiping it down first with a linen cloth and placing the other glass carefully in front of K. K.

"No, thank you, I have seltzer," Kate says, and smiles. She pulls out her liter bottle of Vintage seltzer from her big silver Fendi bag (her mother bought one for each of the girls last week just because she thought it was the greatest bag—lightweight, goes with everything, perfect for summer!) and takes a sip. "So, K. K.," she says, trying to focus now on getting K. K.'s apartment ready to go to market rather than worrying about what the other doormen must think, or people on the board, for that matter, seeing Anthony, after a dinner at Nobu, sauntering into the lobby with his tanned arm around K. K., only to reemerge the next morning in his crisp gray uniform with the white stripes down the sides, his cap covering his dark eyes. "Remind me of the renovations you did. Everything, right?" Kate says.

Throwing her arms across the table like Quinn on *Glee* when she gets cut from the Cheerios because she is pregnant, K. K. announces, "I hate this building more than you can possibly know! Honestly, you can't imagine the people who I thought were my friends but turned out to be the biggest losers."

"Oh, I can imagine," Kate murmurs, and takes a peek at the yellow legal pad Anthony has just slid over in her direction. There's a handwritten list of the renovations K. K. and her ex clearly invested a fortune in before their marriage took a dive: Poggenpohl kitchen with automatic cappuccino and espresso machines and a 124-bottle, thermoelectric wine cooler; one bedroom changed into a windowed, walk-in dressing room; all new Crestron system, new hardwood floors, new windows, Rainhead shower . . . On and on; there is not an inch of the apartment that hasn't been redone.

"Wait, you *can imagine*? What do you mean?" K. K. is saying, and lifts her head to look at Kate.

"Well, I just—" Kate gestures toward Anthony, who's standing behind K. K. and massaging her shoulders now. "K. K., I'm not saying I agree with them at all, but you can't be shocked that they may be a little, I don't know, taken aback—you live in a fancy Park Avenue co-op . . ."

"Taken aback because Anthony and I are a couple? 'Taken aback' is an understatement," K. K. says. "You wouldn't believe some of the icy looks I've gotten, not to mention the shitty things that have been whispered into the ears of the co-op board. And I mean vicious! One of my best friends in the building is on the board, and I talked her into telling me what she's been hearing these past three months or so since Anthony and I have been together. You'd think this was, I don't know, Fargo!" K. K. says, naming perhaps the only small town she has ever heard of, thanks to the Coen brothers' famous film.

Then she really begins to spiral.

"This is New York City—don't these idiots have better things to do than pass judgment on me and my wonderful boyfriend? Who gives a shit if he didn't go to college? So what if his father works as a security guard at MoMA? Do I care? The co-op board is insane."

"Babe, don't let them get to you," Anthony is saying.

"K. K., let's just get you out of this building so you don't have to deal with it anymore, okay?" Kate says. "Maybe you can even move to the beach for the summer?"

"Your shoulders are so tight, you gotta relax, babe," Anthony says, and kisses K. K.'s ear.

"Okay, K. K., let's focus on getting your apartment on the market and you out of here, okay? When can I come in to do photographs and floor plans? I imagine it's easier for me to do that while the girls aren't here?" Kate says.

But K. K. doesn't hear her. She is now in a total meltdown. Kate takes another sip of her seltzer.

"Just try and imagine what it's like to live with these nosy, narrow-minded, judgmental morons," K. K. says.

"How dare they! I've got the money, I pay my mortgage and maintenance on time and don't vacuum naked at four in the morning blasting Lady Gaga, so who the fuck does the board think they are?"

"Come on, chill, K. K.," Anthony advises her. "Do you want me to make you some herbal tea or something?"

"No, I *don't* want tea. You know what I want? I am going to hire a lawyer and sue the board," K. K. says defiantly, rubbing her toes.

"Let's not go there," Kate says. "Listen, let me take care of selling the apartment, and you can start over somewhere totally different—I bet you'd love Tribeca or the West Village, even," she says hopefully. Because she already suspects that if K. K. tries to buy in another building like this on the Upper East Side—where the board members and even the super of her co-op might be contacted by the boards in buildings where she wants to buy—well, let's just say the Upper East Side is a very small town in New York.

"Whatever. If I could move out today, I would," K. K. says. She has calmed down a bit, and takes a sip of her freshly squeezed juice.

"Not me, babe. This place is a palace," Anthony proclaims, gesturing with a dramatic sweep of his arm.

And there you have it, Kate thinks to herself, as she gathers her seltzer and her Fendi bag, blows a kiss to K. K. and Anthony, and walks out the door.

■ ■ ■

As Kate strides past Leon the doorman on her way out, he hisses softly, "So how is the happy couple?"

Kate doesn't respond, and walks out to find a taxi herself. Her phone rings, and she can't find it in her bag, then notices she didn't put the cap back on the seltzer all the way and that it's fizzing all over her workbook and her Louis Vuitton makeup bag. Where is her phone?

"You know the Fiermans?" Isabel begins, when Kate finally finds her phone. "The ones who were so obsessed with having a Park Avenue address before their daughter's bat mitzvah so that the invitations would say Park Avenue on the back of the envelope?"

"Oh yes," Kate says, and has to laugh. "Only in New York—did you find them anything?"

"Well, nothing fabulous, clearly, but they're so desperate, they're taking a back apartment, and I mean back—as in facing walls on the second floor of a building, a two-bedroom, not even a classic six. With three kids!"

"They don't care?" Kate says.

"They're thrilled!" Isabel says. "Can you imagine? All she cares about is that the back of those hand-calligraphed invitations say 465 Park Avenue."

"It's one for the books," Kate says. "Okay, I need to go find a taxi, I'm dripping. Talk to you later," she says, and gets into a taxi, air-conditioned perfectly, thank goodness, because she can deal with only one meltdown on this steamy summer day.

■ ■ ■

Sitting in a Burger Heaven near Bloomingdale's with her best friend Steven Bauer, Kate picks at his curly fries, and he sticks his fork in her Greek salad, having tired of his turkey club. She has been best friends with Steven since they were twelve years old, when he transferred to Horace Mann from a prep school in Greenwich with both legs in casts from a water-skiing accident that summer. His mother, Binnie Bauer, became a legend in the school (even written about years later in the senior yearbook) because she had all of Steven's third- and fourth-floor classes in Tillinghast (the oldest building on the Horace Mann campus, filled with lovely high-ceilinged classrooms) moved down to the basement of the building, because Steven couldn't possibly walk up, and it was too many flights for the gentleman who accompanied him to school to carry him.

Despite his broken legs, Steven became an instant hit at Horace Mann. All the girls ran to carry his backpack, fetch him a Coke out of the cafeteria vending machine, walk him to the car Binnie had pick him up every day because he couldn't get on the school bus. He and Kate became best friends instantly. Years later, they went off to Penn together, living (by coincidence, or fate, you might say) two flights away from each other in the freshman dorm. By junior year, they were living in neighboring town houses on Pine Street—Steven's window was literally perpendicular to Kate's, and instead of calling her, he would often yell out the window to her or open his window and play one of her favorite songs to get her attention, like "Total Eclipse of the Heart" if they were depressed about breakups or "Pour Some Sugar on Me" if he wanted her to come out with him that night. They had one "hot night" together, as they called it—a long, long kiss to Meatloaf's "I Would Do Anything for Love," but that was it—they much preferred to be best friends.

Kate takes another French fry now and contemplates getting a milkshake.

"So Pippa is over?" she says.

"You know what," Steven says, "I can't be bothered. She was fine when it was casual, and I mean fine, not great, fine, she was fun. I don't need her spending the morning with me, I barely want her sleeping in my bed all night, but it would be too awful to ask her to leave. Come nine a.m., I want her out!" He loosens his tie and fixes his suit jacket, which is slipping to the floor. "Oh, they're all the same, they all turn into such stalkers. Whenever we have sex, the entire time she's yelling 'Oh my God' and 'It feels *so* good' and then when she's about to, you know, she screams in a sort of staccato machine-gun way 'I love you, love you, love you . . .' I feel like I'm in a bad porno movie every time we have sex. It's like all I want to say is, 'Would you mind shutting up for like two seconds so that I can pretend that I'm actually having sex with a girl who is not incredibly annoying?' I mean, do girls think guys like this sort of behavior?"

Kate is now laughing hysterically. No one can make her laugh like Steven does. Her mom and sister always know when they are on the phone together because they say her whole voice changes. "At least you have a lineup of suitors," she tells him now. "I've got no one."

"First of all, Kate, that is absolutely not true—you refuse to go out with anyone—that Charlie Marcus guy, and Paul Frank's cousin, who you decided not to see after all, just because you weren't in the mood to meet someone new. There's a lineup of guys who are dying to go out with you. But you choose not to because you're too busy spending all your time watching old movies at your parents' house and going to Atlantic Beach to sunbathe by your pool."

He motions to the waitress to bring over another Coke.

"I need you to try and move on from Scott," he says. "You know you're getting nowhere with him. Surely your mother and sister tell you the same thing."

"Everyone does," she says, "but I don't know what to do—why is he like this?" she says, and starts to cry. "I mean, it's been so many years, what is he waiting for?" Her tears are falling into her Greek salad, and she wipes her eyes with her hand. "I hate that I keep crying over him."

"Oh, Katie," Steven says. He is the only person who has ever called her Katie, and he only does it when they are alone together. "I don't want to say this because it sounds like a cliché, but he has commitment issues. The guy fell in love with you the first night you met at Smoke's. It isn't that he doesn't love you, he just needs to get his own life together and figure out who he is before he gets completely overwhelmed by you and all the Chase women. I'm sure it's no surprise to you to hear that the women in your family are a lot to handle—any guy who chooses you is choosing a whole family. Scott will come back, I know that, but you need to use this time to get out there and be sure this is what *you* want. And anyway, you'll look more attractive to him if you're out there and happy, not moping around in your pink bathrobe and slippers."

"I haven't heard from him since he called me in April . . . so it doesn't look like he's coming back—this is the longest it's ever been."

"Katie, you need to go out, come out with me."

"I know."

"Don't say 'I know.' Please commit to me, we'll do something Thursday night, let's go somewhere decadent and drink ourselves into oblivion. Or, I know, I'll have a party at my apartment next week—you can come over early and we can put together the music and drinks." Steven lives in a huge five-room postwar in the East 60s, on the nineteenth floor in an apartment with the most magnificent terraces the Chases have ever seen in a five-room apartment, or in most apartments, for that matter. The wraparound terrace is close to 1,500 square feet. Steven is currently a commercial real estate broker, very successful, following an equally successful stint in entertainment law, which was not as interesting as he'd hoped it would be, though he did get to take Katie to the Grammys a few times in L.A. Steven also comes from a great family—after Greenwich, they lived at 820 Park, and they own the magnificent Seamann Schepps, whose exquisite jewels the Chase ladies drool over and borrow for major events in their life. Elizabeth once sent Tom to pick up close to one million dollars' worth of jewelry for the three of them to wear to an event—he had to get it at closing time at five on the dot and return it the next morning before they opened.

"Yes, let's do that, I need a good night out," she says.

Kate looks at Steven now, cropped black hair, an adorable, slightly devious smile (they always said a young John Cusack would play him in a movie, though his personality and sense of humor, they sometimes joke, veers more toward John Malkovich in *Dangerous Liaisons*). He has a power over people, girls in particular, and the whole city is in love with him. But Steven himself could take it or leave it. Kate sometimes thinks how easy things would be if they could just fall in love with each other, but it was not meant to be.

"So would you like to be my date for Sam Siegal's wedding in March?" she asks him. "I'm one of the bridesmaids, obviously." He and Kate and Sam have known each other since they were at Horace Mann together, and he'll be at the wedding anyway, so she'd rather just go with him.

"Absolutely," he says. "Now finish your salad, you barely ate a thing."

Her cell rings; it's her sister, wanting to know when she'll be home.

"I'm leaving soon," Kate tells her. "Everything okay?"

"Yes, tell Steven hello."

While Steven pays (never once in their long friendship has he ever let her—or any other girl or group of girls, for that matter—pay), Kate thinks about K. K. Pearlbinder and her unpredictable choice of a boyfriend, and then wonders why she herself can't give anyone else a chance.

Her BlackBerry vibrates now: it's her brother, texting about his idea to take a leave of absence from school for a while to work on his series for HBO. What does she think? Though she suspects her parents will be horrified, the e-mail she sends Jonathan reads: *Let's talk about, sort of feel like yes! You only live once.* Then she adds, *I'm with Steven, will ask him, and have to tell him about HBO—he'll be so proud of you!* Jonathan worships Steven—they met, after all, when Jonathan was a toddler. On his bulletin board in his bedroom at the Chases' he has a photograph of himself and Steven at freshman visiting week at Penn, Jonathan not even ten years old, leaning against Steven in a little sport coat and bow tie, playing some sort of thumb game. Kate realizes then that the one person she knows who would tell Jonathan to go ahead with that leave of absence from school would be Scott, whose fondness for risk-taking she knows all too well.

She and Isabel (and don't forget Michael, she reminds herself) are going to have dinner with their parents tonight, as they so often do, but first Kate's going to take a quick bubble bath, she decides after she kisses Steven goodbye on the corner of Lex and 62nd and climbs into a taxi for the ten-minute ride home, yelling "Vile!"—their favorite word—out the window.

Poised in the hallway outside her apartment, wishing that the hallways were air-conditioned—they get so hot—she searches her bag for her keys. It's like going into a black hole, she thinks—candy wrappers, lipsticks that have fallen out of her makeup bag, business cards, a brush, a tiny umbrella her mom makes them carry "because you never know!" Then she hears Isabel's voice and, a moment later, a deeper, male one—Michael is already there, she thinks, there goes my bath. She rings the bell, leaning against the pale blue striped wallpapered hallway as she waits for Isabel to open the door for her. Eyes closed, she imagines herself for a moment still living here, only alone, Isabel off with Michael, she herself completely and totally unattached, stepping into her thirties—high-heeled shoes and all—then forties . . . Then she snaps out of it and says to herself, *Oh, you sound like* When Harry Met Sally—*you're being ridiculous.*

Isabel answers the door, looking terribly excited. "We've got company," she whispers into Kate's ear. There, sitting on the living room sofa next to Michael, a bottle of Poland Spring in his hand, sitting up straighter than she's ever seen him and bouncing his left knee, is Scott. Kate feels her cheeks turn bright red, and her heart starts to beat in what feels like all of her chest and even her stomach. As Scott gets up and slowly comes toward her, that familiar feeling that can only be defined as, well, the deepest sort of desire she's ever experienced, she thinks, *Oh, if only I could be hard-to-get, and stand here staring at him coldly, and say "What are you doing here?"* but she knows he never intends to hurt her, she believes in him, she believes in her heart that he is in love with her, that has always been why she keeps giving him one more chance. So now, as he stands staring at her intensely, running one hand over her hair and down the back of her head, sending chills everywhere, and then wrapping his long, strong arms around her in the middle of her living room, well instead of standing like an ice cube, Kate finds herself completely bewitched all over again. The smell of his shampoo, the sandpapery black stubble around his jaw, the sweetness and intensity of his dark gray eyes. She thinks, for a moment, if only I had stopped to get a blow-dry . . .

"I just needed to get it together," Scott's whispering in her ear. "Will you forgive me, again?" he nearly begs.

And as quickly and as easily as that, Kate and Scott are back together. A few hours later, they sit at Elios on Second and 84th (her parents and Isabel and Michael have their date without her), an heirloom tomato salad for her—though she can barely eat, she is so excited—mozzarella and prosciutto for Scott, followed by boneless white-meat chicken scarpariello, always well done, for Kate, spaghetti bolognese for him, and Elio's perfectly buttered string beans. Normally Kate loves to see all the boldface names who eat here, so she can report back to her family and sometimes to Page Six as a sighting, but tonight she barely glances at Gwyneth Paltrow, there with her brother and mother at a front table by the bar, and Woody Allen and Soon Yi, there with another couple. All she can think is "Make this time be it, make this time be it," as though she is Dorothy at the end of her favorite movie,

The Wizard of Oz, clicking her red shoes and saying again and again, "There's no place like home."

Kate and Scott and Isabel and Michael are at an early movie a few nights later—*Up in the Air*, which stars George Clooney, one of Kate and Isabel's favorite actors ever since his days as Jo's boyfriend on *The Facts of Life* (in fact, their godmother, Claire Callaway, played Jo's mother!). As the four of them settle into their seats toward the back of the theater, an enormous tub of buttered popcorn nestled in Kate's lap, she thinks about how happy she is; how just totally right it feels to be there with Isabel and Michael, how many movies they've seen together over the years, how many dinners out or ordering in Chinese at the girls' apartment, weekends at the Chases' summer house in Atlantic Beach where they rode bicycles, sat on the beach, and barbecued and drank frozen margaritas. Kate is just so incredibly happy; she flutters every time she even hears Scott's name.

On the movie screen now, George Clooney, as a corporate assassin, is as dreamy as ever. (Kate's good friend Sherri Zeegen from Penn, in fact, who works in Hollywood for the company that produced the TV show *ER*, once called her to report that George Clooney had just phoned her desk—and they shrieked excitedly, like schoolgirls, over what it was like to hear George Clooney's voice coming through Sherri's telephone! Even his voice is enough to make her melt!)

Her phone vibrated in the darkness of the movie theater

now, and Kate holds it up to see that it's her client Danielle Liston; she and her husband own a small but very successful manufacturing company. Kate knows why Danielle is calling, and she doesn't want to speak to her, not now. She knows all about Danielle's beloved Dandie Dinmont terrier, who, though smart, loving, and gentle as can be, weighs twenty-three pounds, three pounds over the twenty-pound limit imposed by the co-op board of the Park Avenue building where Danielle and her husband want to buy a nine. Snuggling up to Scott, resting her head on his shoulder and savoring the feel of his fingers threading through her hair, Kate tries to focus on George Clooney packing his suitcase on the screen and not Danielle's slightly overweight dog. And when the movie is over, and she and Scott and Isabel and Michael walk to the Shake Shack on 86th Street for burgers and fries, she returns Danielle's call and listens to her voice get higher and higher.

"Newman is the sweetest dog there is," she starts, "it is LUDICROUS to put him on a diet just to satisfy the co-op board's ridiculous rules. He's afraid of his own tail, what difference is three pounds going to make? Maybe I'll just say he is bloated at the board interview."

Kate laughs. "But we have to do whatever it takes—you won't be hurting Newman, can't you just stop feeding him table food for a bit, or let him run around more?" Kate says. "No one is more obsessed with dogs than I am, but you certainly aren't giving up Newman, and I know you are dying for this apartment, so shut his mouth!"

"I guess I can tell Yola no more sausage and potatoes for Newman for breakfast. Oh, he is going to be so mad at me," Danielle says. "I know, I will order him the Nectar Cafe egg whites I eat every day—with turkey bacon. Atkins it is!"

Crossing 86th Street, holding hands with Scott while her other hand holds her phone up, Kate says, "Perfect—what's not to love?!" And a moment later she hears Danielle's sigh of surrender.

"Done," Danielle says.

"And off you will go to your nine!" Kate says.

"We better."

"Absolutely," Kate says, and hangs up.

"Who the hell is Newman?" Scott says, laughing, opening the door to Shake Shack. "Don't you *ever* stop working?"

"Only occasionally," Kate teases him, as he kisses her lips. They wait in a long line that stretches, as usual, all the way out the door and onto 86th Street. Thinking only of how starving she is, Kate is happily surprised when Scott tucks her hair behind one ear and whispers, "I love you." He's not outwardly sentimental, and although he is incredibly passionate and affectionate, he saves that for very private moments. It took him a year to say "I love you" to her, and he did it very matter of factly, which she loved, because she knew how much he really meant it.

"Me too," she whispers now. *Me too me too me too.*

CHAPTER ELEVEN

Isabel

Sky High Condo

Lincoln Center area/60s west. 8 rooms, 4 bedrooms, 3 baths. 54th floor in luxury condo has panoramic city views and top amenities. $7.225 million—negotiable.

"Hi, Dad," says Isabel, throwing her arms around her father. "You look wonderful, as usual." And he does. Today he wears a pair of trim, pressed khakis and a pale blue button-down (always Ralph Lauren; their favorite place to shop is the magical Rhinelander mansion on Madison and 72nd Street); his distinguished silver hair has been freshly cut, and he smells of peppermint mouthwash. She thinks suddenly of her father smelling the same way as he tucked her into bed when she must have been no more than four years old, saying good-bye before he went out to a cocktail party with their mother. Elizabeth, before she went out, always smelled of Chanel No. 5, and this, of course, became both daughters' favorite, and signature, scent.

"You too, sweetheart," her father says. "You and Michael are the first to get here. Let's go sit in the library."

They are all having brunch at the Chases', and Michael is making Elizabeth's favorite omelet; he and Isabel bought the ingredients—tomatoes, peppers, feta cheese—at Eli's on Third Avenue on their way over, and in the vegetable aisle, Michael said, "I should consider myself pretty damn lucky to be getting your family. You know, coming from the family that I do . . ."

"What do you mean?" Isabel said. She's never actually met Michael's family in Oklahoma, though she's spoken to them over the phone a number of times, and they've always sounded perfectly friendly, and of course they'll be at the wedding. It's odd, though, she's thought, that they've never come to New York to meet her, nor have she and Michael flown out to Oklahoma, but Michael has explained that this is simply the way he and his family are with each other; a once-a-year visit at Christmastime is what they've all grown used to and are comfortable with. And actually she's thrilled with that—her mother would always tell her daughters, "Marry a man whose family lives in another country, or better yet, marry an orphan." And she meant it.

"You know what I've told you about my parents. They're good people, but they're . . . how should I say this without sounding mean . . . they're detached, somehow. Kind of emotionally distant. I don't think they can help it," Michael said.

"Well, you couldn't be more different, so I don't care a bit," Isabel said, and squeezed his hand.

By this time they had paid and were walking back uptown on Park. And even though the streets were crowded with families on their way to brunch or the park, Michael leaned in and kissed her like they were on their first date.

"Want some coffee?" her father is asking now.

"I'd love some," Michael says. He turns to Isabel, "You?"

"I'll wait," Isabel says. "I'm dying for a bagel, though. Isn't Kate supposed to bring them?"

"Kate's not coming," announces her mother as she enters the room and enfolds Isabel in a hug. She's wearing slim-fitting black pants and, to offset the slight chill of the October morning, a cashmere V-neck in a gorgeous shade of burnt orange, with a Susan Wexler necklace cascading down her neck in an explosion of burnt orange crystals. Susan Wexler is a longtime friend of Elizabeth's who sold her ten-room at 1010 Fifth and moved to Palm Beach after her divorce, and Elizabeth took a huge portion of her commission in jewels for her and the girls. Of course, she neglected to tell Tom what she was up to, so when the apartment closed and she handed him the check, he couldn't figure out why the commission was so small.

"She's not coming? Why not?" Michael says.

Her mother says nothing but shoots Isabel a look. "What?" asks Michael, looking back and forth from Elizabeth's face to Isabel's. "Did I miss something?"

"No, no," Isabel says. "Mom and I were just thinking about Scott and Kate. . . ."

"Yeah, it's so great that they're back together again, right?" Michael says.

"Well, let's just hope it lasts," says Elizabeth.

"Why do you think it won't?" But before her mother can respond, Isabel's father walks back into the room with a steaming American flag mug that he hands to Michael.

In a little while they all move into the kitchen, where Michael starts making the omelets. Then her father takes Isabel aside and back to the library; he wants to show her the opening of one of his favorite Hitchcock films, *Notorious*, a newly reissued Blu-ray of which he's just purchased. Tom's obsession with new carries over of course to movies—he now has triplicates, sometimes quadruplicates, of every great movie ever made—tapes, then DVDs, then newly remastered DVDs, now Blu-rays. "Cary Grant and Ingrid Bergman in a love story that's also a thriller, you can't beat that," he tells Isabel.

"Can I borrow it so Michael and I can watch the whole thing?"

"Take this one," he says. "It's the DVD. Michael should really see it, especially because he's an actor. You should really show him all the old films, they don't make them like they used to."

"He'll love it!" she says, taking the DVD. Her father smiles and sits down to read the Arts and Leisure section of the *New York Times*, his favorite, and Isabel goes into the kitchen to continue the conversation with her mother and set the table.

"So what did Kate say?" Isabel asks her.

"Just that they were exhausted and wanted to stay home," Elizabeth says.

"That's weird, isn't it? Kate never likes to miss a family brunch."

"I don't care what they do, as long as he doesn't leave her again."

"I know," Isabel says, and takes a pile of placemats from her mother.

"Anyway, how's it going with the countess?" Elizabeth asks, obviously wanting to redirect the conversation. She arranges silverware on the four placemats, then pulls out a chair for herself.

"Well, it's a little odd, I guess . . ."

Elizabeth, ever-alert for nuances that concern the business, is immediately interested. "Odd like what?"

Sitting down at the table, Isabel says, "Everything I show her, she likes. No, not likes. *Loves! Adores!* She gushes, she swoons. She whips out her phone to call Fritzie—that's the count," she says, in response to her mother's questioning look. "And then she gushes to him, too. But nothing ever seems to come of it."

"Hmm," is all her mother says, but it's clear she's carefully considering all of this. "No comebacks?"

"Nope. And the places she wants to see are all over the map—literally," continues Isabel. "Uptown and down, east side and west. Old and dripping with charm, new and dripping with sophistication. She wants it all."

"Wants it all but maybe doesn't have the money to buy it? Do you think she's maybe not for real?"

"Well, I don't know, she buys me lovely presents and she always comes in her white stretch limo—I know no one here uses limos anymore, but it seems fitting for her, she always seems so known and liked everywhere we go . . ."

"Maybe she has an allowance from the count that enables her to buy gifts, but not the reserves to buy real estate. This Fritzie might have her on a short leash because, well, who knows why. And so she likes to look at all these apartments, just to convince herself that she has more freedom than she actually does." Elizabeth hesitates. "But I could be wrong, of course. . . . Unfortunately, the person who would probably get the best read on the situation is Teddy, but we can't really trust him anymore. He's dealt with lots of enigmatic people and has a special—let's call it affinity, for them."

"That's because he's an enigma himself," says Tom, who's joined them at the table now.

"Mom," Isabel says, "what's going on with Teddy, anyway? Or have you stopped trying to figure him out?"

"Well, we still don't have much to go on, except that he's really in with LEX." Elizabeth shrugs.

"Do you think he wants to go work for them?" Isabel asks.

"Then he should go and work for them," Tom says, and shakes his head.

"I agree," Elizabeth says. "But something's keeping him from doing it, and that's what's driving me crazy."

"I'll tell you what it is. After all the hard work he's put into getting us Luxury Estates, maybe he wants to wait around until the announcement's made and get all the glory and the business that's to come."

"I can't say I'd blame him," Elizabeth agrees.

"So then what, exactly, do you think he's up to?" Isabel says.

"Jonathan password-protected our computers so that he can't look up our leads on clients and listings anymore. I don't know what else we can do," Tom says.

"Anyway, enough of him," Elizabeth says. "I just thought of something for the countess. You know my new listing, the condo in the Millennium Tower?"

"101 West 67th?" Isabel knows it's an exclusive on the fifty-fourth floor, with 360-degree views. "Yeah, it's fabulous," she says.

"I think you should show it to your countess. Why don't the three of us meet at the apartment next week? Let the countess see it. And let me meet her and see what I think of her."

"Perfect!" Isabel says, and, at that moment, Michael brings over breakfast and they all sit down to eat.

Because Michael has to work on his lines for a call-back tomorrow at the Cherry Lane Theatre in the West Village, Isabel spends part of the afternoon—which turns out to be a perfect fall day, the leaves already turning a golden orangey brown—

walking around the Central Park Reservoir with Dixie, whose playful romping is always such fun for her. Despite the beauty of the day, Isabel feels a tiny bit sad—all the Chase women do when fall comes; there is something about the end of summer, the change of season, that makes them nostalgic.

On the way home, she stops for a quick latté at Yura on Madison, and then crosses over to the Corner Bookstore on the east side of the street with Dixie snuggled in her arms. All the Chases love the quaint, old-fashioned charm of the store and consider it "their" place—the bell rings when you open the door, they all have house accounts, and it's the only spot in all of New York where Elizabeth cannot speak on the phone. On a small hand-painted sign on the door, in beautiful red script, it reads, "Cell Phones Are Not Permitted."

Isabel picks out a book of old movie stills for her father, and a gorgeous, lavishly illustrated volume on Coco Chanel for her mother. Like Elizabeth, both girls are believers in "no-special-occasion" presents; sometimes, Isabel thinks, those are the sweetest and most meaningful of all.

Her apartment is getting dark when she returns home around five thirty; Kate is still not home, and it feels quiet. She must still be with Scott. Isabel calls just to make sure, and Kate tells her that they are having a snack at the bar at JG Melon, so not to wait for her to order Chinese, their usual Sunday-night dinner if they are not out with their parents or at the Chases' home having Elizabeth's chicken cutlets or Tom's spaghetti with meatballs. Isabel can hear the happiness in Kate's voice even in their twenty-second call.

Later, Isabel orders in shrimp and garlic sauce and a wonton soup from Our Place on 79th, making sure there will be enough for Kate just in case she's hungry when she gets home, then applies a Bliss oxygen mask to her face and gets in bed early to reread *Hotel New Hampshire* by John Irving, an all-time favorite she hasn't read in years. In the background, her iPod is playing Billy Joel's "She's Got a Way"; he, too, is one of her all-time favorites. The whole family goes to his concerts every time he's in New York, and they always get the best tickets because he also happens to have been a client of her mother's years ago. The new books from the Corner Bookstore are on her nightstand, because even though she isn't ready to open them, she loves the way books look arranged on a nightstand. There is nothing worse, she feels, than seeing an apartment that doesn't look lived-in. Dixie snores beside her, and every now and then Isabel rubs her pink belly. The only good thing about Kate not being home is that she gets Dixie. When the two girls are home, they alternate whom she sleeps with. Maybe they should get another puppy, Isabel thinks as she looks at the clock—

11:32. Still no Kate. She puts on her Elizabeth Arden Eight Hour Cream—a tradition passed down from Elizabeth's mother; hers sits in a beautiful jade glass jar by her bed—turns off her lamp, and goes to sleep, thinking how happy she is that Kate and Scott are together again.

First thing at the office a few days later, Isabel gets a text message confirming the information she's been so diligently seeking. Yes, Kimby Bennett delivered her twins at Lenox Hill Hospital at the end of August. It's taken Isabel a while to track down and verify this information: the babies, both boys, are named Blaine and Maximilian. They were a little underweight at birth, not uncommon for twins, of course, and spent some extra time in the neonatal unit, also very common. Now Kimby and her sons are back in the same apartment on East 83rd Street that Isabel knows the Bennetts are eager to leave; it was too small for a family of four, and it is definitely going to be too small for a family of six.

Isabel has a couple of hours before her next appointment, where she's meeting a new seller about to list what sounds like a darling mint-condition pied-à-terre at 125 East 74th Street, a beautiful little prewar on a tree-lined street. The owner, a sixtyish woman who has decided she wants to leave New York for San Francisco, where her son and three grandchildren live, has wooed Isabel with talk of a wood-burning fireplace, two bedrooms, and a Juliet balcony off the living room. Isabel decides to use the time until she heads over there to shop for a gift for the Bennett babies. She hasn't heard from them since that doomed showing so thoroughly sabotaged by the seller back in April, but Isabel's sources have also confirmed that the Bennetts haven't found a new place yet. Which means that they are still looking.

She tells her mother her plan, and calls Kate, who is on her way to show on East End. "Can you come shopping with me when you're finished?" she asks her sister.

"Would I ever say no to shopping?" Kate teases, and they arrange to meet at Promises on Second Avenue, their favorite place to buy baby gifts because they will monogram and hand-paint just about everything. They pick out two charmingly old-fashioned wooden rockers for the Bennett baby boys and a pair of pretty flowered hairbands for the girls, so they won't feel left out when a gift arrives for their little brothers. (Isabel spends over three hundred dollars, but her parents always taught them to be generous with presents, especially when it comes to clients.)

After the mini shopping spree, Kate jumps in a cab to get to her next appointment—a wreck off Fifth and 67th—and Isabel walks to 74th. She's arranged for the gifts to be sent directly to the Bennetts. When the Bennetts get in touch to thank her—and Isabel feels quite certain that they *will* thank her, how could they not?—she'll mention that she would *love* to help them in their apartment search, and if they ever think they might be in need of her services, she hopes they'll give her a call.

Michael phones excitedly now from the set of *Law & Order SVU.* The makeup artist is on a break and he has a little downtime, so he's able to call Isabel with the good news: he got the part at the Cherry Lane! "I think this job is a sign," he tells her. "Even though it's a tiny part, not much bigger than this one today on *Law & Order,* I still think it's a really strong sign about the future." And Isabel can't help but think that he's right, and even if he isn't, she loves that he is so damn optimistic!

The apartment on 74th Street is a huge disappointment. Not that it doesn't have great bones—quite the contrary, it has amazing bones—the disappointment is that the seller thinks the apartment is in wonderful shape and should sell accordingly, when all Isabel sees is peeling paint, an ancient kitchen, a bathroom that hasn't been touched in decades.

"It's also, I'm sure you know, the location," Alyssa Ostrow says as she follows Isabel around the apartment, practically stepping on her heels in her enthusiasm. "The location is perfect—near the museums, the park, shopping—everything a person could possibly want. And then of course there's the balcony—" She gestures to the tiny outdoor space that would definitely be an asset were it not cluttered with empty planters and a bag of soil that's been ripped open, its contents strewn everywhere.

"Yes, Alyssa, the location is perfect," Isabel agrees, "but I have to say it needs quite a bit of work. We can't price this at a 'mint' price."

"You mean a little paint job and a some freshening in the kitchen and bath? I would hardly call that 'quite a bit of work,' as you say."

"The kitchen," Isabel says evenly, "everyone is going to gut. The bathrooms, too." Isabel is impressed with her own conviction—so like Elizabeth, she thinks proudly.

"A gut?" Alyssa seems shocked to hear this. She scurries into the kitchen, with Isabel just behind her, and rummages around in the cupboard. Isabel is puzzled until the bottle of Johnnie Walker Red comes out, and the ice is tinkling in the glass. Despite the fact that it's not even noon yet, Alyssa Ostrow apparently feels the need to pour herself a stiff one. "Can I get you a drink?" she asks.

Isabel shakes her head no, and tugs the straps of her black Chanel bag over her shoulder. "Why don't you think about what I've said," she suggests. "I really think we need to lower the price, or you could do some minor renovations—I have an amazing team that could do it for you quickly. But you'd need to skim-coat and paint the walls, you need to replace things that are falling apart, new tiles on the floor—I just don't think it makes sense. The price is the issue. Oh, and you have to clean off your balcony—it's a great selling point, but you can hardly tell it's there." She takes out her business card and leaves it near an overflowing ashtray on the table; in fact there seem to be overflowing ashtrays everywhere in the apartment. In addition to all its other woes, the place reeks of cigarette smoke, an odor that, Isabel knows, is extremely difficult to eliminate and a major turnoff for buyers. One of Kate's best friends from Horace Mann—Ben Meier—virtually stole an apartment in Carnegie Hill because not only did the apartment reek of smoke through and through but the seller sat in her chair in the kitchen at every showing, leaning over her Formica table like she was about to tell a big secret, her wrinkled face looking even more pruney in contrast to the bright yellow laminated wallpaper, sucking each cigarette like it was a piece of chocolate, licking her lips and saying how she couldn't wait to move to Florida to golf. Ben, desperate to live in a prewar in Carnegie Hill (he grew up in the rental building at 1085 Park) was a closet real estate broker, spending lunches at his finance desk perusing and redoing floor plans (Kate nicknamed him Frankie Floorplan). This apartment was the one for him. It was in a Rosario Candela building (the best of the best), the proportion of the rooms was incredible and grand, the ceilings were close to ten feet, and everyone else walked in and walked right back out. Not Ben. He got it, and then he bought it.

Isabel stops for a second now to say, "Thank you, Alyssa, speak to you later!" and then thinks to herself, Ben is actually very good-looking, hysterically funny, and wickedly smart (albeit a bit of a hypochondriac, à la Woody Allen). She makes a note to herself to ask Kate if he is still single; she thinks she has a girl for him.

Out of the apartment, finally! Isabel doesn't bother waiting for the elevator, but takes the stairs down to the lobby and then hurries out into the October sunshine. What a relief to be in fresh air!

As she walks back to the office, she thinks about utterly deluded sellers like Alyssa.

Isabel's thoughts are interrupted by her cell. "Hi, Kate," she says to her sister. "The place on 67th is a disaster? Well, let me tell you about the apartment *I* just saw—" Isabel has a call waiting. "Wait, I'll call you back, okay?" she says, before answering the second call.

"Isabel?" says a quivering female voice.

"Yes," Isabel answers. She doesn't immediately recognize the voice and didn't look at the number when it rang.

"Isabel, it's Alex! Alex Fein."

"Alex," says Isabel. She is not happy to hear her voice, not at all. "How is everything?" she wills herself to say.

"Terrible!" Alex says plaintively. "Totally terrible! You won't believe what I've had to endure."

"What happened?" Isabel asks her. "Did the deal fall through?"

"Fall through?" Alex is practically screeching. "Isabel, you have no idea!"

"What happened, Alex?"

"Well, you know how much I loved, loved, loved the apartment," Alex says. "But there was just one little thing—"

"Yes?" Isabel says. She remembers just how picky Alex was, and how this apartment had been, in her words, absolutely perfect.

"Well, when Brad and I were on vacation in Aix-en-Provence, I found this amazing suite of painted eighteenth-century furniture. An armoire, a bureau, two nightstands, two bergères, and a gorgeous desk. I'd never seen anything like them outside of a museum. And Brad bought them for me as an anniversary gift."

"Sounds beautiful," Isabel says, waiting for the point of the call.

"It is!" Alex wails. "But the master suite in the new apartment wasn't quite big enough to accommodate all of it, and I really didn't want to split the pieces up, they're just so stunning together. So I thought I would have the bedroom enlarged just a *little* bit. Which meant some work on the hallway, of course. And as long as we were doing that, it seemed to make sense to add some built-ins, as well, and to reconfigure the closets. Then we decided the master bath really needed some alteration. The colors were all wrong for the new furniture."

Which was not going to be in the same room anyway, thinks Isabel.

"So I found the architect and the contractor, and everything was perfect, until I discovered that the building has summer work rules and so this job, instead of taking just a few months, was going to drag on for close to two years. I've already sold my place, and guess what, I'm pregnant! I can't afford to have my life on hold for two years, Isabel, I canNOT!" Alex says, suddenly sounding tearful. Isabel imagines her stamping her foot for punctuation.

"What an ordeal," Isabel says. She knows the building on Fifth—and knows all about its draconian rules, especially those governing renovation. She would never have let Alex buy there without first making sure she understood just what these rules would mean if she ever wanted to have any work done on the apartment.

"Oh, Alex," she says. "How horrendous. Your broker didn't tell you about the work rules in that building? Anyone who knows anything about that building knows that the work rules are horrific. I would never have let you buy there without telling you that. You poor thing."

"Oh, Isabel, this is such a mess. I never should have done this, you never would have had me in this situation.

An unbelievable ordeal! And it's not over yet. My place sold in a heartbeat, and it's already in contract. So *now* what am I going to do? Brad's mother says we can stay with her. She's got a huge ten at 983 Park, but the truth is"—here Alex lowers her voice—"that woman hates me and always has. The feeling's mutual, clearly, I mean who in their right mind likes their mother-in-law? There's no way in hell I'm staying with her! No! But the baby's due in February, that's only four months away. I've got to get an apartment before then," she whines, and Isabel again imagines Alex Fein stamping her skinny foot.

"Do you want me to help you find one?"

"Could you?" Alex says, her voice suddenly meek and pleading.

Isabel is silent for a moment before she replies, just to make poor Alex Fein twitch. Oh how she would love to say, *I'd sooner see you living in a tiny postwar than help a vile, whiny, disloyal client like you!* But Isabel is not Elizabeth's daughter for nothing, and she understands completely that, as delicious a moment as this well-deserved revenge might be, it's simply not worth the many possible repercussions. To say nothing of a nice commission and teaching Alex a good lesson—never leave a Chase!

"Of course I can help you," Isabel tells her. "I'll go through all the listings and see what I can find that might be right for you—and won't need an ounce of work, of course."

"Oh God, thank you, Isabel," Alex says, the relief in her

voice palpable. "This really means a lot to me. I know you must have been upset when I suddenly turned around and bought from someone else."

Upset? *Livid* is the more appropriate word. But Isabel says nothing, and Alex goes on, "And you know what? Maybe this is all going to work out in the end anyway. I'll buy an apartment through you—someone I can trust, someone who still has some integrity."

Oh, the irony of that comment, Isabel thinks, and says, "Thank you." She begins to walk faster. She can't wait to tell her mother and Kate about the Alex Fein development; she imagines Kate imitating Alex Fein's whiny voice— "Poor Alex Fein!"

When she arrives at the office, her sister and mother are there, sharing a Cobb salad and a turkey sandwich in Kate and Isabel's office and a mint lemonade they picked up at Le Pain Quotidien. They always eat in there; they have an extra desk, where Elizabeth sits. Tom usually comes in and gets his food, but goes back to eat at his own desk. They share lunches every time they are in their office together, their favorite being from June to September—when their Carnegie Hill CSA food co-op begins. As members, they pick up every Tuesday afternoon at the church on 90th Street the freshest, most amazing fruits and vegetables trucked in from local farms, and Elizabeth and Cecilia make a huge salad with all the ingredients, a surprise each week—heirloom tomatoes, ten kinds of lettuce, bunches of radishes with the mud still clinging to them, yellow cucumbers. . . . "We ordered enough for you, too," says Kate as she bites into a sour pickle now.

Isabel puts her bag down and takes a plate and some salad. "So the apartment on 67th was really awful?"

"Awful is an understatement" Kate exclaims. "They had ferrets!"

"What's a ferret?"

"I don't even know. Mom thinks they're illegal in New York, actually—they look like little rats. There were lots of them, running all over, I didn't want to walk in. Some of them used a filthy litter box, and the rest used the floor as their bathroom. It was the most vile thing I've ever seen—can you imagine showing that apartment?"

"Ewww, I just shuddered!" Isabel says.

"Oh, and there was no refrigerator—none! Apparently it had broken, and the owner never bothered to replace it. Said she ate out all the time anyway."

"I can see why," Elizabeth says dryly, joining the conversation after a quick call about a board package.

Kate says, "What kind of people live like that—I mean, the list of problems goes on and on. Do you mind if I finish this?" she asks, holding up half of the turkey sandwich. "I'm starved."

"Sure," Isabel says. "I'm still nauseated from all the cigarette smoke in the apartment I just looked at."

"Too bad the ferrets didn't kill my appetite!" Kate teases. "Where was there smoke?"

Isabel tells them both about the 74th Street listing, and

Kate reminds her of Ben Meier. "I know!" Isabel says. "I kept thinking of him—too bad he already bought—this apartment is for him!"

Elizabeth is thrilled when Isabel finally shares the tale of Alex Fein. "Hah! She got what she deserved! I love the way you handled it."

"Mmm," Isabel says with a mouthful, "I thought you two would get a kick out of that."

Their assistant Ben Boylan walks in to tell Elizabeth that Raizy Haas is on the phone about the Stanhope. Ben is a tall young man in his late twenties or early thirties, the kind of man whose age you cannot tell. He shaves his head, wears black-rimmed glasses, and is every bit as deadpan as the girls are bubbly. Ben looks like he should have been cast in John Hughes's *Breakfast Club*, one of Kate and Isabel's favorite movies.

Raizy Haas is one of the most powerful women in the real estate development business. Number two at Extell, wears her hair in a stick-straight, shoulder-length bob with a row of bangs straight across her eyebrows like an exquisitely cut lawn. She has piercing blue eyes, china doll pale skin, and despite being quite thin, is in a constant battle with her weight. She once called Elizabeth at three in the morning Dubai time whispering, "The best thing about Dubai is that I've lost ten pounds!"

"Where's the call?" Elizabeth says. "My cell is in my hand." She clutches her cell as if it were the hand of a two-year-old ready to make a run for it.

"She said it went straight to voice mail, and Violeta has been paging you, you didn't hear?"

"No, okay, I'm coming in." Elizabeth is representing one of the most expensive and spectacular trophy properties in all the city—the $28.5 million last-remaining full-floor residence at the Stanhope hotel, converted to the highest-end luxury building and renamed "995 Fifth." The apartment, which takes up the entire sixteenth floor of the building, spans 8,300 square feet, with seven bedrooms, even more baths, and sweeping views of the Reservoir, the Metropolitan Museum of Art, Central Park, and all of the West Side from each major room—the living room, dining room, library, and sitting room, and even the kitchen.

Elizabeth is waiting for the okay from Raizy to have it decorated; as ludicrous as it may sound, as an empty space, it's almost too big for people to imagine. When she or the girls show it, buyers often stop and say, "Wait, what room is this?" Elizabeth and the girls agree that with a property like this, it's worth it to spend the money to help buyers differentiate the rooms.

Elizabeth wants to hire the hottest architect in the city, JP Forbes Jr., a 6'2" black-haired, blue-eyed "hunk" (as Kate and Isabel and all their friends call him) in his late thirties, who was just featured in a four-page spread in *Town and Country* at his home on Lower Fifth, with his beautiful young wife and twin three-year-old daughters. He looks like a cross between Jon Hamm and Clive Owen, two of the Chase girls' favorite actors. Kate once met him at an event in the penthouse at the London hotel and, after spending hours talking to him and drinking Bellinis, was devastated to learn he was happily married, especially since he was the one and only other boy she got a flutter with in all the years since she met Scott.

"I got the go-ahead," Raizy says. When not in the mood for chitchat, Raizy cuts right to the point. "You better make this worth our while, Elizabeth." Raizy and Elizabeth have gotten very close in the three or so years that Extell has been giving her so many of its "trophy" properties to sell. But she rules, as Elizabeth says, with a velvet glove.

Before Elizabeth can respond, Raizy says, "Okay, Elizabeth, gotta run, my plane is boarding, I'll be back in New York City tomorrow, we need to speak about something at 535 WEA," and then click.

Elizabeth walks back into the girls' office and does a little dance. "We can hire JP Forbes for the Stanhope!" she says. "Which one of you is going to come with me to meet him?"

"Fabulous," both girls say together. And then, because they both have huge crushes on him, they say, "We'll both come!"

Elizabeth turns to leave. "I have to go show uptown, I'm going to be late," she says, so Isabel follows her out to tell her that Michael got a small role in the Edward Albee play at the Cherry Lane.

"And it was written about in Page Six today!" she says.

"That's fabulous," Elizabeth says. And even though she

secretly worries about his having chosen what she and Tom consider a rather unstable, albeit totally glamorous, career, she says, "Michael is going to do very, very well, I know. And his looks sure won't hurt him either!"

Isabel grins.

Two days later, Isabel is walking along West 67th Street, on her way to the fifty-fourth-floor apartment she and her mother are going to show Delphine. The day, bright and without a cloud in the sky, is quite cold for mid-October (although there are always some days in October when the temperature is in the forties, the Chase ladies never prepare their closets in time, still clinging to their summer colors), so this morning Isabel had to rummage madly under her bed to find a Ralph Lauren cable cashmere sweater (purple—their favorite color!) and a pair of Ralph Lauren black wool pants. If only she didn't store her coats at the cleaners, she thinks, but thankfully she finds a cream cashmere Portolano wrap—the Chase ladies have them in every color, thanks to their relationship with Francesca, one of the owners of the company.

Her mother is already at the apartment; she was showing at the El Dorado on Central Park West and went straight there. Isabel gets a call from her on the way over. "I'll wait for Delphine in the lobby," Isabel tells her. "We'll meet you up there." And just as soon as Isabel reaches the building, she sees the long white limo and then Delphine stepping gracefully from it, one highly shined cowboy boot placed down on the pavement before the other.

"Isabel!" she calls. *Iz-a-BELLE* is how it sounds. Everything always sounds better with a French accent, Isabel thinks. Today, above the trademark black cowboy boots, the countess wears an ankle-grazing sable coat so exquisite she has never seen anything like it. She and Kate both have fun black mink bomber jackets, gifts from their mother, and Elizabeth has a collection of furs, but none of them have anything like this. Fur used to be reserved for the absolute coldest days when you felt too frigid to even stick a toe outside, but now New York women wear fur from October till May. Under the coat, worn open, Isabel sees a glimpse of something long and chiffon, in a chic geometric pattern of yellow, black, and cream. The countess's long, flaxen hair has been done up in a loose topknot with appealing little tendrils escaping to frame her face, and delicate, diamond-studded gold hoops adorn her ears.

"My mother's already upstairs," Isabel says, after the two women perform the quick, double cheek-kiss that is as much Delphine's signature as her cowboy boots. "We'll meet her there."

Linking arms with Isabel, the countess sails regally past the pair of doormen—both of whom, it seems, can't help staring at the willowy, fur-clad blond—and toward the elevator. As they step inside, Delphine says, "I can tell you are wearing the perfume," and leans over toward Isabel's neck. "It is enchanting on you. But then, what wouldn't be?"

"Mom and Kate loooove it —Mom put it on the other day when she was at my apartment, and it smelled divine on her," Isabel says.

Delphine says, "I am very much looking forward to meeting her."

"Oh, she is looking forward to meeting you, too," Isabel says as the elevator makes its swift ascent to the fifty-fourth floor. The elevator arrives, and there is her mother, smiling.

"So good to meet you, finally," Elizabeth says.

"And you," says Delphine, taking Elizabeth's hand and clasping it with both of her own. "I've read about you in the *Times*, and I can't help but admire women like you who are so successful. I only wish I were more ambitious. And you're even more beautiful in person than you are in the photographs."

Elizabeth smiles, saying, "Thank you!"

"I'm sure you know by now how much I think of your daughter. She's a jewel. But of course you don't need me to tell you that."

"Well, I must thank you again!" Elizabeth says, flashing Isabel a smile. "The truth is, I have three amazing children."

"And I hope to meet the others, too," says Delphine. She lets go of Elizabeth's hand and shrugs off her sable coat. "Here," Elizabeth says, "let me put that down for you."

The views of the apartment are simply breathtaking—west across the Hudson, which today sparkles like glass; south at the Statue of Liberty; north and east at the park. The place is flooded with so much light that Elizabeth, who compulsively turns on every light and lamp in all her listings and has taught the girls the same, has left them all off here. It is one of the few apartments where extra light would be completely unnecessary. The floors have been done in a glossy brown lacquer, so dark it is nearly black. The kitchen has a stainless steel industrial-looking center island that Delphine coos over, a Viking range, two Sub-Zeros and dishwashers—everything one could want in a kitchen. "The owner was a serious chef," Elizabeth says.

"Fritzie loves to cook! He's an amateur, of course," Delphine says with a charming giggle. "But what an amateur! I could get very, very fat if I did not remain vigilant!" She pats her washboard-flat stomach lightly with her manicured hand.

"I'd love to meet your husband sometime," Elizabeth says. Her voice is casual, but Isabel knows from experience that her comment is anything but. "He sounds like such an interesting man. And of course it would be so useful to get his reactions to the showings as well. After all, you're both going to be living wherever it is that you end up buying."

"Oh, I would love that as well!" Delphine says, with what sounds like utter sincerity. "But he's just so busy! Right now, he's in Dubai. Very high-level project, you know."

"And just what is it that he does?" Elizabeth asks.

"Well, Fritzie does a little bit of everything—banking, finance, light industry, global marketing. He's a true Renaissance man." Just then Delphine's cell phone rings, and she begins talking, very animatedly, in German.

"*Ja, ja*," she says, nodding her head enthusiastically, though of course the person at the other end can't see her. "*Jawohl!*" she adds, with emphasis. She is quiet for a moment, and then the voluble torrent of words resumes. Isabel, who took a couple of excruciating semesters of German in college, can make out a word or two here and there—*flugzeug*, which she remembers is airplane, and *autobahn*, which is the superhighway—but mostly the conversation passes right over her head.

Delphine snaps her phone shut, and they continue the showing; Elizabeth's question remains unanswered. They view the three bedrooms and baths: the master suite, with its full-size dressing room that features leather-lined closets extending from floor to ceiling, and an exquisite spa bath with the requisite double vanity, separate shower (this one a double rain head), and oversize deep soaking infinity tub surrounded by a huge window. The countess loves it all.

When Delphine asks to "make a pee-pee in zee little girls' room?" Elizabeth whispers, "Very charming, but there is definitely something off."

"You think so?" Isabel says.

"She is very elusive."

"Yes, I guess so."

Then Delphine reappears from the bathroom. "Ta ta," she sings, grabbing her sable. "Isabel come, let's go, I must run. Elizabeth, what a pleasure," and in a flurry of kisses and perfume she is gone.

■ ■ ■

Neither her mother nor Kate is at the office when Isabel gets in (Elizabeth stayed at West 67th; she had back-to-back showings there, and Isabel doesn't know where Kate is), but she has plenty to do. There's a message from Kimby Bennett—that was quick!—and another from Alyssa Ostrow (the owner of the smoke-filled 74th Street mess), both of which she needs to answer. And she has an apartment in mind for Alex Fein, but wants to discuss it with her mom before she calls Alex.

A few hours later, Isabel hears the tinkling of her mother's charm bracelets as she walks into the office. She puts her charcoal Carolina Herrera jacket and matching colored python bag on her chair before calling out, "Isabel! Did you order lunch?"

"Not yet—Mangia for a change?"

"Yes, I don't care what, I'll just have some of what you get, and get Dad a tuna, I guess."

"Should I order for Kate, too?" Isabel yells.

"No, she's out."

"Client?" asks Isabel, who is about to phone the restaurant for their lunch.

"Yes, new ones. A couple just moved here from Texas. They both have big jobs in finance. I think they were referred by her friend Kevin from Penn."

"So, let's talk about Delphine," Isabel says later, as she and her mother sit across from each other at Elizabeth's desk, sharing a broccoli quiche and a grilled chicken wrap. Tom's tuna is sitting on his desk; he's at the bank.

"Well, she's evasive. But thoroughly charming about it," Elizabeth says. "It's hard to say, really. She could be politely liking everything but hasn't yet found what she really wants, or, as I've said, she could be just extravagantly wasting your time."

"I know." Isabel sips from a plastic cup of iced tea, with the extra wedges of lemon they always get floating like ice cubes.

"But the truth is, you're getting to see magnificent properties that you might otherwise not see, and she's certainly fun to be with."

"And the presents!"

"Things could be worse. I would certainly play it out," Elizabeth says, as she takes a bite of quiche. "The husband, I can't figure. 'A little bit of this and that' usually means a lot of nothing."

"I know, and I'm showing her some of the toughest buildings in the city—"

"Well, with her I think you should stick to condos and town houses. Or you could just make a joke, like, 'If you do decide to buy a co-op, Fritzie will have to do full disclosure on all his finances, and of course show up for a board meeting!' I just honestly think even if they have all that money, you're never going to get their cooperation to show it to a board."

"You're right."

Her mother continues, "She may not understand how things work in this country."

"I'll try and talk to her," says Isabel, but then she's distracted by the high-pitched barking of what sounds like a small dog. Dixie? she thinks hopefully, although Dixie is of course at her mother's, where the girls drop her every day to play with Lola, Roxy, and Dolly so that she's not alone. As she gets up to see—for any dog would be a treat to see—she nearly bumps into Violeta, and a messenger with a dog carrier behind her.

"Isabel?" Violeta says. "This guy says he has a delivery. For you." Her expression is one of utter bafflement.

"For me?" Leaning down to peer inside the carrier, Isabel discovers that it's not one but two shih tzu puppies! "OMG!!" she squeals. "Mom!!"

"It's from a Countess Ho-man von heren—," the messenger says, stumbling over the name.

"That's all right," Isabel says, addressing both the messenger and Violeta. "I know the sender." She just left the countess's company; when and how did she manage to find these puppies, and arrange for them to be delivered to the office? Unless the countess really does possess some sort of magic. At this moment, Isabel half believes that she does.

"OMG, what are these little angels?" asks her mother as she walks over.

"A little gift. From the countess." Isabel signs for the "package" so the messenger can leave, and takes out the frantic puppies, who lick her face, her ears, her neck.

"Oh, give one to me!" says Elizabeth, and then to the puppy, "You're so delicious, you could be Dixie's sister! Oh, look," she says, "there's a note."

> Dear Isabel, I know you are a lover of these small dogs and I thought your Dixie might enjoy having a little companion. Of course, when I found the right one, I had to buy two! They are very good-tempered and their breeding is, of course, impeccable. With affection, Delphine.

CHAPTER TWELVE

Elizabeth

Prime Chelsea Loft

Artist's loft; private keyed elevator leads to this large live/work space, open and light with north and south exposures, oversize windows, 14-ft ceilings. Bring your architect. $2.15 million.

Elizabeth is in a taxi on her way to meet Bart Schneider at a loft that he's bidding on in Chelsea, against her better judgment and despite her repeated advice that he look elsewhere for something more suitable. It's mid-November now, and some of the windows and trees with lights are just beginning to show the twinkling mood of Christmas. The city looks so alive again.

After irritating Elizabeth for months with his indecision and almost daily phone calls, the exasperating Bart Schneider has finally opted to buy a loft a convenient three blocks from his art gallery. Elizabeth has—after trying her best to convince him that this property is just too problematic—very reluctantly helped the sale along. As far as she's concerned, the only thing the property has going for it is "proximity," something she'd strongly suggested early on and which Bart had flatly dismissed. Like many buyers, he'd begun his search with a strong idea of what he wanted in his dream apartment—something that would reflect his success and his world-class lifestyle—only to see that idea change over and over again. When he first began looking, he was sure he wanted a duplex (he claimed to love climbing a flight of stairs to get to his bedroom), then decided a duplex didn't matter, but the apartment must be not only completely renovated and in totally move-in condition, but furnished as well (a near impossibility in New York). Then it was a town house with a parlor floor that had at least twelve-foot ceilings to display his artwork, and then a town house became too hard to tend to, a simple apartment, facing any direction but south (would fade his art collection), unfurnished (someone else's taste would never match his), until, alas, he settled on a loft he found on StreetEasy.com and forwarded to Elizabeth saying, "This is the one." It had been renovated in the 1980s and had glass brick dividers, two bathrooms, and two bedrooms carved out on either side of the rectangular space. The place was in shabby condition at best; it would need at least half a million in work, she guessed. Bart, always looking for a challenge, decided that he wanted to take on yet another project. This decision of his to move forward proved an old saying of hers: "Buyers are liars."

He is, unfortunately, Elizabeth reflects, one of those overachievers who believes that everything he does, every decision he makes, can't come easy. Despite the fact that his gallery is a tremendously successful one and that he employs ample staff to help him, he insists on working nonstop and micromanaging everyone and everything. Elizabeth has to admit to herself that there were a few times when his incessant phone calls and demands of her time made her seriously consider giving him to another broker in her office. But there was something about Bart that kept Elizabeth working with him. He was kind, unlike Lance Roberts who, as Elizabeth expected, was discouraged from making an offer by the co-op board of 860 UN Plaza, who'd heard about his bad behavior and refused to allow him or any of his relatives to live in the building. The good news about that was that she never heard from Lance Roberts again.

Bart's offer of $1.7 million on a $2.1 million asking price had been presented and, much to her surprise, accepted rather quickly and easily at $1.8 after only two rounds of negotiations. But of course Bart had contingencies. He insisted on a building inspection (fair enough), but then wanted time for an architect to study the space, drawing up plans so that Bart himself could determine if the space actually could be reconfigured to suit his idiosyncratic needs. But he was all cash, and that was appealing, and it seemed as though he was the one lone offer in the apartment's nearly two years on the market. The only hiccup—the sellers put a three-week deadline for the contingencies to be met.

As her cab turns down 25th Street, Elizabeth's cell rings again, this time with a number she doesn't recognize. A not particularly friendly voice says, "Elizabeth? It's Roberta Green from LEX."

Elizabeth tenses for a moment when she hears LEX. The most recent development with Teddy is that his once competitive, edgy relationship with Christopher McKinnon has evolved into an exceptionally close friendship. The two brokers lunch together at least once a week, usually at Del Frisco's or Fred's at Barneys—although this, in and of itself, isn't anything out of the ordinary. Elizabeth and her best broker friend, Barbara Fox, have regularly lunched together for years, but their friendship goes way, way back and stems from multiple things in common, like a love of animals—Barbara has her own charity called Woof and a brood of at least ten rescue dogs at any given moment; they both sit on the Real Estate Board of New York's ethics committee, and they both love a good glass of champagne or a frozen margarita! Elizabeth and Tom also frequently double-date with Barbara and her divine husband, Jimmy Freund, a Horace Mann alumnus and a real Renaissance man. Teddy Wingo and Christopher McKinnon, on the other hand, had been enemies until about a minute ago, and the only time Teddy referred to him was to talk about Christopher and the "trashy" women he dated. And so Elizabeth finds herself utterly bewildered by the recent turn of events.

"I'm calling because I have somebody very interested in your listing at 33 East 70th," Roberta begins, referring to a

$9.5 million four-bedroom, three-bath co-op that Elizabeth has had an exclusive on for nearly two years, before she herself found a buyer with the right financials.

"Oh, I'm sorry, but we actually just have a signed contract," she informs Roberta, wondering who gave out her cell number and why—she never gives it to brokers unless she is doing a deal with them, or has booked a showing.

"I understand that you sold it yourself," Roberta says, her voice now tinged with a bit of contempt. Her inference is that because Elizabeth is representing both seller and buyer, there might be a conflict of interest.

Elizabeth chooses to ignore this—it is none of Roberta's business.

"Well, I'd like to show it if the contract isn't fully signed."

If the contract were fully executed, Elizabeth would no longer engage this broker, but the truth is, the buyers have signed but the seller has not, so she says vaguely, "If anything changes, I'll let you know, or you can follow up with one of my daughters tomorrow." She suddenly gets a peculiar feeling that Roberta knows more than she should about this particular deal.

"But has the *seller* signed?"

Now Elizabeth feels certain that Roberta somehow knows that her seller has yet to sign the contract. "He's returning from Paris. And then coming into Manhattan to sign the documents."

"Well, if he hasn't *yet* signed, I'd like to arrange a showing. My buyers are intimately familiar with the building. They used to live there in a larger apartment and then moved farther downtown."

"How long ago?" Elizabeth asks. "When did they move?"

"Oh, probably ten years ago or a little more. They're very keen to return. So who knows, maybe they'll pay more than your buyers."

The empty apartment had been listed at $9.5 million in March 2008, just before the financial crisis. Even though New York City real estate saw some fluctuating prices, Elizabeth's seller, Maxwell Glenn, then eighty-six years old, wanted to maintain his price. An exceedingly wealthy inventor of a certain kind of pulmonary respirator, he'd made a fortune licensing it to a French medical conglomerate. Maxwell Glenn also happens to be one of the most handsome octogenarians Elizabeth has ever seen. He met Ondine, his most recent, much younger French wife, on one of his business trips to Paris. Ondine's an elegant Parisian who insists they spend at least four months a year in her enormous flat on the Ile Saint-Louis. Not a fan of Manhattan, she convinced her husband to buy a mansion in Bedford, picked through his furniture, discarded half of it, and left his apartment on East 70th completely empty. Beyond this, the couple refused to stage the empty apartment with furniture and artwork that would highlight its features, which might be a reason why the apartment has seen very little activity. But then six weeks ago, Elizabeth got a call from a nuclear radiologist named Ai-Ling Chua; her husband is a business consultant for the Chinese government. They saw her ad for the apartment in *Avenue* magazine, made an appointment to see it, and negotiated the price down to $9.23 million. (Though the Chases don't do much print advertising anymore, Elizabeth and Tom are longtime friends of the president and publisher, Julie Dannenberg, whose magazine goes only to the finest buildings and hotels.)

"So when would you have time to meet us over there?" Roberta persists, knowing that until Maxwell Glenn signs the contract, Elizabeth is obligated to bring him any offer that's presented.

"Let me look at my schedule." Elizabeth opens her Day-at-a-Glance—the big black old-fashioned book where she keeps all of her appointments, client notes, phone numbers, etc.—and peruses a list of appointments and apartment showings until she sees an opening at 5:00 p.m.

"Five o'clock isn't optimum because of the light, but I guess it will have to do," Roberta tells her.

"That's the earliest I can show it," Elizabeth says, trying to sound cordial.

There is a long, awkward pause, and then Roberta says, "My buyers saw the apartment two floors below when it came on the market a few years ago. And decided not to buy it. How about if I told you now—and they've instructed me to do so—that they'll pay $200,000 more than your outstanding contract? All I need to do is see the contract, and then they'll make their offer."

"That's ridiculous," Elizabeth tells her. "I can't show you the contract. You know that's not done. In all the years I've been in the business, no one has ever asked to see a contract in order to outbid it."

"Well, the business is changing, what can I tell you?"

"You're welcome to see the place at five o'clock, and if your buyers are still interested, make me an offer tonight. I'll call my client in Paris. And if your offer happens to be higher than the one I have, then I'm sure he'll seriously consider it."

"Fine," Roberta says. "We'll see you there at five."

When Elizabeth calls Tom to tell him, he agrees that Roberta Green probably was given private information, and that Teddy is without a doubt the source—presumably for some kind of kickback. Although Elizabeth doesn't remember telling Teddy the agreed-upon selling price of the East 70th Street apartment, he must have looked at their deal sheet. Elizabeth has the disturbing feeling that Roberta already knows the price agreed on between Ai-Ling Chua and Maxwell Glenn.

"When is Barrington's announcing they've selected us as their New York City brokerage house?" Tom asks her.

"Violeta wrote to them, and they said probably next week."

"I think we need to look into Teddy's correspondence," Tom says, referring to Jonathan's offer to try and hack into Teddy's e-mail.

"I know I said we needed to wait until the Luxury

Estates announcement is made, but now I'm thinking that maybe we should have tried to look into his e-mail a long time ago," Elizabeth says. "I just worry that he could sue us for breach of privacy."

"Well, at this point I think we need to take the risk, and I think we should do it now," Tom tells her.

Just as Elizabeth is getting out of the cab to meet Bart, her phone rings again. It's her friend Carol Goodman, the board president at 860 UN Plaza, the building where Lance Roberts wanted to buy an apartment.

"Are you sitting down?" Carol says.

"Just going to meet a client. What's going on?"

"Guess who sent a letter to the board threatening a lawsuit for discrimination?"

"Oh, no, he didn't!"

"Oh, indeed he did."

"Oh, I never should have gotten involved with him," Elizabeth says. "He has no case, he never even applied to your building."

"I know, but we got a letter from Nixon, Kerin & Tainiter, which is a pretty big sign."

"Oh, please," Elizabeth says. "He probably has a friend there who did him a favor. Don't worry, I'll call Lance. The only way he'd have a prayer of a case is if he'd actually gone through the application process."

"Well, let me know what he says."

The nerve! Elizabeth thinks when she gets off the phone. She is reeling, between this, the call on 33 East 70th, and Teddy. And to think that she's on her way to deal with yet another lunatic!

With his architect, interior decorator, a contractor, and a "paint consultant," Bart Schneider is pacing the apartment frantically when Elizabeth walks out of the elevator into the 2,200-square-foot loft space. Southern light is streaming through a bank of windows, and she can see how dirty the place is. It reminds her of a gigantic version of a railroad flat in the East Village, or a football field with banks of windows on either end of a long, windowless space that has been minimally divided.

"Thank God!" Bart says when she walks in the door. Though Jewish, he's one of those tall, lanky, very patrician-looking blue-eyed men who could easily be confused with a high-born WASP. He went to St. Paul's and then Princeton, and then Princeton again for graduate school in art history. He's superbly educated, with an overactive brain that doesn't stop thinking. Elizabeth can tell he's very upset, and wishes he was not so insistent about buying this apartment that she just knows is wrong for him. The irony is that all he seeks is her approval, and he's not listening to her now.

"I'm so glad you're here, Elizabeth."

Bart's consultants are standing together in a group behind him, watching the exchange.

"There are big structural problems here," Bart announces and goes on to explain that several wall joists are bad and that one of the walls in the apartment is actually in danger of collapsing. The hired engineer comes forward and makes his case with diagrams and drawings.

"Okay, anything else?" Elizabeth asks calmly.

Pointing to the ceiling, where there's water damage, Bart says, "It's not cosmetic. The ceiling is rotted all the way through."

Elizabeth turns to the contractor, introduces herself, and asks what it will cost to repair the structural problems. The man hands her an itemized list with the figure $132,000 at the bottom.

"So you'd like me to call the listing broker and tell them that you want to reduce your offer?" Elizabeth says to Bart. She purposely doesn't mention the figure.

Bart says, "That's right, by a hundred and thirty-two thousand dollars."

Elizabeth shakes her head. "You already got an amazing deal on this place, Bart. They'll probably get their own expert in here for a second opinion."

"They can if they want," Bart says.

"Look, Bart, as you know, I think this is the wrong apartment for you—but for the first time in our relationship, you're not listening to me, so I have to protect you from yourself. The broker told me the other day that there's somebody else who wants to buy this apartment, and has indicated that they'll pay more than you."

Unsurprisingly, Bart looks miffed. "Then let them do that," he says, though without real conviction.

Looking around the run-down loft, whose renovation Elizabeth knows will end up costing more than what the consultants estimate, she says, "I *told* you not to buy this apartment, Bart. When you buy a place like this, something that hasn't been updated in years, you expect to spend a lot of money on renovating it. The seller might, *might* split the difference with you, but I wouldn't even begin to assume—"

"Well, then, I guess we won't have a deal," Bart interrupts, with a bit too much confidence, Elizabeth thinks.

She shoots him an unhappy look, reflecting on all the time he's wasted by calling her nearly every day. Bart is the sort of person who probably would begin a litigation just to have one. He's one of those people who has everything but never believes that what he has is enough. Elizabeth is seeing a different side to him, and she doesn't like it.

His face is bright red; he's clearly very agitated.

"Listen, I have another appointment," Elizabeth says as she looks at her watch. "So I'll call the broker and let you know what the sellers say."

Bart's mood suddenly changes. "Can you just stay a few minutes and see what my architect's come up with? It's really wonderful."

"Bart, why don't we wait and see if we can keep the deal together? There's a very good chance that we can't."

"I don't agree. I think they'll come to their senses," he says.

"Well, I'm glad you're so optimistic. I'll let you know when *I* know." Bart moves closer to her, as though wanting some kind of hug or handshake. "I've got to go. I have another appointment," Elizabeth tells him for the second time.

Once she's riding the slow, dilapidated, trembling elevator down to the ground floor, she wonders why Bart has no issues with the elevator. The elevator is a real problem. Oh, well, this is all going to fall apart anyway, and she decides she'll pass Bart on to someone else in her office, maybe Lorelei Lyne, who can put up with anybody.

On her way back uptown she hears Billy Joel's "My Life" playing on her cell phone. This is one of Jonathan's favorite songs; he's programmed her phone to ring with it whenever he calls. She assumes he's calling from home now. Though she'd been vehemently opposed to Jonathan taking time off from school because she worried that he'd never go back, in the end, she'd said yes when everybody else in the family—even Tom—supported it. And so she's come to see it, as the rest of the Chases do, as a once-in-a-lifetime chance for Jonathan.

"Hi, Mom," he says. "Just spoke to Dad. I have this program I just downloaded and copied onto a DVD. If you install it on somebody's computer, it basically monitors every key stroke a person makes. If I install it tonight, tomorrow when Teddy goes to the office and signs on to his personal e-mail, we'll have a record of his user name and password. And then we can start digging."

"It's as easy as that?"

"Yup. We just need to read through the transcripts of

key strokes until we find what we're looking for. It could take a while, but it's definitely doable."

Elizabeth is silent. She considers herself to be highly scrupulous. And even though she's agreed with Tom that it is time to hack into Teddy's e-mail, a part of her still feels weird about it; it's not illegal, but she feels it is somehow not right.

"Mom, I think we really have to do this," Jonathan is saying.

"I know."

"Why don't you just give me a key to the office, and I'll do it," he says.

"Okay, I'll give it to you when I get home," Elizabeth says.

"Love you," Jonathan says, and hangs up.

Roberta Green, chubby and totally frumpy, raven-haired with no makeup, thick glasses, and dressed in a navy blue jumpsuit, arrives at the empty four-bedroom, three-bath on East 70th Street with Barry Kessler, a sixtyish, nervous-looking man. Having once been a resident of the building and thus already familiar with the particular layout of the apartment, he moves through the high-ceilinged rooms briskly, confirming that the apartment is in excellent condition. Approaching a large living room window and peering down on Madison Avenue for a moment, he takes a deep breath and turns to Elizabeth.

"It doesn't take me long to make up my mind."

"Sounds like you'd made up your mind long before now," she says. There's something between a raffish grin and a smirk on his face. She feels an aggressive self-promotion about to begin and deflects it by saying, "So I understand you once lived in this building, Barry."

"That's correct."

"And why did you move?"

"Kids went to college. Our apartment was slightly bigger than this one. And we didn't like the empty-nest feeling. So we downsized. But now we're expecting a grandchild, and we want more room again. My wife and I—we loved it here." Massaging his hands, he says, "Look, I'm prepared to offer 9.43 million." Roberta nods as though she is his walker in *Best in Show.*

Two hundred thousand dollars more than her accepted offer from Ai-Ling Chua and her husband; Elizabeth is taken aback for a few moments.

"Well, I'm happy to present the offer as soon as my seller returns from France," Elizabeth says. "But in the meantime, I'd like to see your financials. I need to be sure they're still suitable for the co-op board."

Looking impatient, Roberta now says, "He's already lived in this building."

"Roberta," Elizabeth says, "you and I both know that finances can change in a day, let alone ten years. I'm sure they're fine, but I'd like to see them."

"Yeah, it's changed—he's richer now," she says.

Oh, Elizabeth hates this woman's guts. So she pretends she is not there. "Barry," she says, "I certainly think my seller will take the best offer. But I must show him your financials before we speak any further."

"So what do you need, exactly?" Roberta asks.

At this point, Barry interrupts. "Roberta, I'll take care of this. I know what she needs. I would assume you do, too—you've been a broker for over twenty years." And then he shakes Elizabeth's hand, thanks her for her time, and says, "I expect to hear favorably from you." And then he walks out the door.

Barry reminds her of an old client of hers, Adam Kamenstein, who was looking at prewar co-ops asking between $13 and $20 million. When one particular listing came up in a building that required a minimum of three times liquid after closing, Elizabeth felt compelled to ask him what, exactly, his liquidity was. The girls were sitting next to her on her sofa in the library as she had the phone conversation, and they heard the client on the other end of the line.

"Oh, I just can't bring myself to say the number out loud," he told Elizabeth.

And Elizabeth said, "Well, give me a hint." She had been working with the client for quite some time, and they had a friendly, flirty rapport. As he started hinting, she began motioning with her hand, flicking all ten fingers out at once, over and over and over again, as she balanced the phone on her ear, until the girls counted to 100 million.

In fact, this turned out to be no exaggeration at all, and,

happily for both the client and Chase Residential, in the end he bought a triple-mint fifteen-room on Fifth Avenue for slightly less than $30 million!

Tonight is movie night with the whole family, including Jonathan. They order in a couple of extra-cheese pizzas and then gather around in the library to watch *North by Northwest*, one of the family's all-time favorites; Elizabeth especially loves the famous opening scene where Cary Grant is having lunch at the Oak Room at the Plaza just before he's abducted.

Kate and Isabel are sitting in club chairs that they've rearranged to face the television screen. Jonathan is lying on his back on the Oriental rug, eating extra-salty pretzels as Roxy, Lola, and Dolly stand on him, kissing his face. He's grown his hair longer; it's become curly and tousled. Elizabeth thinks it's flattering, that it brings out his cheekbones and his gorgeous green-blue eyes. She's been so thrilled to have him back home, hearing the patter of his feet at two, three, five in the morning as he shuffles out of his room in his boxers into the kitchen for a snack of pickles or those salty pretzels, or to make himself a cup of coffee. And she loves seeing his door closed in the morning as she leaves for work, knowing he will probably sleep till noon, sometimes two, and then will come out, yawning, in his blue plaid boxers and a worn Polo teddy bear T-shirt, yelling, "Mom!" She even hides the Vico bills from Tom—Jonathan has been ordering in his favorite salad and Spaghetti Vico nightly, and they like to throw away the evidence quickly before Tom catches them. Tom is more of a believer in balancing your checkbook, and spending only what you can afford. Elizabeth, a "more is more" kind of woman, is all about indulgence, especially when it comes to her son.

CHAPTER THIRTEEN

Kate

Perfection on CPW

70s west/7 rooms. Turn-of-the-century building, 3 master bedrooms with en suite baths, new EIK, solid oak floors. Wine cellar, full-service cooperative. $7.3 million.

Oh, my God!" Kate says into her phone. "Don't tell me you took three Ativan before your board interview! Andy, are you kidding me?" Rushing up Madison Avenue in four-inch Manolo stilettos to meet Scott for dinner at Vico, one of the family's favorite Italian restaurants on 92nd and Madison, she pulls her black cashmere coat closer together with one hand to shield herself from a horrible November wind. She is too rushed to stop and actually button her coat. Andy Candel graduated a year ahead of her from Penn, and shares a very successful legal practice in the city with his father. The SoHo apartment he wants to buy is in a very cool, very downtown sort of building, one that has a different feel from so many of the apartments she sells on the Upper East Side. In addition to its loftlike open space, it has soaring windows, twelve-foot ceilings, and a hot tub in the master bath; Andy had described the property as "basically perfect" for him, and Kate is horrified to think he just may have lost it.

"Tell me what you talked about at the interview. Maybe it's not as bad as you think," Kate says hopefully.

"I'm screwed. Totally," Andy insists. "Things were going fine, I think—we talked about my financial package and clearly they were happy with it, and then, after a while, we somehow, I guess it was my fault, got onto the subject of Sarah Palin, and well, I just couldn't—"

"Oh, no! How did you get on the subject of Sarah Palin? We went over this—you never talk politics during a board interview! Never! Oh, no!" Kate says. She likes Andy a lot (they tutored inner-city kids in West Philadelphia together in college, and both of them volunteered at a local animal shelter in her junior year) and he is just one of those utterly likable people. But how could he be such an idiot!

"I know, I know," Andy is saying, "it's just that I was so nervous before the interview, and I didn't want to have a drink and then smell like a bar, so I figured a little extra Ativan would only make me feel even more relaxed. I guess I got a little *too* relaxed."

Kate moans and ties her coat—what street is she on? Only 87th; there are no cabs and she's walking as fast as she can, regretting her heels.

He continues, "After I told them that if Sarah Palin were ever elected president, I'd seriously consider moving out of the United States, preferably to someplace in the Caribbean, like, maybe, Turks and Caicos, they—"

"No!" Kate says. "No, no, no! You didn't!"

"Well, I did, and then I started talking about Bristol Palin and how she and her ex should have used birth control, and then—"

"Oh, Andy!" Kate interrupts him as she arrives at Vico. "I'm laughing and crying for you! I'm walking into Vico now, I'm very late for a dinner, can I call you back in an hour and a half or so?" She feels badly hanging up, but there is unfortunately nothing she can do now. Scott is sitting at the table, nearly finished with a glass of red wine already.

"How about if I e-mail the board an apology, and then send them like . . . maybe . . . a really good bottle of wine, a nice French Bordeaux, umm, maybe a Château Mouton Rothschild . . ."

"I don't know, let me think about it and ask Mom," Kate says. "I'll call you later."

Settling in at their table for two at the restaurant, Kate looks over at Scott seated across from her, wearing a blue-and-white-checked button-down, perfectly worn jeans, and a pair of lightly scuffed loafers.

"I got you a glass of wine," Scott says, and she is dying to just lean across the table and kiss him. But instead she sits down, sips her wine, and tells him about Andy and his ill-advised remarks about the Palins. Scott laughs. "So there goes that?" he asks.

"If I had to guess, I'd say yes. Poor Andy, I love him."

"Let's order, I'm starved," Scott says.

"If I have the balsamic chicken, will you get the Rigatoni Siciliana, and we can split it? And I don't feel like a salad," she says.

Sal, their favorite waiter, takes their order, and then asks about Isabel and the rest of the family, who have all been coming to Vico since Kate can remember. "She's getting married," Kate reports, smiling, and Sal smiles back and says, "*Congratulazioni*!" He sends over the dashing owners, Nino and Genero, motorcycling "cool guys"—who she, Isabel, and Jonathan have grown up with—to say congratulations as well.

While Scott is eating his buffalo mozzarella with tomato, and Kate is drinking her second glass of Montepulciano, her BlackBerry begins to vibrate. It's Isabel, who's sent an e-mail about a showing she finished late in the day. She asks Kate to guess what was in the condo's oven when her client opened it. Kate has no idea, but Isabel's answer comes a moment later: "Books! An oven full of books!" "HA!" Kate writes back, and shakes her head. And then Isabel e-mails back, asking her to guess again, this time about what was in one of the cabinets in the master bath. Kate's shocked by the answer, which turns out to be a 9mm pistol. "UGTBK" she types back—*You've got to be kidding.* "The buyers, a young couple from Great Neck, got a great kick out of it," Isabel e-mails her.

"What's going on?" Scott says. "Your sister?"

"Yes, she was showing an apartment today and her clients opened the medicine cabinet and there was a gun in it!" Kate says, and dips a piece of bread into a small plate of olive oil.

"Don't read into this any more than what I'm saying, but you and your family are in touch every single minute," Scott says. "I don't know, maybe it's because I'm a guy and my two brothers are out in San Francisco and Seattle and I'm just not into checking in with them and my parents every five minutes, but you guys are together like, ninety-nine percent of the time, and you're on the phone or e-mailing when you're not. I mean, don't you get tired of each other? Ever?"

Shrugging one shoulder, Kate says, "My family—the five of us—has always been the center of my life." She and Scott have had this conversation before, of course; in fact, it's a conversation she's had with nearly every man she's dated for more than a few weeks. *The center of my life.* She and Isabel have always said that if they could, they'd be living in a family compound of sorts, an enormous apartment large enough to accommodate all of them—their parents, Jonathan, Isabel, future husbands, wives, someday, their children, and all the dogs . . . they are soul mates, the Chases.

"I honestly don't know any other family like yours," Scott says. "Don't you ever worry about being suffocated by it?" His face, angular, with ruddy cheeks and that stubble she goes crazy for, wears an expression of vague bemusement; a moment later, he looks at her affectionately, then leans over and kisses her mouth.

"Suffocated?" Kate says. "Never!" Kate, the hopeless romantic, believes that in all matters of the heart, you can never have too much love.

By the time their *tartufo* comes, she feels Scott staring at her, so much so that she just wishes they were home alone. When the check arrives, he reaches for it quickly, and when they walk out the front door he pulls her close. "There's something I want to talk to you about," he says, and for an instant she feels dread.

"Okaaay?" she hears herself say softly, and then in her head, *Don't do this again, please.*

"Well, don't faint or anything, but—I'm thinking about going back to school," Scott tells her.

She stops in the middle of Madison Avenue, right in front of the 90th Street Pharmacy, the mom-and-pop drugstore where the Chases have had a family account for decades, and shrieks, "OMG!"

Scott smiles a very shy little smile, sort of crooked and as though he is trying to conceal it. She sees his dimples and wants to kiss them. "In fact, I've already taken the LSATs and sent in my law school applications to NYU, Columbia, and Fordham. I did pretty well on them!"

"I don't even know what to say," Kate says. "When did you study? I'm speechless!"

"No, you're not," Scott says, and she sees that he's

laughing at her. "I think you and your sister haven't stopped talking since the day you were born!"

"You aren't the first to say that," Kate says. She holds his arm tightly as they walk east toward her apartment. The side streets on the Upper East Side are dark and quiet and nearly deserted on this chilly autumn evening, except for the occasional dog walker. She is always so thankful that her whole family paper-trains and they don't have to be out walking the girls at all hours of the day and night.

"So?" Scott is asking her now. "Thumbs up or thumbs down for the law school applications?"

As if he hadn't already heard her joyous shriek of approval. "Umm, let's see," Kate says, as if she needs time to think this over. She jumps up to give him a kiss and screams, "Yesss!"

"Sorry, what did you say?" Scott teases.

"Should I scream louder?!" Kate says and kisses him again.

"Don't you want to know what I got on my LSATs?" he says, pretending to sulk.

"Oh, please, I know you well enough to know that you probably got pretty close to perfect."

"One seventy-six out of one eighty," Scott says casually. He's an innately modest person, Kate knows, but she can see that he's really excited. She imagines Scott with his book of practice tests in his un-air-conditioned bedroom last summer, sitting on his unmade bed with stacks of art magazines on his floor, a box of Hershey bars and bottles and bottles of Coke, some half-empty, concentrating intently on endless pages of short-answer questions, biting one pen, another in his ear, contemplating this change of direction. Although Scott could have lived in the city (his parents offered to get him an apartment dozens of times), he chose to live with his friends in Brooklyn, in a shabby apartment filled with furniture and sets of dishes and mismatched silverware they got from their families. In all the years she has known him, he's never seemed interested in the life he grew up with, on Central Park West, in a beautiful prewar duplex where a dirty pair of jeans left on the floor was put back in its proper place two hours later, clean and pressed. Now his laundry sits in a bag on his floor, piling up weeks at a time, to the point where he sometimes buys a new set of boxers before taking the bag to the cleaners. She can't ask him why—she did once, but Scott wasn't one to discuss matters like that; when she asked him something complicated, something he didn't want or wasn't ready to discuss, he answered with a look and then a short but firm kiss that said "enough."

They've arrived at the awning of her building now, and just before they step into the small lobby, Kate presses herself against his chest, resting the side of her face in the soft wool of his navy jacket.

"Tell me," she says, because she just has to know.

"Tell you what?"

"Tell me what made you decide to take the law boards, to even *think* of going back to school, to law school in particular. I mean, you've been out of school for ten years now. Away from all that studying, taking notes, writing papers—"

"You're saying it's going to be hard."

"No, I'm not saying that at all—you can do anything, I know—that Phi Beta Kappa key I found in your sock drawer still impresses me, even though I know it doesn't impress *you*," Kate says.

"You're right—I *don't* care about that," Scott says, smiling.

Kate runs her finger between his heavy, dark brows, tracing a scar whose origins he doesn't recall, only that it was sometime during the several summers he worked as a lifeguard at Brant Lake Camp in the Adirondacks, where her brother Jonathan went years later.

"Scott, I'm serious, why *did* you decide to take the law boards now?"

"I don't know, Kate, I just think it was time for me to grow up, I guess," he tells her.

She smiles, and says, "One more question."

He starts to pull her inside. "You mean the inquisition is ending?!" he teases.

"Yes, last one! With LSAT scores like that, why didn't you apply to Harvard and Yale? Or Stanford?"

"Because I know a certain girl who doesn't like to leave home," he says. "Now let's go inside, you're shivering."

Kate smiles.

"Entertainment law," he whispers seductively into her ear now. "Or maybe intellectual property."

"Keep talking, funny boy," she tells him as they get in the elevator.

It's Allison Silverman-Cole who wakes her up early the next morning, calling to report the good news that she and her cheating husband, Chip—boyfriend of Honey Baer—are now officially divorced. "Yay for me!" she says. "And I'm in a buying mood, that's for sure."

"Wonderful!" Kate says, reaching over a sleeping Scott for a sip of water and to look at the clock on the night table, which reads 7:32. Thank goodness Allison woke her, Kate thinks. And she realizes, too, how utterly excited and hopeful she feels this morning.

"So let's go apartment-shopping," Allison says, "the sooner the better."

Kate hasn't heard from Allison for at least two months, despite the follow-up e-mails and phone messages she's left for her. The last few showings Kate took her to hadn't gone well at all. This was no fault of Kate's; she just left them feeling Allison had perhaps too much going on to focus on real estate. At one, Allison refused to remove her shoes before entering the apartment as requested by the seller because, Allison whispered to Kate, she hadn't had a pedicure in three weeks and was mortified at the thought of showing her tootsies in public; at another, a large apartment she seemed to love, she was turned off by the co-op rules that relegated dogs, as well as tenants in wheelchairs, to the service elevator. Kate agreed—and it wasn't even an A-list building! Sometimes in New York, the less impressive a building, the snobbier it is.

"I'm so happy you called," Kate tells Allison now. "I promise to send you some listings later today—there are some good things on the market for you." *And please please please don't bring Jessica Prettyman this time, unless she is now, in fact, your lesbian lover!*

"Oh, and BTW, you won't have to call ahead to see if the seller had any avocados," Allison reports.

"Really?" Kate says as Scott opens his eyes and smiles at her. "How come?"

"I've been seeing this fantastic acupuncture doctor in midtown, and my allergies have disappeared."

Smiling back at Scott, Kate says, "Really? But haven't you been allergic for years?"

"The guy's an MD, and he's in practice with all these other MDs in a holistic wellness center."

"Oh, Allison, that's so amazing, such a relief for you." Scott kisses her throat, then makes his way down to her belly button. "You're tickling me!" she whispers.

"What?" says Allison.

"This three-bedroom on Central Park West," Kate says. "I know you prefer the Upper East Side, but I think you're going to love it, trust me!"

"Trust *me*, Kate," Scott whispers in her ear. "You can, this time, I promise."

And despite the past, all those years of on-again, off-again, back-again, every instinct she has at this moment tells her to trust him completely.

The owner of the Central Park West co-op insists that brokers observe her children's "napping hours," as she calls them, so show times are Monday through Friday from 9:30 to 11:30 (so the children can be fed a proper lunch before their nap) and then from 3:00 to 4:00 (so potential buyers can be long gone before dinner and bath). And so Kate and Allison Silverman-Cole arrive at 3:40 and learn from the co-broker, Stacy Crocker from Douglas Elliman, that they have just twenty minutes until bathtime. While Jessica Prettyman is not present for today's showing, Allison has instead brought along her cousin, an imperious woman in her late forties named June to whom Kate takes an immediate disliking. These clients! No one can make a decision anymore without a committee!

Stacy Crocker, who looks to be no more than twenty-five, opens the door and says, "Hi, I'm incredibly busy, can you show yourselves around? I need to make some calls." She takes out her phone like she is taking out an emery board to file her nails, and sits on a bench in the entrance gallery, dialing away.

Kate wonders, How do brokers like this get listings like this?

Cousin June leads the way into the kitchen first, which irritates Kate, because Elizabeth taught the girls to always start a showing with the living room.

"I have to say the kitchen is a *major* disappointment," Cousin June observes sourly.

"Really?" Kate says. "I think it's a great kitchen." She points out all the top appliances, the custom white wood cabinets with gorgeous chrome hardware, the backsplash of subway tile behind the Viking. All new, made to look old, Kate's favorite.

"What this kitchen *doesn't* have is a window with a decent view," Cousin June says. "Honestly, who wants an eat-in kitchen that overlooks a courtyard?"

"Actually," says Kate sweetly, "the kitchens—and often the dining rooms, for that matter—face courtyards in most prewar buildings. When the architects designed them in the 1900s, only the servants used the kitchen, and the dining rooms were only used in the evenings, when beautiful curtains were drawn and no one cared about the light."

Allison runs her hand along the marble counters. "I do love this marble," she says. "The new me wants all clean and white. And I really don't care that much about the view from this one room."

"Suit yourself," Cousin June says. "But don't blame me when you wake up one morning and realize you've made a big mistake."

"All right, let's go to the bedroom wing, totally private off the entertaining space, as it should be. A very classic layout," Kate says. When they get to the first bedroom, they find the seller's three-year-old marching around naked except for a ski hat with long black cotton braids hanging down on either side.

"Hello, there," Kate says, smiling at him. That's a Marc Jacobs hat, she realizes.

"Little boys aren't supposed to be greeting strangers without their clothes on," Cousin June notes. "Where are your pajamas, young man?"

Taking Kate aside, Allison whispers, "June's daughter was kicked out of Andover last week for not only smoking pot but passing it around to all the sophomores as well. Hence, the mood."

Each bedroom has enormous walk-in closets, and two of the bedrooms (the master and a second) overlook Central Park. When they enter the one bedroom that doesn't, Cousin June puts her hands on her wide hips and says, "Oh, this will never do. Look over there—you can see the housekeeper's reading a book as she irons. Talk about depressing!" From the third bedroom, you can indeed look into an apartment in the building across the street.

Kate sighs and says, "June, if Allison wants to see no one at all, she's going to have to move out of the city—sometimes, in some rooms, you do see into other buildings! And this is one of the best buildings on Central Park West." And then she adds, because she knows Allison is obsessed with *Us Weekly*, "Guess who lives here? Michael Douglas and Catherine Zeta-Jones, John Lithgow, and—"

"Who cares?" Cousin June says. "The view out this bedroom window is not acceptable."

There is no point in further discussing the matter with Cousin June.

"I don't know," Allison is saying, "if you're paying, what, how much is this?"

"Asking $7.3 million."

"Well, for 7.3 the views should all be spectacular, shouldn't they?"

Nothing is perfect, no matter the budget, Kate thinks. If clients are spending $7 million, they moan, *Oh, if only I could afford eight, eight would get me the apartment of my dreams.* And then at $8 million, there are more items that just "won't do"—spacious postwar apartments ruined by eight-foot ceilings; apartments where you must walk through a dining room to get to the kitchen, or past a maid's room to get to the kitchen, or where one bedroom is off the entrance gallery as opposed to being in the bedroom wing. Kitchens that can't be opened up on to maid's rooms. The list goes on. There have been apartments that clients of Kate's have adored, and then on a third showing at 2:45 in the afternoon, when they are about to make an offer, they hear an explosion of little voices shrieking and they peer out the window of the master bedroom to see that the $4 million condo they've fallen in love with faces the school yard of P.S. 6.

Kate's phone rings. It's her sister, all excited, calling to tell her that she's figured out the song she wants played as she walks down the aisle at her wedding.

"What is it?" Kate says.

" 'Uptown Girl,' " Isabel says. "Hasn't it always been

one of our favorite Billy Joel songs? Jonathan suggested it!"

"It's the perfect song!" Kate says approvingly. "I'm in the middle of a showing, love it, call you later."

Although, disappointingly but not surprisingly, Allison Silverman-Cole has no interest in pursuing the three-bedroom on the Upper West Side, Kate will receive an excellent piece of news soon enough. After a quick early-morning call to Andy Candel, her friend who was high on Ativan at his board meeting, she learns that after the expensive wine she and Elizabeth had okayed him to send to the board, along with an apology they encouraged him to write ("Sorry, should never mix politics with pleasure!"), Andy passed the board. They will never know if it was the $750 bottle of Chateau Mouton Rothschild or the fact that the SoHo board either had a sense of humor or were all Democrats!

Sarabeth's on the Upper East Side has always been Kate's favorite place for brunch. She either gets the blueberry pancakes or designs her own omelet with tomato, mushroom, and Gruyère, and devours the scones and hot biscuits that come on the side with their melty butter. Today she is sitting at the big square table at the front of the restaurant that feels like a private booth, with Scott's parents, Michele and Ian Lansill. It's the first time she's seen them in a very long while. The four of them have had a few dinners together over the years, always at Michele's request; oddly, in the past, Scott seemed not to want Kate to spend much time with his family and, more often than not, turned down invitations to have dinner with the Chases, causing Kate a little heartache each time. (Kate and Isabel have agreed that this must have been a reflection of Scott's fear that his parents or the Chases might mistakenly think that he and Kate were actually serious about each other.) And so Kate was both startled and thrilled when, earlier in the week, Scott asked if she'd like to have brunch with Michele and Ian.

Her mother bought her a beautiful pink V-neck Ralph Lauren cashmere sweater at Bergdorf's just for the occasion; and just a moment ago, Michele happened to compliment her on it.

"Unlike me," Scott tells his parents now, "Kate puts a lot of thought into what she wears—in fact, she and her mother and sister make shopping a second career. You wouldn't believe the size of her bedroom closet or how many pairs of shoes she has!" Lifting her hand gently from the table, he momentarily raises it to his lips—right there in front of his parents—and Kate is astonished. She almost wonders who she is sitting next to!

"If everyone cared about their wardrobe as little as you do," his mother teases, pointing downward to his scuffed-up suede Nikes, "the fashion industry would be in huge trouble, not because you don't always look adorable, but because you never buy anything new!" Michele met Scott's father in the 1970s while she was at medical school and he was a trader at Bear Stearns. She is a very attractive woman, small, with dirty blond shoulder-length hair, a perfect nose, and Scott's gray eyes. She wears very little makeup and is dressed simply but elegantly in a gray cashmere sweater, charcoal gray pants, and a Hermès scarf tied around her neck. Kate doesn't know all that much about her, as Scott doesn't talk about his parents all that much, but she does know that Michele is "always counting calories." For as long as he can remember, Scott said, she's had a calorie book in their kitchen that she consults before every meal. During one particularly drastic diet, she even took to weighing her food on a mini scale! Luckily for Michele, she has three sons; Kate can only imagine what eating issues a daughter of Michele's would have. And she can't figure out why she's always dieting—she must be no more than a size six—but perhaps, Kate reconsiders, that's because of her diligence!

Today, though, Michele is indulging in a big cheesy frittata. What Kate does know is that Michele is one of the most popular clinical instructors in psychiatry at Bellevue Hospital, where she's taught for twenty years. Kate has no trouble believing this. From the moment they sat down at the table together, Michele has been as warm and friendly as can be to her. As has Ian, who, hugging her enthusiastically, whispered how happy he was that she and Scott were together again. At that, Kate actually blushed with hope.

CHAPTER FOURTEEN

Isabel

The Comeback

Walking along Fifth Avenue in December is like stumbling onto a magical kingdom of sorts, Isabel thinks to herself. New York is just sparkling with Christmas—the enormous, dazzling tree at Rockefeller Center (Isabel and Kate have been watching the tree lighting ceremony on TV since they were little); the spectacular light show that washes over Saks Fifth Avenue; the Cartier Building, wrapped like a red present and topped by a giant red ribbon; the windows at Tiffany—miniature marvels, studded with jaw-dropping jewels—and then the Christmas windows at Bergdorf's, Barneys, and Lord & Taylor.

Isabel, her mother, and her sister have always been in love with Christmas. She thinks back now to their family holiday traditions, the horse and carriage ride through Central Park she still remembers, she probably no more than seven years old, with Kate and Jonathan and their godparents, Tom and Claire Callaway, who came in every Christmas like Santa Claus. Their father showed *Miracle on 34th Street* every year on Christmas Eve in their living room on the big screen—an actual ten-by-twelve-foot movie screen, framed by electrically operated curtains, upon which a real movie projector would play the film. Kate always tells Jonathan that she remembers being seven years old, lying on her mother on the sofa watching the movie, her mother eight months pregnant with Jonathan, and she felt him kick inside her stomach and screamed with excitement, "Isabel, Isabel, come quick, the baby likes the movie!" and Isabel, who was arranging the butter cookies around the cup of tea they always left for Santa in case he got hungry and thirsty during his travels, came bounding over to feel Jonathan move, both girls so excited for the baby they had been begging their mother for, for years.

And this year she takes special delight in the season—so many good things are happening. She and Michael are engaged; Michael's play is opening soon; Kate and Scott are back together. They love having Jonathan home—the original five, they always call themselves. He has been writing incredible material for the series that he hopes will be developed by HBO (they know because he prints out rewrite after rewrite for them daily, each one saying "from New York, December 13 edit, 3:32 a.m.," and then, "December 13 edit, 4:47 p.m.") and he calls them frantically, asking, "Did you read the one from last night yet?" "No, I was showing all day, will read tonight," Isabel may say, and he says quickly, excitedly, "Good, good, throw that one away, I changed it, it's much better, I'll e-mail you the new one."

It's been such a busy season, too: this week alone, Isabel has had four straight days of back-to-back showings, two open houses, and an elaborate handholding and prep session with a wealthy client and her girlfriend for their upcoming interview with a prospective co-op board. (The Park Avenue building in question is notoriously stuffy and straitlaced; Isabel is a bit concerned about how the prospect of a gay couple is going to appear to them.) Plus there is Alyssa Ostrow, who has miraculously decided to renovate—sometimes you are surprised by a client—and who phones Isabel daily with a progress report. (Isabel has actually been consulting on this and has been able to recommend the Chases' hunky painter George Trapierakis and their amazing contractor Brendan Flanagan.)

Alex Fein is active again as well, and she has been reduced to the mousiest of clients, meekly agreeing to see whatever apartments Isabel can arrange to show her. As her pregnancy advances, her irritating perfectionism seems in decline; or perhaps, Kate points out, it is simply a matter of desperation. She made an offer on a lovely four-bedroom condo at 47 East 91st Street. While it's not as over-the-top as some of the properties Alex had coveted in the past, it does have an uncommonly large master suite consisting of a bedroom, adjoining sitting room, and a bath with a deep soaking tub. The floors are white oak herringbone, the moldings custom-carved. It's a lovely, serene space, and best of all, the eighteenth-century furniture that Alex so can't live without will fit just perfectly (she knows, because she brought in her designer to measure every piece against every inch of the apartment!). Now Alex and Brad are just waiting for their closing date.

In between all these appointments and showings, Isabel and Kate and their mother have managed to do a little wedding shopping together: they've returned to Beth at Bergdorf's to swoon over dresses and try on shoes. Isabel has no need for a wedding planner; her mother and sister will help her plan the perfect wedding.

And if all that weren't enough, just last Saturday evening Isabel's parents hosted an intimate engagement party for her and Michael in the private room at the restaurant Daniel. After midnight, the two sisters—each in a glittery, black-sequined Vicky Tiel dress, Isabel's a plunging halter with a flowing silk skirt, Kate's strapless, short, and skintight—climbed onto a table to sing to Jefferson Starship's "We Built This City on Rock and Roll" for the family's sixtysomething closest friends. By two o'clock in the morning when the last of the guests teetered out into their waiting cars, the women collapsing on their dates' arms, a light snow had started to fall on the city. Isabel and Michael spent the next twelve hours in bed, sound asleep.

Today, a cold December morning with a hint of snow in the air, Isabel, Kate, and her mother are Christmas shopping together, part of their annual holiday ritual. The Chases buy carefully chosen gifts for their most important clients, and selecting these gifts is great fun for the girls. They're strolling up Fifth Avenue together now, talking and laughing—three beautiful women in matching black tuliped Burberry coats that look like ruffled dresses. They get a little kick out of dressing alike sometimes; in fact, Elizabeth bought the coats as gifts for her daughters last Christmas. They always turn heads when they wear them.

The first stop is Saks Fifth Avenue, where Elizabeth spends considerable time at the La Mer counter on the ground floor with their favorite salesperson, Francis. "Oh, you and the girls have to buy our new suntan lotion," he says. He never sells them anything they don't need or he doesn't believe in. They have been working with him for years, and the sight of him, tall, lanky, light blue eyes, short salt-and-pepper hair, glasses he wears at the tip of his nose, always makes them excited—they won't shop the first floor on his days off. In turn, when Francis sees them coming, he always yells, "There are my girls!" In addition to the three La Mer suntan lotions they buy and the regenerating serum ("Great for your face when you sleep, and also to put on before your makeup, makes your face pop!" he says, and then, "Rub in upward circles and don't forget your eyes!"), he takes them to the Chanel counter (where they buy three bottles of No. 5), the scarf counter (a Pucci scarf for a client), and then to buy a red Nancy Gonzales clutch for another client.

Next they go to the shoe salon on the eighth floor—a department "so big it has its own zip code"—where their favorite salesman, Phillip, has several selections all ready for them, each in their size. "How are my three favorite ladies in real estate?" he sings out when he sees them. "Elizabeth, I have the perfect pair of Jimmy Choo boots for you for your showings—on sale, of course, as resort just came in . . ." The girls squeal, about both the sale and the thought of the resort collection, always their favorite. He continues, "They have a nice kitten heel, just under two inches—I worry about you climbing the steps of town houses in stilettos." Elizabeth laughs. "So, did your clients buy the house on West 13th?" Phillip has clearly read the blurb in the *New York Times* about Elizabeth showing an $11 million twenty-four-footer in the West Village.

For resort wear, he has a rainbow of wedges and sandals; for showings in the city, an array of the fall/winter collection, all 40 percent off—dozens of classic Louboutin pumps and Jimmy Choo suede booties. Eight pairs of shoes later—four for Elizabeth and two for each daughter—she tells the girls, "Christmas is coming early!" as she hands Phillip her Saks card for all of them and asks him to messenger them to her home.

They stroll up Fifth Avenue to the Bergdorf's men's shop next—cashmere Loro Piana scarves, Hermès ties, and a light blue Vilebrequin bathing suit patterned with little pink whales for Tom that Kate and Elizabeth pick out, along with an ice-blue cashmere bathrobe.

Exhilarated and starving, they stop at the restaurant on the third floor for their absolute favorite salad in the city—the Bergdorf Gotham salad and ice-cold lemonades—before making one last quick stop, at Argosy 59th Street, a classic antiquarian book and print emporium that's been there for decades. Elizabeth decides she'd like to buy Tom a vintage 8" x 10" photograph of Marilyn Monroe, one of his all-time favorite stars. It's a stunning black-and-white photo of a young seated Marilyn, wearing only a white terry-cloth bathrobe, smiling her trademark come-hither smile. "This was taken on the set of *The Seven Year Itch*, wasn't it?" Isabel asks the salesman.

"That's right," he says, clearly impressed by her knowledge. "How did you know?"

"The robe," Isabel says. "I remembered she wore it in those scenes where she's leaning out the window. My sister and I were raised on old films, and this is a favorite." Actually, Tom, at age twelve and living in Queens, got on a subway and sat directly behind Marilyn Monroe and Joe DiMaggio at the world premiere of *The Seven Year Itch* at the Loews State Theater in Manhattan! The girls' favorite detail about the film was how Marilyn put her undies in the freezer because her apartment was so hot—their mother did the same thing in her un-air-conditioned first apartment in New York when she was twenty-one years old. She had moved here with their "Aunt" Sheila from Pittsburgh, the day they graduated. Elizabeth grew up in a sleepy suburb in Pittsburgh on a street called Darlington Road, and she and her best friend Sheila used to have sleepover dates in shorty pajamas on her parents' porch. She shared a bedroom with her older sister Bobby and fell asleep every night holding her hand until she was six, when Bobby, age twenty-one, got married and moved to the house next door, leaving Elizabeth with her brother Mike, their parents Sam and Hilda, and a staff of four including a cook, housekeeper, driver, and a laundress who specialized in making pickles. (The ceramic barrel they used to make pickles is currently a waste basket in the master bedroom of the Chases' beach house).

When it came time to go to college, Elizabeth enrolled at Syracuse University, not realizing that New York didn't necessarily mean *the* New York. After her first drive from campus to the city (five hours without traffic), Elizabeth transferred back to the University of Pittsburgh, where Sheila went, and the day the girls graduated, with copies of *The Best of Everything* in their brown suede pocketbooks, they boarded a plane to New York City.

Their first apartment was on East 80th Street, a tiny one-bedroom where they slept with a box of pretzels between their beds, kept their undies in the fridge, and grilled tuna melts with an iron. When Elizabeth's mother came to visit and discovered her ironing her suit for work, she cried. After that, Elizabeth had a mailing carton with a return label, and she sent all her ironing back to her staff in Pittsburgh.

Elizabeth, in the tradition of her own beloved mother Hilda, will not let the girls iron! She has them bring their clothing over as needed for Cecilia to launder and press, and they are returned in white waffle monogrammed laundry bags and garment bags, perfectly ironed.

With the Marilyn photo in hand, the three Chase ladies are finished with their excursion. In the taxi home, Isabel asks, "So I still haven't found a Christmas present for the countess." Yet another person on her list whose gift seems elusive. "Any suggestions?"

"What do you get for someone who truly has absolutely everything?" Kate asks, a cliché, but the truth. Isabel thinks, with a little surge of joy, of their new puppies from Delphine, which she and Kate have named Daisy and Lilly—names that sounded so adorable with Dixie—and smiles.

"What's going on with her these days?" Elizabeth asks.

"Nothing new," Isabel says. "She's still asking to see more properties. And she wants to go back this afternoon to the town house on 82nd that I showed her."

"Did she say she'd bring her husband?"

"She didn't mention it, but I'm sure not."

"Maybe a spa day . . ." Elizabeth says. "We'll think of something."

"Shoot, I have to jump out here," Isabel says. "Meeting Delphine, I'll call you after!"

"It's your first comeback with her," Elizabeth reminds Isabel. "That, at least, is hopeful!"

As Isabel walks to her showing, her cell rings. It's Lawrence Bennett.

"Hi there, how's everything?" Isabel asks. "And how are all the twins?"

"Everyone's great," Lawrence says, "though of course the grown-ups are a little sleep-deprived. And by the way, thank you for the gifts. That was incredibly thoughtful of you."

"You're welcome," Isabel says, surprised at his graciousness; it was Isabel's contention all along that Lawrence was the more difficult of the two to win over. In fact, he'd been downright rude on a couple of occasions.

"I was wondering if you might have any other listings to show us," Lawrence is saying. "We're still where we are, bursting at the seams, as you can imagine, so we're definitely still looking."

"Of course I can show you a few things," Isabel says. "I've got a couple of new listings that I think might work very well for you. What's your schedule like?" She spends another few minutes on the phone with Lawrence, and then as soon as she clicks off, she calls her mother to tell her the news.

"Fabulous!" Elizabeth says. "I just walked in the door, the dogs are going crazy. I'll call you back."

As her mind whirls with potential apartments for the Bennetts, Isabel walks by an antiques store she's never seen before and decides, looking at her watch (she has fifteen minutes or so), that there is time to go in and maybe find a little treasure for the countess. She steps into the shop and is greeted by an exceedingly tall, thin man dressed in a tweed jacket and silk bow tie. His posture is a little stooped, giving him the air of a large, slightly ungainly bird. A stork, perhaps.

"May I help you?" His accent is British.

"I'm looking for a gift . . ." Isabel says.

The man laughs, a low, reedy laugh that Isabel finds instantly appealing. "Well, you've come to the right place," he says as the chuckle subsides. She spots it right away—the absolutely perfect present for a countess who has it all.

"May I see that?" she asks the man with the bow tie.

"The nineteenth-century botanical?" he says, pointing to a tiny print. Isabel holds the print in her hands. There, contained by a simple yet elegant gold frame, is a cluster of delicate flowers: pink, blue, and white delphinium, their name rendered in graceful black script at the bottom. "The person I want to give this to is named Delphine," she explains. "I'll take it."

"How perfect!" says the man. As he busies himself wrapping and bagging the print, Isabel takes a peek around—she finds a fabulous crystal-faux-pearl-and-brass vintage Chanel necklace that she grabs. This will be for her mother, and then she chooses a 1970s Yves Saint Laurent goldtone pendant with a "ruby" at the center that Kate will love.

"Come again," the salesman calls in his cheery, British-inflected voice as Isabel leaves. She promises that she will, and next time, she'll bring both Kate and her mother with her, who, she says, "are big shoppers."

As the door rattles behind her, Kate calls to tell her that K. K. Pearlbinder, the doorman-dating client, isn't the only shareholder her doorman is having sleepovers with. He's been cheating on her with apartment 10C, a bigger and better apartment with an additional bedroom and a library!

"Oh, that's an only-in-New York story!" Isabel says.

Isabel arrives at the twenty-five-foot limestone town house at precisely four o'clock, right on time. Delphine isn't there yet, so Isabel uses the time to make some calls: her mother, her brother, and then Alex Fein and Alyssa Ostrow, as well as Lizzy Banks and her partner, Stephanie Silver, the lipstick lesbian couple who are about to go before the stuffy co-op board. Still no sign of Delphine. She's always been so punctual; the few times she's run a little late, she's always called to let Isabel know. Isabel calls her cell, but it goes straight to voice mail. Something is odd.

She rings the bell to see if the exclusive broker, Jed Garfield, has shown up. Jed answers the door and asks, "Where's the countess?"

"I was hoping that she came early and was already here—I haven't heard from her and can't reach her," Isabel says.

"Hmmmmmmm," Jed says to himself.

Isabel tries her again, but Delphine doesn't pick up. Isabel leaves a quick message: "It's Isabel, I'm at the house waiting! It's about 4:20—you're never late, hope you're okay! Call!"

Twenty minutes later, Jed says, "Is this like her not to show up?"

"I'm so sorry, this is most unlike her. I'll be in touch to reschedule when I hear from her. I'm so sorry to have wasted your time."

"Hmmmmmmm," Jed says again, and turns off the lights and shows Isabel out the door. "If it were any other broker,

I'd be angrier!" he says and kisses her good-bye. Jed and Elizabeth are old friends, and he is one of the top town house brokers in the city.

When Isabel gets home, there is an enormous bouquet in her lobby. "This just arrived for you," her doorman tells her. The bouquet—an explosion of pink, cabbage roses, peonies, hydrangeas, and parrot tulips in a big seafoam-colored square glass vase—is so huge, she needs her doorman to help her up with it. Isabel opens the envelope, which is made of thick, cream-colored paper, and reads aloud the note contained inside.

> My dear Isabel,
>
> I am so very sorry that I was unable to cancel our appointment before you went to meet me. I will not try to excuse myself. I went out for a little Christmas shopping this morning and returned home with one of my migraine headaches. These headaches are exceptionally painful, agonizing, really, and they often last many hours. I took my medication and thankfully fell asleep. When I woke up I realized that I'd missed my appointment with you. I've thought about this unspeakable rudeness very carefully and decided it was better to messenger you an apology rather than call. And then I had an idea of how to make up for my thoughtlessness. I managed

to get a hold of Fritzie, and he has enthusiastically endorsed my idea. He and I would like to offer you and your young man a week's stay in our little Parisian pied-à-terre. It's a small place on the rue de Bac, charming in every regard. My assistant will be in touch with you to let you know when the apartment will be free. We of course offer to pay for your plane tickets and will make sure the kitchen is well stocked in anticipation of your arrival. I am enclosing a small photo of the apartment. I will call you tomorrow to reschedule our appointment.

As ever,

D.

The photograph shows an appealing living room outfitted with tufted armchairs covered in wine-colored velvet, and a marble-topped table upon which rests a bowl of chocolates.

CHAPTER FIFTEEN

Elizabeth

Time Warner Center

Columbus Circle Dream. 75th floor with 360-degree views from Central Park to the Hudson River, 4 bedrooms; 5-and-a-half baths; 30 foot living room with separate formal dining room and EIK; 32 feet of windows in two-room master suite. $28 million.

The next morning Violeta announces on the intercom, "It's Bart Schneider again."

"What is this, the third time he's called?" Elizabeth asks.

"The third time *today*," Violeta says. "Yesterday he called—"

"I know, five times. It's ludicrous!" Elizabeth says.

"Maybe you should talk to him again," Violeta suggests.

"Nothing to say. I told him any number of times that

the sellers won't sell to him now, no matter what he offers. I told him there was another accepted bid on that loft. But does he listen to me? No. I told him not to start lowering his bid like that—it's always the kiss of death after you have a contract out."

As she is talking, Elizabeth starts to go through the foot-and-a-half-tall pile of papers on her desk, searching for an exclusive agreement, and the phone rings again. "Violeta, get that please, I have to find this."

"It's Robert Morgenstern."

"I'll take it."

Robert Morgenstern is a hot young developer who left a huge position at a hedge fund to go into real estate. Six feet tall with dirty blond hair and green eyes, he looks like Brad Pitt meets Ferris Bueller (thanks to a constellation of freckles and a terribly mischievous manner). Robert is converting a twelve-story rental building on the coveted corner of 82nd and Lexington into a luxury condominium with full-floor 3,700-square-foot private residences.

"Elizabeth," he says, "it's been too long."

"It has," she says, "and we don't like when we don't hear from you for such a long time. How is 82nd Street coming? The girls and I all have clients for it."

"That's why I'm calling," Robert says, and then she hears him yelling in the background, something about a fantasy football league that night, actually. Elizabeth laughs.

"I'd like to send a car to bring you and the girls over to have lunch and a hard-hat tour—I want you to be the first ones in to see it. We're a few months away still from being able to actually show, but I know no one can help me build the buzz better than you three."

"Love to," Elizabeth says. "E-mail Kate or Isabel, let's do it next week."

"Done!" says Robert. "See you then!"

Elizabeth hangs up and buzzes Ben, saying, "Come in, I can't find the exclusive for 850 Park, did you move it?" And then she calls Kate into her office.

"Good news, Robert Morgenstern is having us for lunch at his new project." Kate does her and Isabel's "woohoo" dance—they both have had little crushes on Robert ever since they met him at the launch of one of his downtown buildings their first year in the business.

"Tell Isabel," Elizabeth says, "and now I need help writing up my new listing. Pass me a pretzel, a very salty one."

The phone is ringing again. It's her client Todd Wolcott, the young hedge fund manager who dropped off the face of the earth after Elizabeth showed him and his wife the loft near the Bowery last spring.

"Elizabeth," he gushes, "I'm sorry not to have been in touch. But it's been a busy time for both of us."

"Don't be silly," Elizabeth says, using a phrase that both her daughters are fond of, though to her it conveys a disingenuous nonchalance.

"Well, this is a good-news call. My wife and I are ready to buy at the building we saw near the Bowery. Believe it or not, we've been mulling it over since April. Of course, we know that the choices are more limited now."

"I do know that quite a few—though not all—of the apartments have been sold, but let me call and see what's left that will work for you," Elizabeth says. Had such a high-end, luxurious building been in a better location, it would be totally sold out by now, she knows.

"Oh, we know exactly what has and hasn't sold," Todd says. "We've checked StreetEasy and have been following its progress on Curbed.com and *The Real Deal.* We know what's available. And we've even been to see apartment 5L—we told the broker from LEX that since you brought us to the building, we felt that you should represent us."

Oh, how delighted she is to imagine Christopher McKinnon's face when the Wolcotts told him that.

"Thank you," she says now.

"We're going to make this very simple for you, Elizabeth," Todd says. "We know the listing price and the selling price of the units. We have friends who live in the building who've purposely been keeping track of the sales. They told us that one apartment in the L-line on a higher floor than the one we saw was under contract at $2.65 million. That the broker, Christopher McKinnon, sold it himself, but that deal fell through. So we'd like you to offer $2.65 million on our behalf."

"I'll call right now," she says, and is soon off the phone.

A moment later, Isabel calls on her way to a showing on Central Park West.

After quickly updating her on the Wolcotts, Elizabeth tells her that Jonathan has hacked into Teddy's computer with the program that reads keystrokes. "So we should be able to find out soon why Teddy's been in such close contact with McKinnon and LEX," she says.

"I can't wait to find out," Isabel says. "And the countess called, finally. We're having lunch tomorrow, and then going back to the town house that I wanted to show her."

"Sounds good!"

"There's something I find a little weird, though," Isabel says.

"Which is?"

"When I first showed her the house, she was in love. We both agreed that it might just be 'the one.' But once I talked to her about rescheduling the appointment, she seemed a lot less enthusiastic. I almost felt like I was pushing her to see it. I can't explain it."

"She's weird, but you have to play it out," Elizabeth says.

"Oh, of course!"

Elizabeth glances at her watch and realizes that if she doesn't leave right now, she'll be late to meet Suzanne Shea at her $28 million Time Warner listing with Suzanne's wealthy Japanese clients. The husband is one of Sony's high-ranking executives.

She's in a taxi on her way over to Columbus Circle when Tom calls to tell her that Jonathan is now monitoring Teddy's computer from home.

"However, Teddy called in to say he'd be working from his apartment for part of the day," Tom says.

"Okay, good," she says.

"Also, Ben printed out the JetBlue itinerary, and it lists only Roxy and Lola on the ticket," Tom says.

"Are you kidding?" she screams. "That's a disaster!"

"I know, you have to call them back."

"Oh my God, I knew I was speaking to an idiot when I booked, she repeated everything ten times and still didn't get it. . . . Oh, I can't do it right now, I'm late for a showing, call Kate, tell her to call JetBlue, give her the reservation number, and—"

The call drops as the taxi goes through the park.

The penthouse at 80 Columbus Avenue in the Time Warner Center is, no question about it, the definition of a "wow" apartment. With unobstructed views of Manhattan and the outer boroughs, it is on the seventy-fifth floor and is currently, elevation-wise, the highest condo in Manhattan. The apartment is all ten-foot floor-to-ceiling windows, the living room thirty feet wide, and the master suite has thirty-two feet of glass facing Central Park. The dining room and two of the four bedrooms offer a panoramic view of the Hudson River. The current owners, Saudis who use a London address, have decorated it minimally in all-white leather sofas and a highly glossed white birch dining table with matching white leather chairs.

The Japanese couple are both dressed impeccably in Prada black. The man is handsome, with thick, jet-black hair, but he is eclipsed by his wife, who has a porcelain-like, ethereal beauty and a grace of movement Elizabeth finds disarming. She imagines Mrs. Watanabe to be highborn, even fantasizes that she might be Japanese royalty. When the woman turns to speak to her to ask about the apartment, she speaks in perfect English. Mr. Watanabe's English is adequate, though not nearly as polished as his wife's. The couple seems to love the apartment, and Elizabeth and her friend Suzanne Shea exchange excited looks. And then Mrs. Watanabe addresses them and says that she and her husband would like to retreat to the master bedroom in order to have a private conversation. They do so and softly close the door.

Suzanne turns to Elizabeth. "Actually . . . there's something I've been meaning to tell you."

Elizabeth nods. "Yes?"

"Anyway," Suzanne says, "I was helping cover for another broker in my office who has a listing in the San Remo and who couldn't meet Isabel and her client, this was last spring. Isabel arrived with this blond woman who was very charming and had a foreign accent."

"The countess with the mystery husband."

"Oh, so she's a countess?" Suzanne sighs. "And married?"

"Yes, his name is Fritzie," Elizabeth says.

Frowning, Suzanne says, "Well, guess what, I saw Isabel's countess again just last week. I knew I recognized her, but I couldn't for the life of me remember from where. And then I—" She hesitates, as though for effect. "Well, you know Donny was born in Ireland," Suzanne says, referring to her husband.

"Of course," Elizabeth says. "How many times have the four of us had dinner together?"

"Well, I'm just reminding you of it because he likes to go to this real dive of an Irish pub way downtown right next to where the World Trade Center was. And on Sundays, I often go with him, and we watch the European football matches with friends."

Elizabeth has no idea where this conversation could possibly be going. "Okay . . ." she says.

"Well, a week ago, we were there with a few of Donny's friends, and one of them, Liam, pretty rough around the edges, was with this woman, the woman Isabel brought to see the apartment in the San Remo. I talked to her, and of course who could forget that strange accent? She was very cozy with Liam, and I just assumed they were a couple."

"Are you sure, Suzanne?" Elizabeth says.

"Oh, yes."

"This is very strange," is all Elizabeth says. At that moment, the Watanabes emerge from the bedroom. Mrs. Watanabe announces that she and her husband would like to go back to Suzanne's office for a discussion about the apartment.

Suzanne turns to Elizabeth with a smile. "That's absolutely fine." And then sotto voce, "You'll be hearing from me later," her smile conveying her excitement over the prospect of co-brokering such an enormous sale.

Elizabeth counts the moments until the Watanabes leave and she can call Isabel and Tom and let them know what Suzanne told her about Delphine. When she speaks to Tom, he promises to call Isabel and relay the news. "By the way," he says quietly, "Teddy's in the office now, and Jonathan's monitoring him."

"Tell me if he comes up with anything."

Her phone rings while she's in a taxi on the way back to the office; the ringtone is Billy Joel's "My Life." "Hi, darling," she says to her son.

"Mom," he says. "I'm in his e-mail. And it's bad."

"What is it?"

"I asked Dad to explain to me about Luxury Estates."

"What about Luxury Estates?" Elizabeth says.

"Well, you're not getting it. It's going to LEX."

"What? How do you know?"

"It's all in the e-mail. I can't pinpoint the exact amount, but a few of the e-mails between Teddy and someone named Christopher McKinnon hint at the fact that they paid Teddy to help them get the account. And Teddy wrote to Christopher to say that the announcement that LEX is getting Luxury Estates will be made next week. They also talked about his commission split. Dad says that means he's planning to go and work for them."

Of course. It all makes sense now. Why didn't she realize this? Elizabeth says to herself. The taxi she's in is heading along Central Park Drive North, veering around a pack of reed-thin runners all dressed in tight black spandex.

"Dad's about to call our lawyer," Jonathan is saying.

"Okay. But is Teddy still at the office?"

"Violeta said he went out to show."

"Thank God you were home to do this for us, Jonathan. I'll see you at the office soon."

"Of course, Mom, anything for the family. I just can't believe this guy. Love you," Jonathan says.

"Love you, too."

"Oh, and I won't see you at the office, I'm going to Best Buy to get the new iPhone, and then I have to go home and write."

Teddy is indeed gone by the time Elizabeth reaches the office. Tom comes out of the office they share, and tells her they can't do anything until they speak with Jeffrey Tabak, their lawyer; Tom's already placed a phone call to him. "Not a word," he says.

"Okay, I figured," Elizabeth says, feeling her eyes sting.

"I'm hoping we'll be able to fire Teddy by the end of the day. Let's just see what Jeffrey has to say."

Thankfully, Elizabeth has a lot of things to distract her, principal among them an envelope from LEX with Barry Kessler's tax returns, which, after numerous requests, his broker was finally able to messenger over to Elizabeth. She opens the package and quickly looks at the income of the potential buyer of the co-op at 33 East 70th Street. In 2007 his net earnings were $1.4 million. In 2009 his net earnings were $990,000. But in 2008, he recorded a loss of income of $800,000.

She looks at her watch. It's 11:30 a.m.; she's meeting her seller Maxwell Glenn at his office at 3:00.

She calls Roberta Green and says, "Well, I'm concerned about the one year where Barry Kessler reported that negative eight hundred thousand dollars. Is he financing?"

"Yes, but noncontingent," Roberta tells her. "Oh, and he'd like to put down a five percent deposit."

"Are you kidding? As you know, Roberta, the deposit is always ten percent."

"Close to five hundred thousand is enough of a deposit," Roberta insists.

"Roberta, the board will see the deposit—a five percent one, which I have seen maybe once in my career—and raise a huge red flag. Why on earth would he do that?"

Roberta apparently pretends she doesn't hear this, and continues as though she is reading a script. "We also want to raise our offer by another hundred thousand dollars. They want to nip the other bidders in the bud, and I imagine this will do it."

"Please tell him the deposit absolutely must be ten percent—and I'll speak to my seller," she tells Roberta.

When she hangs up, Tom tells her that Jeffrey Tabak is tied up in a deposition but hopes to get back to them about Teddy in the midafternoon.

"Oh, God," Elizabeth says, "I just hope I can control myself when he comes into the office."

"Yes, you will," Tom assures her. "You'll be fine."

"What if I just ask him if he's heard anything more from Barrington's and the announcement that we've been selected for Luxury Estates?"

"For what reason?"

"Well, just to see the expression on his face," Elizabeth says.

"Let's just not engage him," Tom says.

Thankfully, Teddy is coming into the building just as Elizabeth is leaving to meet the seller of 33 East 70th at his lawyer's office. Teddy's face is ruddy from the cold, his neck covered by a beautiful purple scarf that perfectly complements his gray cashmere coat. He smiles when he sees her. "I think I might be presenting an offer for that four-bedroom at 784 Park," he tells her.

"The LEX listing?" Elizabeth asks, watching Teddy's face carefully. He recoils ever so slightly, and his expression tightens.

"That's the one!" he says, chipper as can be.

He's cool as a cuke, Elizabeth says to herself. "Well, good luck with it," she tells him.

"So where are you headed?" Teddy asks her.

"Meeting my seller at 33 East 70th. He's signing the contract."

"Wait, who's buying it again?"

Elizabeth watches his face carefully as she says, "A physician and her husband. Lovely couple."

Teddy stiffens and says, "Oh . . . right. Well, good.

I'll see you in a bit," he adds. Elizabeth watches him hurry along, now certain that he knows about the other offer from Roberta Green.

Maxwell Glenn is alone at his lawyer's office; the lawyer is tied up with an emergency and will be back in half an hour, he tells Elizabeth. Minutes off the plane from France, he is wearing a beautiful pinstripe suit and a red Ferragamo tie with navy anchors. He smiles at Elizabeth and extends his hand cordially. At eighty-eight, he's cool, unflappable, and dashing. A real gentleman.

"Sit down for a moment," he says, and when she does, he reaches into a bag and pulls out an orange gift box that she immediately recognizes as Hermès. He hands it to her.

"Oh!!" Elizabeth says. "My favorite—you are the sweetest!"

"Well, just think of it as an early Christmas gift. Please open it."

The box contains three of her favorite enamel bangles in varying shades of pink. "Oh, they are exquisite," she tells Mr. Glenn. "Thank you so much."

"Well, I know that I've only agreed to pay you a three percent commission even though this is a direct deal for you, so this is to say a little extra thank-you."

"I actually have some potentially good news," Elizabeth tells him. "Another buyer for your apartment has turned up—he's someone who used to live in the building. He's offering $300,000 more than the buyers under contract." She goes on to explain about the man's financials, his one-year,

$800,000 loss, and the fact that he owns lots of middle-income real estate rentals.

"Oh, that's not good," Mr. Glenn says. "About the 2008 loss, I mean."

He shifts around in his seat uneasily and says, "Of course $300,000 is $300,000, but it's awfully late in the game, isn't it? I mean, the buyers have already signed. I'd feel like a bit of a heel, but of course, money is money, isn't it?"

Elizabeth lets him think about it for a moment; it has to be his decision.

"Well, I'd like to mull it over and discuss it with my wife. Somehow I don't think I should sign the contract today. I know the buyers are probably expecting it, so why don't you tell them that I was feeling ill and just needed to get home to Westchester."

On his way out, he tells the receptionist to let his lawyer know that he couldn't wait for him, and that he'll call tomorrow and possibly give him different instructions about the purchase and sale contract.

He and Elizabeth ride the elevator down to the lobby in silence, and before the doors open, Mr. Glenn turns to her. "You're getting three percent whether or not you represent both ends of the deal, you know."

"I know."

"Just wanted to make sure," he says, leading the way out of the building to where a chauffeur-driven car waits for him.

She's in a taxi back to the office when Tom calls her. "I

think Teddy is suspicious. Violeta said he came in whispering on his cell phone and then went into the conference room."

"Well, that could mean anything," Elizabeth says.

Tom tells her that Jeffrey Tabak finally did call back and that he offered to handle things himself for now, and asked Tom for the name of Teddy's lawyer.

"Then I think we can assume that Teddy's lawyer has already spoken to Jeffrey and told Teddy what's going on," Elizabeth says.

"Probably so," Tom agrees.

When she arrives back at the office, she immediately looks around for Teddy. "He went out again," Violeta tells her. "And just so you know, Roberta Green has called you twice."

Elizabeth sets down her purse. Then she calls LEX and is patched through to Roberta Green.

"Glad we caught up with each other," Roberta says, though she doesn't sound particularly friendly. "A slight change of plans here."

"Oh?"

"Barry Kessler decided he wants to reduce his offer to $9.2 million."

Elizabeth is startled; this is now $30,000 less than the offer from the original buyer. "You're aware we have higher than that with a signed contract?" she says. "Why on earth would we detour for this?"

"Oh, he did some research on StreetEasy and decided he's overpaying."

"I'll let the seller know, but I imagine this will rule him out. Please pass that on to Mr. Kessler."

"I will," Roberta says, and gets off the phone quickly.

Elizabeth should have realized that Roberta was engaged in unscrupulous maneuvering to ruin her deal, so that Barry Kessler could get the apartment for the same price as Elizabeth's buyers, or even for less. Had Kessler's offer been accepted by Mr. Glenn (thankfully, Mr. Glenn had decided to think about it), they would have had to let the other buyers go, and then Kessler would have found an excuse to lower his bid to the amount that Roberta had just offered, knowing that the original buyers, already rejected by the seller, quite conceivably might not want to commit themselves once again to purchasing the apartment. Teddy clearly was masterminding this, and Elizabeth wants him gone. She no longer even cares about the loss of income or even forfeiting the sponsorship of Luxury Estates; Teddy is toxic. And no matter what Jeffrey recommends, she knows she needs to indeed fire their star broker.

Later, a couple of hours after dinner, Elizabeth, Tom, and Jonathan are still sitting around the kitchen table, staring in disbelief at the incriminating e-mails between Teddy and Christopher McKinnon that Jonathan has so cleverly retrieved.

Kate and Isabel call Elizabeth from their apartment just after 10:00 p.m. to discuss the best way to fire Teddy. They will want to be there when it happens, but then Kate and Isabel realize that they both have early showings the following morning. So only Elizabeth and Tom will be there when Teddy appears. Once this plan is finalized, Tom calls security in the building where Chase Residential has its offices, and notifies them that tomorrow they will be requesting somebody to officially escort Teddy out of the building.

The following day, Tom and Elizabeth get to the office early. Elizabeth knows Teddy was to meet a broker a little after ten to do a board package, so she would like to take care of this first. Once she's at her desk, she decides she wants to fire Teddy herself.

Teddy strolls into the office at ten, a festive red cashmere scarf wound around his neck, his blond locks tumbling into his eyes. Elizabeth discreetly calls down to security and asks them to send up their man.

She can tell by the look on Teddy's face that he assumes some sort of confrontation is imminent. Something about his looks has deteriorated, almost like *The Picture of Dorian Gray*. As he passes her office, smiling his once-endearing grin, she holds up her hand as if to say, *Stop*. He pops his head in. "I need a word with you," Elizabeth tells him.

"Just let me put my briefcase down. I'll be right back."

"I'll come in to you in a second," she says.

She watches him scurry to his desk and immediately pick up the phone.

Hurrying out after him to where she knows he can hear her, she says, "Teddy, hang up the phone." And then she walks into his office and shuts the door.

"I just need to leave word—"

"Put that phone down."

Teddy hangs his head for a moment, looking totally defeated.

"So I understand we're not going to be selected by Luxury Estates," she begins.

Staring at her in bewilderment, Teddy says, "Well, that's not *my* impression."

"Oh, please, Teddy—you've been working against us to pass off the business to LEX, and you succeeded. You should be very pleased with yourself."

He continues to stare at her, but says nothing.

"They've been giving you kickbacks for private information."

Teddy's face colors. "No, they haven't!" he insists.

"So what are they offering you: a better commission split?" Elizabeth asks him.

Suddenly changing his tune, Teddy says defiantly, "Well, as a matter of fact they are."

"Then you should go and work for them." She turns to walk out.

"Oh, Elizabeth," he says, "how did you know about this? Did you have someone look into my e-mails? I know surely you didn't do it yourself."

"This is *my* company," she says sternly, "and it's well within my right to look into the behavior of a broker I believe is jeopardizing our business."

Teddy doesn't seem surprised to hear this. "That's *your*

opinion," he says. "And by the way, if you've read my e-mails, you've actually done something illegal."

Elizabeth somehow begins to laugh. "It's actually not. Unethical, perhaps, but not illegal. You know better than that, Teddy." Outside the glass window of the office, Elizabeth can see the security officer waiting at the reception desk, flirting with Violeta. "So," she continues, "I suggest you clear out your desk and go join your friends at LEX. I've gotten an escort for you."

CHAPTER SIXTEEN

Isabel

Dirty Rotten Scoundrels

Delphine is fifteen minutes late, and Isabel checks her watch for the third time. She can't help wondering if this is going to be like that time at the town house, when Delphine failed to show up but then sent her an extravagant apology afterward. Isabel has just glanced down at her watch, yet again, when one of the waitstaff at Pastis taps her on the shoulder.

"Are you meeting someone, mademoiselle?" he says in a charming French accent.

"I am, but she's late and I'm just beginning to worry—"

"*Non*," the waiter says. "She is right there." He's too polite to point, but he inclines his handsome chin in the direction of a tall, attractive woman seated by herself at a table.

"Oh, no," Isabel says, taking in the big black sunglasses and the cropped, jet black hair. "That's not her."

"*Mais oui*," is the reply. "She recognized you and asked that you join her." Puzzled, Isabel follows him through the busy restaurant, squeezing past packed tables of chic lunchers.

"Iz-a-BELLE!"

Isabel's jaw drops. "Delphine?" she says, astonished.

"*Mais oui*," she says, unintentionally echoing the man who brought Isabel over. "Do you like my new look?"

"I didn't recognize you!" Isabel says, sitting down.

"Everyone needs a change now and then. Don't you agree?" The countess looks around to signal the waiter that she's ready to order, and even though Isabel has just arrived, she doesn't mind; she stares at her menu, which keeps her from staring at Delphine, whose new look she finds deeply disconcerting, though she's not quite sure why.

But when the order is placed—a frisée salad and fries for Isabel, roast lobster with garlic butter for Delphine—Isabel looks up to study her.

The long, straight blond hair has been dramatically cropped in an arresting, asymmetrical cut, nearly shaved on one side, and tip-of-ear length on the other. Her makeup is more dramatic, as well: two bold slashes of bronzer define her cheekbones, her brows have been darkened, and the red lipstick she wears is the color of wine. Glittery flecks of copper and teal sparkle above her eyes. Delphine has added several piercings to both her ears, and now a series of small gold hoops line each earlobe. Her fingers are bereft of jewels, and the only thing encircling her wrist is a new tattoo, a delicate pattern of leaves traced around the equally delicate bone.

"So," Delphine says. "How are things? The real estate business? Your darling young man?"

"Everything's good," Isabel says, sipping her Pellegrino. Delphine's clothes have undergone a similar change in style. She's wearing an elaborate tie-dyed tunic, all runny, swirling colors and voluminous sleeves. Around her neck is a heavy silver necklace—to Isabel, it looks like a bicycle chain—and several odd, even cheap-looking scarves, shot through with metallic thread, the sort of thing you would buy from a vendor on the streets of the city. Isabel casually gazes downward to see the artfully shredded Earnest Sewn jeans, and peeking out from beneath the hems, the trademark black cowboy boots, the only aspect of Delphine she recognizes.

The waiter appears with their order. "That was quick!" murmurs Isabel, and takes two French fries.

"They know me here," the countess says with just a touch of entitlement in her voice. "They know I don't like to be kept waiting."

Isabel nods and keeps eating. "So let's talk apartments!" she nervously begins, trying to stay focused on real estate, while her heart is pounding. "Did you still want to go back and see the house on 82nd Street? I can set it up."

Delphine's gobbling her lobster, butter dripping down her chin (so uncountesslike, Isabel thinks), and the sounds of shells crackling and crunching punctuate the conversation. "Could you?" she says.

"Of course," Isabel says. "Anything else you want to go back to?"

"Isabel, you are so, so kind!" The countess reaches out one beautiful pale hand and lightly touches Isabel's wrist. "I know, Iz-a-BELLE, that I haven't been the easiest client," she says, "and I much, much appreciate your patience, and your kindness, *ja*?"

"Ms. Le Clair?" says a man's voice. They both look up, expecting it to be the manager, but it's not. Two men, whom Delphine doesn't seem to recognize, are standing over the table. She and Isabel study the two men closely. One is wearing a rather shabby blue sport coat, the other an ill-fitting plaid jacket. Both wear sloppy khaki pants and worn-in, thick-soled shoes.

The taller of the two men clears his throat. "Ms. Le Clair?" he says again, for no one has answered. His tone is respectful but somehow commanding. "We'd like you to come with us."

Le Clair? Isabel wonders as she stares at Delphine, who has frozen, hand arrested midbite, a deep flush staining her cheeks and all the way down her neck, until it is hidden by one of her scarves.

"What are you *talking* about?" she says, and her voice reflects a wavering imperiousness.

"We'll tell you as soon as we're outside," the man says, extending a meaty hand to help her up.

The man is powerfully built, and Isabel watches as Delphine takes his size into consideration with a quick up-and-down appraisal. "I think you have made a mistake," Delphine says at last, and drops her hands to her lap. "A big mistake."

"I don't think so," says the tall man. "Now if you'll just get up and come with us, it won't—"

"I. Am. Not. Going. With. You," says Delphine through tightly clenched teeth. "I'm well known here, and I can assure you the manager will throw you out."

"Well known *here* and a lot of other places," says the shorter of the two men. He shoots a glance at his companion and then sighs.

"Where is the manager?" Delphine says grandly. "I demand to see him."

"He's right over there. And I don't think he can help you now, Ms. Le Clair."

"Stop calling me that!"

"Why not?" says the taller man evenly. "It's your name. Or at least *one* of them."

"I'm not going to allow you to insult me like this," Delphine hisses. "I'll call my lawyer."

"Yes, that's a very good idea," the shorter man says. "And as soon as we bring you over to the station, you can do just that."

"Delphine, is there anything I should do?" Isabel says quietly. She looks at the two policemen, who seem so self-assured and unflappable.

Now Delphine has fallen alarmingly quiet. She looks up at the tall policeman and says, "Please let me go," in that soft, girlish voice Isabel knows so well. "Please, I'd make it worth your while. You can just say I . . . eluded you." She blinks a few times, and presses her hands together; given the expression on her face, the effect is supplication.

"Nice try," he says, "but it won't work. And we're getting tired of standing here."

"One last time: get up and come with us," the other urges. "Unless you want us to cuff you in front of the entire restaurant."

The countess's heightened color is drained away, and she suddenly looks deathly pale. It's like the moment in *The Wizard of Oz* when the Wicked Witch of the West dissolves onto the floor of the castle, and all that is left is her hat. Isabel imagines Delphine is already gone.

"That won't be necessary," Delphine says. She stands up, looking very regal indeed, a doomed queen in captivity. "Fine, I'll go with you." She looks down at Isabel, who remains welded to her seat. "I meant what I said before," she adds. "You have been most, most kind. And I don't want you to think I haven't appreciated it."

She moves gracefully through the restaurant with the two men who have come to escort her. A few people look up as the odd threesome passes by, but most barely notice.

As soon as they leave, Isabel feels the spell that had held her there snap. She rushes to the window to see Delphine's final "scene"—as she bows her head, as though meeting her king, to get into an unmarked car, Isabel catches the distinct gleam of silver around one slender wrist. Of all the magnificent things that Isabel had seen or imagined encircling the countess's slender wrist—gold, platinum, rubies, diamonds, emeralds, or jade—the cold shine of silver handcuffs was never one of them.

Isabel's father will read a few months later in the *New York Post* that the countess is, in fact, going to prison and awaiting sentencing. The full story, when it emerges, is quite astonishing. Delphine, a sociopath—albeit a very charming one—had been using a number of credit cards, all stolen, to pay for her extravagant and prolonged spree. And she'd been sleeping with one of the managers of the Dartley, who had done a lot of "adjusting" of her bill and was subsequently fired.

And Isabel will also recall how Delphine once mentioned, in passing, that she detested the color orange; it was the one color she refused to wear, and she even banned tiger lilies from her decor. Ironically, this will be the only color that the colorful sociopath Delphine will see, for her outfit—for as long as the judge who presided over her case in Manhattan Criminal Court decides—will be a neon orange prison jumpsuit.

CHAPTER SEVENTEEN

Kate and Isabel

Mansion on Fifth Avenue

Fifth Avenue/60s. Sprawling 30-room limestone mansion with private courtyard, marble staircase, three ballrooms and WBFs throughout. Soaring ceilings and direct Park views.

Old New York

Not For Sale

Five Months Later

The morning of May 17 Isabel wakes to a downpour. Rain batters the windows, floods the corners, and pools in great, pond-size puddles in the center of the street half a dozen floors below. Normally, she would view such a day as a perfect excuse to curl up with her and Kate's three dogs, a DVD of *All About Eve*, and a bowl of popcorn. But today, May 17, is not an ordinary day—today is the day that she and Michael will be married at the Metropolitan Club, at 7:30 this evening.

The wedding gown is hanging in her closet, in an oversize linen garment bag. The white satin Manolo pumps with their tiny but stunning rhinestone buckles sit demurely in their box. Yesterday, Isabel, Kate, and Elizabeth spent the afternoon at the Kimara Ahnert makeup studio, where they had facials and their eyebrows shaped before going to Alyssia on Madison for waxing and a massage. Today they are ready to walk down the aisle.

The last few months for the family have been magical. Scott proposed to Kate right after the holidays, at Kate's apartment one snowy night in January—January 20, in fact, on Jonathan's birthday. They were on the sofa by themselves after a family dinner at the Palm (Isabel had gone to a cast get-together from Michael's play at a dive downtown), and Kate and Scott were cuddled under a cream-colored cashmere blanket watching *Tootsie.* Kate was lying with her head on Scott's lap, her feet bathed in shea butter and nestled in fuzzy pink socks, and Daisy, Lilly, and Dixie were sleeping on her legs. Halfway through the movie, Scott pressed pause and asked her to make her world-famous popcorn in their Whirley Pop, and when she came back, he was standing next to the sofa with a look on his face that made her stop breathing for a second. What exactly he said that night she has no recollection of, but she does remember that the next moment he was down on one knee with a ring in his hand. Simple, and utterly romantic.

Isabel stares up at the darkened sky now, and then down at the rain-slicked streets of the Upper East Side. Dixie wrestles with her fuzzy lavender slippers and then moves on to the belt of her matching lavender satin robe, which droops, untied, to her ankles.

"Can you believe this weather?" Kate says, carrying Daisy and Lilly, she in a matching pink ensemble; Elizabeth had given both girls nightgown and slipper sets as last-minute gifts, sent over from Bergdorf's sixth floor.

"I know," says Isabel.

"It's hideous hair weather!" Kate says. "I couldn't sleep at all. I left Mom a message at the office, and she called back thirty seconds later—she's been up since five a.m."

Isabel's phone rings.

"I'm so glad I caught you," says Kimby Bennett, a note of desperation clearly audible in her voice. "I really need your help."

"What's going on?" Isabel says. After that call from Lawrence a few months ago, she'd pretty much lost touch with the Bennetts yet again. She *had* shown them a couple of apartments that Lawrence immediately said were "too cramped" or "not our kind of building" or "on a humiliating block"—too close to a firehouse or half a block from the entrance to the subway. The truth was, Isabel fully agreed with these locational flaws. And then there was the nine-room at 21 East 87th Street, right off Madison, that sounded like "the one," but by the time they got their schedules together to see it, it was gone with an all-cash offer significantly over ask.

"Isabel, I'm going crazy!" Kimby says now. "The six of us are crammed on top of each other here, and I hate to use a cliché, but we're like sardines! And one of the babies is a nightmare, so colicky, I can't sleep. I'm losing my mind, and I can't even hire a night nurse to take care of him because we have no room. The other brokers we've been dealing with have just been so difficult. And Lawrence"—here she lowers her voice, as if he might be in earshot—"is driving me nuts." She says the word *nuts* like it goes on forever . . . *nutsssssssss.* Isabel imagines Kimby's eyes fluttering as she says this. "He's so picky!" she is whispering now. "I can't take it anymore. I've lost my mind." Kimby sighs.

"Oh, Kimby," Isabel says, trying not to laugh.

"You have no idea." In the background, a baby starts to shriek. "I stopped nursing so that I could medicate—and even that hasn't helped!"

"We'll find an apartment for you very soon," Isabel promises.

Kimby says, "Call me the second you have something. My breasts are still leaking, it's a nightmare—gotta run!"

"The instant," Isabel assures her, and hangs up.

Kate is in the shower, doing a L'Occitane lemon verbena scrub, when Isabel's phone rings again. "Isabellllllllllll, your cell!" she yells over the sound of running water.

"Where is it?" Isabel says. "I can't find it!"

Kate opens the shower door and peers out. "Somewhere near me, I hear it so loudly."

Isabel finally sees it in a shoe. She's missed the call, but she doesn't bother to check who it was. Their mother is on her way upstairs, the boys are all sleeping after a late night out (they even took Jonathan, just four months legal) after the rehearsal dinner in the private room at Fresco by Scotto on 52nd, and no one else matters right now.

For the next half hour, the apartment is in a frenzy—last-minute packing in the purple monogrammed T. Anthony wheelies the girls are bringing to the Metropolitan Club, shoes, undies, an iPod so they can listen to the *Glee* soundtrack over and over again as they get their hair and makeup done, a bag of sour lollipops and M&M's (no pretzels; Mom will blow up).

Their assistant Ben has given them each a list of all the wedding vendors' cells, just in case they can't find them anywhere. "Kate, where did you put it? It was right on the kitchen counter this morning!" Isabel yells. On the list are cell numbers for the photographer (Terry deRoy Gruber, whom they hired on two simple merits—he is from Pittsburgh, and he did the wedding of Catherine Zeta-Jones and Michael Douglas), videographer (*Access Hollywood*, thanks to Isabel's good friend Christine Fahey), music (DJ Cassidy, the biggest DJ in New York, who does events for everyone from Beyoncé and Jay Z to Jennifer Lopez and President Obama's inauguration ball), "set design" (the one and only Preston Bailey, who also did Donald and Melania and every Oprah event she throws), and the five-piece orchestra (Gail Curtis).

The buzzer rings to announce that their car is downstairs. The girls will go to the Metropolitan Club first because they are getting ready there, and the car will go back to get Tom and Jonathan later.

By the time they get outside, with Dixie, Daisy, and Lilly, in little pink raincoats, going for their own holiday at Elizabeth and Tom's, the rain has stopped and the sun looks like it is frantically trying to peek out of the clouds.

Kate tells the driver to swing around to her parents so they can drop off the dogs, and then they are off!

The Metropolitan Club is located on the corner of 60th and Fifth Avenue. When you walk into its circular courtyard behind the large wrought-iron gate, it feels as though you've stepped right back into the late nineteenth century, the time it was built. Thomas, the club's head of events, is there to greet them and take them to their suite, where he says that Valery Joseph and Kimara Ahnert are waiting to do their hair and makeup, that someone has sent over three enormous bouquets of lilacs (Scott and Michael), and that a reporter from the *Post* called to see if they would let any photographers in (absolutely not!). They will later appear in the wedding pages of *Town and Country*.

Their suite faces the park, each bedroom with a king-size canopy bed and an enormous living room with a fully stocked bar and plates and plates of food Thomas has had sent up in case they are hungry. A few hours later Tom and Jonathan arrive, stunning in Ralph Lauren tuxedos, and they all nibble on club sandwiches and French fries, except for Elizabeth, who has one more pound to lose, she says, before the Vicky Tiel looks just perfect.

Isabel's wedding dress is a princess-style Badgley Mischka with a tight beaded top and a huge tulle skirt worthy of Cinderella. Kate wears a strapless sweetheart Vicky Tiel in the palest pink lace with a skintight corset top and slight A-line skirt. She and Scott have decided to marry as well that evening, in the first double wedding the Metropolitan Club has ever hosted.

At just about seven o 'clock, Thomas comes up to give the family a final rundown of the evening. The wedding ceremony will take place on the first floor—the wedding party will descend the enormous *Gone with the Wind* red velvet staircase and walk down the aisle, a white satin runner with rows of cherry blossom trees enveloping it like a secret garden. The bridesmaids—there are seven—will wear pale pink strapless gowns to match the cherry blossoms, and the flower girl, Kayla (Christine Fahey's daughter), wears a baby pink princess dress and a tiara of flowers in her hair.

After the ceremony, guests will go up the staircase to the third floor for cocktail hour. Then dinner and dancing back downstairs in the rich red ballroom, all overlooking Central Park. Classic New York.

Soon they hear the delicate sounds of Gail Curtis's harp. There's a light tap on Isabel's shoulder now; it's Thomas, signaling that the bridesmaids and groomsmen are down the aisle, along with the flower girl. Tom, Isabel, Kate, and Elizabeth, in that order, descend the magnificent staircase, giggling, as notes of "Moon River" from *Breakfast at Tiffany's* quiet the crowd, and as they step off the stairs to begin down the aisle, the old-fashioned bridal march begins. The crowd of just under two hundred is a blur of smiles, waves, and tears, and the family looks up to see Isabel and Kate's baby brother Jonathan, the best man, of course, with a shy, excited smile they haven't seen on his face since he was five.

Scott and Michael step down to hug Tom and Elizabeth, who then give one last squeeze to their daughters before handing them to their future husbands.

The ceremony is fast. Rabbi Posner from Temple Emanu-El says the prayers, the four say their vows, the glass is broken. They kiss quickly before turning their gazes—Kate and Isabel so giddy they both have their hands over their mouths—toward their guests, who all stand and clap wildly as the family walks back down the aisle.

The wedding is a fairy tale. The couples walk out to Billy Joel's "Uptown Girl," followed by a first dance to Frankie Valli's "You're Just Too Good to Be True." Terry deRoy Gruber, on a ladder to capture an aerial shot, takes the most exquisite black-and-white photograph (which months later will adorn the walls of Bergdorf's bridal salon) of Isabel and Michael twirling on the dance floor; Jonathan, with his girlfriend Jen leaning against his chest, a glass of champagne seemingly slipping from his hand; Scott holding Kate up to reach his lips in a kiss; and in the background, blurry enough that only the family will know who they are, stand Tom and Elizabeth, holding hands.

Thomas has arranged a sampling of every item served that evening to be sent up to the family's rooms after the wedding, from each of the hand-chosen buffet stations: sushi, caviar, Peking duck, dumplings, steak frites, shellfish, and homemade pasta, followed by dessert, a parade of minis that will be passed around like cocktails to the dance floor—ice cream cones, brownie sundaes, crème brûlée spoons, milkshakes, coconut snowballs, s'mores . . . "After all," Elizabeth had confided to Thomas, "I've starved myself for months—I'm treating myself the moment I unzip my dress!"

The Sylvia Weinstock cake makes its own entrance toward the end of the evening, in the shape of, appropriately, a Park Avenue prewar co-op, complete with the "wedding cake" layers of terraces at the top; tiny windows, moldings, and a white-gloved doorman standing at the lobby entrance, all molded from white fondant and spun sugar. After the cake cutting, Kate takes Isabel's hand and orders the boys to go sit down. As all their bridesmaids gather around them on the dance floor like the Supremes' backup dancers, DJ Cassidy plays the first chords of Cher singing "The Shoop Shoop Song (It's in His Kiss)," and Kate and Isabel serenade their husbands—in one of the sexiest and most adorable wedding dances ever, the guests all say.

The last song of the evening is Frank Sinatra's "New York, New York." Jonathan and Jen and Tom and Elizabeth are still on the dance floor, singing, arms around each other, and Isabel and Kate are sitting on Michael and Scott's laps. As they finish their glasses of champagne and get ready to go upstairs for the family's private after-party, they hear a woman's voice say, "Those Chase girls are too, too much! Don't you think they should be on TV or something?"

"TV?" a man answers. "Those girls should have their own show!"

And that, the girls can't help thinking, is a fabulous idea!

ACKNOWLEDGMENTS

The real joy in writing this book was going back in time, to a world where all was innocence and pure happiness. Above all else, this is a novel about love for the divine power of the Family, with a capital F. "There Is No Place Like Home."

To our Family, who is all that matters; all the men who put up with us as we wrote draft after draft, always promising "this is the last edit" as we were on deadline at 3 a.m. again and again. Ian, the man behind us all, whose fascinating life and love of old films inspires so much of our lives and these stories, and to our favorite of all your many edits—"*No one* in New York calls it a. . . ." To JP and Rob, who allow the three of us to speak fifty times a night after spending all day together—you are both saints, even if we don't ever tell you that! To our purest loves, our little boys, Chase and Cooper, whose innocence, laughter, and happiness light up our lives every second with love. To Muffin and all our girls past and present, Fluffy, Daisy, Lilly, Lola, Roxy, Dolly, and Dixie. And to our guardian angel, Jonathan, to whom this book is dedicated. "You're in My Heart, You're in My Soul. You'll be my breath should I grow old." Love You.

To our incredible agent at WME, Dorian Karchmar, who never gave up on us as the years passed with no manuscript . . . for her endless support, brilliance, wisdom, and love—we could never ever have done this book without you. To our HarperCollins Dream Team: the divine Claire Wachtel, our amazing, inspiring, brilliant soul sister editor, who along with her Wizard of Oz, Jonathan Burnham, bought us after a whirlwind meeting one afternoon in 2005. Thank you for understanding that "we never met a deadline we couldn't change!" To our other favorite girls at Harper—Kathy Schneider for her support and fabulous-ness; Elizabeth Perrella, for each little edit after edit; Leah Wasielewski; Leslie Cohen; and Tina Andreadis.

To our best friend and partner in crime, Steven Bauer, whose wicked sense of humor and love for our family has helped keep us standing. To Valerie Feigen and Steven Eisman—you have been with us through it all and will never let us sink—we love you. To our bulldog in Prada, Danielle Anderman—from this core greatness grows. And last, but never least, to the mighty Horace Mann and our favorite English teacher, Dr. David Schiller, who gave Samantha her first and last C plus on an English paper, and thus inspired an English major: for all the great books you taught us that inspired our own voices and for your wise and heartbreaking answer to why we can't be HM students again, "You can never go back."